BAD WOLF

Bad Wolf Chronicles - Book 1

Tim McGregor

Perdido Pub
TORONTO

Perdido Pub
6 Lakeview Avenue
Toronto, Ontario, Canada

Publisher's Note: This is a work of fiction. Names, characters, places, and incidents are a product of the author's imagination. Locales and public names are sometimes used for atmospheric purposes. Any resemblance to actual people, living or dead, or to businesses, companies, events, institutions, or locales is completely coincidental.

Book Layout & Design ©2013 - BookDesignTemplates.com

Bad Wolf / Tim McGregor. -- 1st ed.
ISBN-13: 978-1484903209
ISBN-10:148490320X

For Mom

Speak of the wolf and his tail appears.
—Dutch Proverb

I

THE WOLF MOVED THROUGH the trees, nose to the ground. Down from the mountain and out of the primordial darkness towards the lights of the city. It skulked through a hole in a fence, pads heavy on the worn pavement. Past a leaning stack of pallets and into a lot that stank of gasoline and men. Jaundiced light beamed from the poles haloed in the light drizzle. The rain dampened the stink of the ground and turned it sour.

It kept to the shadows, winding through the yard to avoid the lights. It wasn't far now, the smell it was after. Prey. It caught the scent from a mile away and tracked it from the slope of the dead volcano down into the city.

It was close, the thing it tracked.

The dogs came after, a clumsy pack of pokey ribs and ravaged hide following the lead animal. A Rottweiler and three pit bulls, a Doberman and a sleek Siberian Husky. Others of no discernible breed and still more of such bastard mix they were barely dogs at all. Heads low and single file, the dogs followed the lobo's path step by step. The pack snorted and snuffed, sometimes snapping at one another but none barked, none made any unnecessary noise. When the hunt was on, they stifled the raw instinct to bark and ran silent. The lobo taught them this and they had learned it the hard way. The pack was down in numbers because two ill-mixed breeds couldn't help themselves and barked on a hunt. The wolf killed them both, snapping their necks in its enormous maw. The troop was learning. Dogs barked, wolves did not.

They were hungry but the wolf had taught them how to hunt as a pack. First the small woodland animals darting across the forest floor and then bigger prey. At night, always at night. But this night was different and all to an animal knew it. The wolf hunted even bigger prey bigger this night. Something slow and stupid and easy to kill.

TWO boys and a gun. How many terrible nights have started this way? The gun was an old bolt action rifle. A 303 Enfield with a walnut stock and a battered scope. Lifted quietly from its dusty rack in Owen's grandfather's house. Owen held the gun now, sliding the bolt forward to reveal the loading gate, showing it to the other boy.

"Just lemme shoot the fucking thing." Justin was fifteen and impatient about all things. He drained his beer, also stolen from Owen's grandfather, and crushed the can.

Owen looked at him with contempt. "You gotta learn how to load it first, dumbass. Maybe you ain't ready to wear the big boy pants."

"Come on. Before those things run off."

They were hunkered down under the steel bridge that spanned the Willamette, the dark riverwater moving slowly below them. Empty cans of Pabst scattered around, two fresh ones sweating cold in the plastic bag. The air was warm, pushing the stink of the river up the banks.

Owen had seen that old Enfield in his granddad's cellar since he was seven years old. Once, when he was ten, he pushed a chair up to the wall and climbed up just to touch it. The black metal was cold to his fingers but the wood felt warm. His grandfather had caught him just as he was trying to lift it from its cradle and Owen had gotten a sharp crack over the ear for it. After that the old man kept the basement locked but Owen never forgot about the gun. Now that his grandfather rarely left his bedroom, Owen took it whenever he wanted. Justin wanted to shoot it so they got the beer and the gun and headed down to the river. There were raccoons and cats down there among the broken bikes and appliances dumped from the roadside and the boys had taken to shooting at them late at night. But tonight was different, tonight they got lucky. "There were dogs."

God knows where they came from. Six, maybe seven. Hard to tell at this distance. Big and mangy looking. Strays for sure. They swarmed over something down in the weeds, scrapping over it. Teeth snapping and jaws popping. Feeding time.

Justin tossed his can away. "Lemme shoot already."

Owen handed him the rifle. "Here".

Justin rolled onto his belly in the dirt, aimed and fired. It was that quick. He jumped back at the recoil and whined. Owen watched the dogs bolt away then circle back. They sniffed the air then tore back into the thing in the weeds.

"Fuck are they eating down there?" Justin looked through the scope, watching them feed.

"You missed."

"You're fat."

Owen took the rifle back and lay on his gut in the dirt. He put his cheek to the stock and squinted down the scope. He recalled everything he knew about firing a rifle, all of it schooled from a Punisher comic book. Draw your aim, hold your breath and squeeze the trigger slowly. Bang.

He jolted from the kick but quickly re-aligned the gun and looked down the scope. One of the dogs was flopping in the weeds, twitching in a spastic fit. "Shit," he said. "Did I hit it?"

The dog was still by the time they walked down there. It wasn't dead, just lying on its side, tongue flat on the ground and peppered with dirt. It panted, the ribcage undulating up and down. The boys stood over it, watching it die, neither horrified nor repulsed. Justin spat on it.

"Lucky shot, is all."

Owen smirked, watching the dog's legs kick. Justin moved on, trampling down the weeds. Looking to see what the dogs were scrapping over.

"Fuck me."

Justin lurched away and puked. Owen stepped up and saw what was there. Limbs. Legs and feet. An arm. The core of the body had been chewed up and eaten. There wasn't even a face. All of it pulled apart like jerky by the hungry dogs. Owen backed away from it and looked around. The dogs were long gone.

2

JOHN GALLAGHER SMILED AS he pushed the shitbag up against the chain link. The guy looked antsy and sweaty in his green parka, and that made Gallagher happy. Few things were as satisfying as watching the eyes of some screwhead when he realizes his world has turned instantly to shit.

Gallagher had been with the Portland Police Bureau for sixteen years, the last eight as a detective with Homicide Detail. And nothing topped working homicide. Ninety percent of the job was braindead boring but the other tiny percentage of piecing together murders and tracking down shitbags was unlike anything else. The methods one chose to pursue the job were key and John Gallagher led more with his guts than his head and that had consequences. His internal file was stuffed fat with reprimands, warnings and final warnings about his aggressive methods but all of that was balanced against a clean closure rate. The complaints and threatened lawsuits from banged-up suspects were silenced by a clean evidence trail that pinned the son of a bitch to the wall. Just like this shitbag in the parka.

"Hey man, we just wanna talk", Detective Roberts said, holding up his palms. Roberts was older than Gallagher, clocking down this side of fifty. Cautious and methodical. He hated working with Gallagher and the feeling was mutual. Fourteen hours earlier, they had been at the hospital, looking down at a woman who had died shortly after arrival. She had been beaten and tossed down a flight of stairs in some godawful tenement in No Po. They went to work looking for the woman's boyfriend and voila. Now the part Roberts hated, playing peacemaker off Gallagher's wolverine schtick.

"Wasn't me." The man in the parka clucked his teeth with impatience. "Go piss on somebody else's life."

"We will, chief". Gallagher pushed him one more time. "Soon as we're done pissing all over yours".

"Fuck you."

Parka Man walked away. He bumped Gallagher's shoulder on the way and that was all it took. Gallagher smiled.

Oh Christ, thought Roberts.

Gallagher kicked the man's knee out and he collapsed inward. Parka Man hit the sidewalk bald, found Gallagher's knee on his throat.

"Fucking kill you, bitch", was all Parka got out before he choked.

"See, a bitch is why we're here, chief." Gallagher jammed his knee into the man's windpipe. Still smiling. "You put your woman in the hospital yesterday."

"Fucking told you. Wasn't me."

"How original."

"Easy, Gallagher." Roberts scanned the alley for onlookers. "There's people around."

Gallagher ignored him. "Your woman died in hospital yesterday after you stomped her face to hamburger. You know what that means, chief? Your ass is mine."

The man seethed through clenched teeth. Gallagher hauled him up. "On your feet, asswipe."

Parka Man sprang, cracking his skull into Gallagher's nose. Blinding pain.

Roberts flinched, then reached for his service issue. Too slow, too old. The man barreled into him like a tackling sled. Roberts hit the ground hard and Parka Man stomped on his guts then ran. But he didn't get far, hit full freight by Gallagher. Face to the pavement. Gallagher pummeled the guy mercilessly until he curled into a ball to protect himself.

Gallagher let up, caught his breath. "Roberts", he hollered, "you want a turn?"

No response. Detective Roberts was still on the ground and he wasn't moving.

LIEUTENANT Mike Vogel was trying to get off the phone but the damn thing kept ringing. He had big, meaty hands with thick fingers and his cell phone looked like a kid's toy in his big mitt. How he pushed those little keys correctly was anyone's guess. Vogel was a monster with

Popeye forearms and a huge trunk. With his shaved head and permanent scowl, he still looked like the wrestler he was twenty years ago. He was spry and agile for such a big guy and back then, the old-timers in the amateur leagues all agreed he was the best thing to come out of Multnomah county in a long time. His professional tag was Bone Slab Vogel, which he prided himself on. It had a nice horror movie ring to it.

The Lieutenant kept a picture from his glory days, framed and hung on his office wall. Twenty-two years old with a full head of hair, spandex pants and lace-up boots, the whole deal. His press kit photo, Bone Slab posing for the camera with muscles flexed and fury in his eyes.

There was another picture of Bone Slab Vogel floating around the offices of Central Precinct. This one showed Bone Slab shaking hands with Hulk Hogan himself. Big smile, oiled biceps and locks flowing. The problem was the shiny pants Bone Slab was wearing at the time. No word of lie, they were bright red with sequins. His manager's idea. Someone in the Homicide Detail had found this photo, framed it and now it moved mysteriously through the office. Sometimes it hung in the main hallway, other times in the kitchen, always askew like it had been hung quickly. A couple times it hung in the men's room on the main floor and once in the women's bathroom, where it remained undisturbed for a month. Vogel would gripe about it, threatening to smash it but then it would disappear for a while again, waiting like some phantom to reappear in some other location.

Four months after that photo was taken, Bone Slab Vogel was wrestling an unschooled amateur in Tacoma when everything went bellyup. Bone Slab took a boot to the kidneys and landed wrong. The amateur launched himself from the turnbuckle and dropped on him full tilt. Two cracked vertebrae and Vogel never stood straight after that. Four months convalescing and three months smoking bongweed and killing time. An uncle stopped by to talk him out of his funk. He suggested becoming a cop. Do something good.

"Come on. You're gonna miss it." Detective Latimer hovered in the doorway, waving at his Lieutenant to shake a leg. Latimer was a Homicide veteran and a stickler for punctuality. He personally had hung the picture of the red-sequined Bone Slab a dozen times.

Lieutenant Vogel flattened the phone to his collar bone. "Can't you do it without me?"

"You gotta bring the cake out," Latimer said. "Not me."

Vogel snuffed, then finished his call. He hated these things; birthdays, promotions and retirements. The retirements most of all now. Two detectives, one Homicide, the other Fraud, had both clicked over into retirement and needed to be replaced. And here he was unpacking a cake to celebrate the last day for yet another cop. Detective Alex Papadopoulos was a solid workhorse that Vogel didn't want to lose but Papadop's wife was ill and he'd crossed the early retirement line three years back. So Papadopoulos needed to take care of his family and now the Lieutenant was down two bodies in one unit. Not good.

The Ouzo melted the bottoms of the Styrofoam cups. Toasts were made, the Lieutenant said a few words and Detective Papadopoulos got choked up. The retiring detective said a few words himself, admitting that he was dreading what the day after would bring. How does one not go to work after grumbling about it for thirty years?

After the cake was gone, the Lieutenant took him aside and asked about his wife. Papadopoulos said they were taking it one day at a time. The man was scared, that was plain enough. Who wouldn't be? Vogel knew that Papadops had a huge family but he reminded him that he had family here too and if there was anything they could do, just call. Papadops thanked him

Both men's eyes became dewy and both became ashamed but, thank God, someone was already tugging at the Lieutenant's sleeve with a problem. It was Bingham.

Detective Bingham pulled him away to speak privately. Whatever it was, he didn't want to spill it in front of everyone else and ruin the party. Bingham was young for a detective and good looking to boot. His nickname around the office was the Panty-Atomizer. Poof.

"What is it?"

"Roberts is in the hospital," Bingham said, keeping his voice low. "Not sure how serious it is."

"What happened?"

Bingham shrugged. "He was with Gallagher."

Gallagher. Vogel gritted the name between his molars. He was going to murder that son of a bitch.

DETECTIVE Roberts lay in a hospital bed in with his left leg elevated, the kneecap shattered. He'd injured that same knee when he was seventeen playing for the Lincoln High Cardinals. That was 1975, when Ford was President and American helicopters were being pushed into the Gulf of Tonkin. Shattering the same knee thirty five years later, Roberts was screwed. What the hell was he going to tell his wife? Work would be the worst. He'd be chained to a desk and the only thing Roberts hated worse than paperwork was computers. And all of it because of one fucking prick.

"Gallagher."

"Pardon me?" The nurse leaned over him to check the ECG, her chest at eye level. He smiled at her. "Nothing".

Roberts forced his eyes away and cast about for something else to look at. He caught sight of a face looking in through the window. Roberts raised his fist, middle finger straight up.

GALLAGHER watched the nurse fuss over Roberts. She was pretty. When Roberts flipped him off, Gallagher waved back, all friendly like. "Fuck you too, hoss," he said.

"I should snap your neck in two." Lieutenant Vogel came up the hallway and looked down at Gallagher. He probably could too, one handed. Gallagher was solid and built to punish but the Lieutenant stood five inches over him and outweighed him by a hundred pounds. To Gallagher, Vogel always resembled that bad guy in the Spider-man cartoons. Not as dapper as the Kingpin of crime, but Vogel was a tank who could drop anyone. With or without the red sequined tights.

"Once, just once, I want to find you in the hospital with your head stomped in. Not your partner." Vogel's nostrils flared wide, something he did when he was mad. "What happened?"

"Asshole tried to rabbit. Put Roberts down pretty hard."

"And you had nothing to do with it, izzat it?"

"I was trying to collar the shitbag." Gallagher looked back in on his partner. Former partner, whatever. Roberts looked old, hooked up to all those machines. "How was the party?"

"Good. Too bad you missed it."

"We were on our way when we spotted douchebag in the parka." Gallagher looked back at his boss. "Did Papadops have a good time?"

"He wondered why you were AWOL."

"I'll catch up with him later, say goodbye properly." Gallagher chucked at Roberts. "What are you gonna do with him?"

"What can I do? Bench him for the duration. Which he'll hate."

"Yeah, well. Life sucks."

Vogel felt his stomach turn to ice, that same feeling he used to get before he laid the boots to someone in the ring. "What the hell am I gonna do with you?"

"Quit saddling me with partners. Let me work alone."

"What you need is a goddamn leash." Vogel unwrapped a piece of gum, tossed it in his mouth. "And a psychiatrist to boot. When's the last time you talked to the staff therapist?"

"Don't. I will eat her alive."

"How about early retirement? Think of it as a favor to me."

Gallagher chinned the nurse in Roberts's room. "What are the chances she's single?"

THE Pettygrove Bar and Grill was on Stark Street, just off Second Ave. It had been a cop bar since the very beginning and that would never change. Situated two blocks from the site of Portland's first police precinct, the Pettygrove was the first watering hole a cop came across after a shift. The interior was dark, the wood mahogany and although smoking was verboten in bars since the nineties, the smell of it clung to the walls like a phantom cloud. The pictures on the walls were all of cops. Newspaper photos mostly, going all the way back to grim faced sheriffs in big moustaches.

Gallagher came in through the side door and scanned the room. Papadopoulos held court at a central table, flanked by detectives who had ended their day early. Gallagher ordered a round for the table and paid up. As he waited, he looked over at the now retired homicide detective. Papadop had been Gallagher's first partner when he moved from Assault/Injury to Homicide and he remained a mentor after all this time. Papadopoulos had a gentle way about him, not the hard shell most cops had. Not like Gallagher either. People talked to Papadop, opened up and spilled the beans. The old man was genuinely interested in people and what they had to say, no matter what they'd done. Their sob stories and their improvised justifications for their heinous acts. Gallagher couldn't stomach it but he learned from the old man that if you just let people talk, they'll gladly hang themselves on the rope you trail out to them.

Jesus. He was gonna miss the old man.

They'd finished the round and Gallagher ordered again. Papadopoulos protested, saying he had to get home but yet didn't move when the drinks came in. Of the cops at the table, all of them had been schooled by Papadop and none wanted to see him go. Latimer and Bingham subdued when Gallagher sat down, the party mood dampening. They didn't like Gallagher and Gallagher just grinned at them, liking it that way.

"You really know how to kill a mood, huh?" Detective Sherry Johnson had five years under her belt and she hardly ever smiled. Johnson never said a nice word about anyone, cop or crook. For this reason, Gallagher liked her. It didn't take much to wind her up and watch her tear on a rant about how she's up to her eyeballs in assholes and does anyone have a rope to pull her out.

"We call that Irish charm," Gallagher said. He distributed the drinks from the waitress's tray.

"Irish charm? I thought that was being shitfaced."

"That too." Papadopoulos lifted his drink. "Opa."

Gallagher looked at the old man. "You really going through with this? What are you gonna do with all that free time?"

"Anything I want to. That's the point isn't it?"

"You gonna leave me with these knuckleheads?"

Johnson snorted and ordered him to go fuck himself.

Papadopoulos laughed and said, "Don't be a hard ass, Johnny. You could learn something from these knuckleheads." He mopped at a spilled drink with a coaster. "What happened with Roberts today?"

Gallagher went into the story, exaggerating his actions as heroic and minimizing his own stupidity at violently provoking the perp in the first place. He wrapped it up by passing the buck onto the Lieutenant, claiming Vogel should know better than to anchor him with partners. Who needs them?

"You do, that's who." Papadopoulos leaned in, man-to-man like. "The best thing you can do is partner up with someone exactly opposite of you. They'll catch the things you miss. Make you a better cop too."

Gallagher rolled his eyes. "You're drunk."

"Yes sir." Papadops leaned back, completely content. "But I don't have to go in to work tomorrow. Do I?"

3

DETECTIVE LARA MENDES STOOD inside Super Fast Travel, a tiny travel agency and wire transfer place on the 4300 block of Sandy Boulevard. Broken glass crunched under her foot no matter where she stood. The front desk was trashed, everything swept to the floor. Two smaller desks behind it were untouched. Lara scoured the floor for anything useful, anything left behind by the assailant. Her hair swung loose and she tucked it behind an ear but found nothing in the broken glass on the floor. She hadn't really expected to. She looked over at the woman sitting in the chair and wiping her eyes with a tissue. She had been assaulted, which was why Lara was here. Lara had worked the Sex Assault detail for three years now and although she hated to admit it, it was wearing on her.

Irena Stanisic sat in a hardback chair that Lara had righted for her. Her left eye was beginning to swell and the blood on her lip was gelling. Four of her press-on nails had been torn off. She realigned her torn skirt, smoothing the fabric down under shaky hands.

"This is my fault," Irena said. "I kept meaning to upgrade the security, get one of those buzzer lock thingies for the door. But I kept putting if off, you know? And now look at this."

"This wasn't your fault, Irena." Detective Mendes knelt eye level with the woman. "No way, no how."

"Can I go home now?"

"Officer Rhames is going to take you to the hospital," Lara said. "You need that eye looked at. And they need to run a rape kit too. I'm sorry."

"God." Irena shuddered at the thought of it. "I just want to go home."

"I know, but it just takes a few minutes. And we need it. Oh, and do me a favor, don't wash your hands until then. The nurse will scrape under your fingernails. Okay?"

Irena looked at her hand. "What fingernails?"

Lara patted the woman's arm and straightened up, feeling her knees click. Lara was thirty-six but days like this made her feel older. Eleven hours into her shift and she was bone tired but there was still work to be done. She stretched, trying to wring out the sore spot in her lower back.

"There was a gun," Irena said. She looked up at Lara.

"The man who assaulted you had a gun?"

Irena shook her head. "No, he took ours. We keep one in the drawer."

"What kind of gun? Make, size?"

"I don't know. It's silver and shiny. My dad got it for me."

Lara perked up, hopeful. "Is there a permit for it?"

LARA Mendes stepped out to the street, dinging the old fashioned bells inside the doorway. Two blue and whites were up on the curb, the uniforms talking quietly amongst themselves. The dusty Crown Vic she snagged from the motor pool was parked further down. Leaning against it was Detective Kopzyck, a Captain America type with a toothy grin and tattooed biceps. His sleeves were rolled up even now, yakking into the phone. Kopzyck was a pill who had zero talent in the empathy department. For exactly that reason, the Lieutenant had partnered him up with Mendes, hoping something would rub off. So far nothing had. Kopzyck was arrogant and mouthy but Lara tolerated him without complaint. She hated complainers.

They did have one thing in common though. Both knew that Homicide Detail was hurting for active detectives and both wanted to cross the shop floor into that department.

Detective Kopzyck saw Mendes coming out and ended his call. "You get anything more out of her?"

"Maybe," she said. "Hop in."

Lara slid under the wheel, Kopzyck dropped into the passenger seat. She slotted the key into the ignition but didn't turn it over. "How did she describe her attacker?"

"White male, thirty to forty" Kopzyck shrugged. "Twitchy, face full of meth scabs."

"He tossed the place after he attacked her. But there was little cash on the premises and less than twenty dollars in her purse."

"He's a methhead looking for money. Big news."

"He took a gun." Lara looked out the window, her hand still on the key. "They kept one on site, he finds it and takes that. Why?"

"So he can jack some other poor fucker for cash."

"Or he could just pawn it." She looked at him now. "He's an addict on foot. How many pawn shops in the vicinity?"

"There's one down Sandy, Lucky something. But the dude who owns it, he's straight. Hell, dude calls us when something fishy comes in."

"And the other one?"

"That dump further south from the Lucky, near the Sally Ann. That dude will move anything. What's his name, Hair something?"

"Herrera."

MARTIN Herrera sat behind the mesh cage of Magic Man Pawn Brokers. One hand on a Slurrpy, the other clutching a remote. Mounted to his left were a bank of monitor screens. One was a security cam, broken, and the others played daytime TV and cheap porn. Herrera never got rattled. It was a point of pride, a line in his personal sandbox. Even with two cops shooting dumbass questions at him.

"I don't deal in guns," He said, slurping on the straw. Bored. "You want a piece, the gun shop's round the corner."

Lara stood before the cage. Kopzyck behind her, fiddling with the camera equipment. She looked past the proprietor to the junk piled even higher behind the cage. Some of it tagged, most of it not. "I'm just asking Mr. Herrera. I have a suspect looking to pawn a gun he stole four blocks from here. Quick money."

Herrera shrugged. "Told you, nobody come in with a gun. In fact, no one 'cept you come in at all today."

"Look at me."

He dragged his eyes from the porn and tilted his head back to give the impression he was looking down at her. Mussolini used to do that, because he was short. He'd seen that on the History Channel. "Yeah."

Lara leaned on the counter. She could smell the guy from here, rank sweat and stale clothes. "I can always get a search warrant. We'll come back and toss the place. God knows what we'll find then. It's up to you."

Herrera just smiled. "Good luck getting probable cause. Now if you don't mind, you're scaring away my business."

"Hey, does this work?" Kopzyck held a dusty Pentax.

Lara held her tongue. She turned and headed out the door.

Out on the street, Kopzyck caught up to her at the car. "You know he's gonna ditch that gun soon as we drive away."

"Yeah, probably."

He held his hands out, palms up. "Where you going? Let's toss the place now and get what we came for. That fat fuck won't say shit."

"Don't start with that. Let's go."

"Jesus, Mendes. Unclench already. Sometimes you gotta get creative with the probable cause. Drop a dimebag on his floor and bingo. We toss this dump and find our popgun."

"And have it blow up in our faces when his lawyer smells a rat? No shortcuts, Chris. No dirty busts."

"Think outside the box, Mendes. For once. You gotta adapt as the situation changes."

Lara dipped back into the car. "No. I don't."

Chris Kopzyck pointed an index finger to his head and mimicked blowing his brains out. Lara lowered the passenger window and leaned over. "Are you riding with me or do you want to adapt your way back to precinct?"

A WEIRD buzz thrummed through the fourth floor cubicles of Central Precinct. Lara felt it all the way back to her desk. She figured it was a good bust or maybe a clean confession issuing from the interview box. Maybe it was just another office party like the one yesterday, a retirement sendoff in Homicide. A retirement in Homicide meant there was a vacancy. She shook it out of her head and hunkered down to write up the incident report and witness's statement.

Twenty minutes later Kopzyck buzzed her cubicle and asked if she could send him her report so he could sign his name to it and send it off. She said no and he started bellyaching about how much he hated writing them and her reports were always done so well. When she still refused, he went into a long complaint about time management and pooling resources. Lara couldn't take anymore so she packed up her work to take home.

"You guys hear what happened?"

Detective Latimer leaned an elbow on the cubicle wall, looking at them like a schoolyard kid with a big secret.

"You got laid?" Kopzyck turned the page on his newspaper.

"Roberts got hurt. He's in the hospital." Latimer handed her a greeting card. "Sign this."

"Is he okay?" Lara opened the card, saw the signatures crisscrossed everywhere and looked for an empty space to sign. "What happened?"

Latimer told them what he knew and Lara passed the card on. Kopzyck shook his head and laughed. "Gallagher. What an asshole."

Latimer took the card back and moved on, hunting down more signatures. The floor was quiet, the lull before the shift change. Lara packed her homework and Kopzyck drifted back to his desk and they spoke no further. Both were thinking the same thing; one more drop in the unit.

Someone's getting moved up to Homicide.

Kopzyck headed out, not bothering to say goodbye. He wanted a drink at the Pettygrove. See who was there. Maybe he'd learn more about what happened and if the Lieutenant had anyone in mind to fill the vacancy. He knew he had a good shot at it. Lara Mendes? Not a chance.

OWEN couldn't take it anymore. It had been two days since they shot that dog near the bridge. Two days since they saw that thing in the weeds. He had watched the news, listened to the radio and skimmed the newspaper. No mention of a body found by the river.

Run. That's what Justin had said. Owen wanted to call 911 but Justin said no. Just get the fuck out of here. They didn't do anything wrong. This was not their problem. Somebody else will find it. Just book.

Owen did what he was told. He didn't talk to Justin the next day nor did Justin call. He played PS2 and didn't leave the house. He kept checking the news, expecting the police to kick down his door any minute. He imagined the cops digging the bullet from the dead dog and tracing it, all CSI-like, back to him. He peeked out the windows, expecting to see a SWAT team creeping up to the house and bursting inside.

But they didn't. Nothing happened and that was worse. Maybe the cops found it but didn't call the press. They were sneaky fucks like that. Maybe it was still out there, the body rotting in the sun.

Owen got his bike and rode it down to the river. He just wanted to take a look. He rode off the bike path into a dirt rut and glided into the shadow of the bridge. Everything was dark. No flashing lights, no cops, no yellow police tape.

It was still down there. Waiting to be found.

He turned around and pedaled home as fast as he could, as if that thing out there would rise from the muck and come after him. He shut his bedroom door, snatched up the phone and just held it for a long time. Justin would kill him. Fuck him. He punched 911.

4

THE ALARM WAS SET EARLIER than usual so Lara could finish her work over breakfast and still have time to shower. She tried not to think about what Latimer had said, about the deficit of working bodies in the Homicide Detail. She washed her hair and put on some nice clothes. Nothing fancy, just something a little smarter than her usual work fare. Telling herself the whole time that she was being silly. Appearance wouldn't make a difference in the Lieutenant's eyes. Still.

She got to the office and squared away the work she'd finished. Three cubicles down, someone was laughing and talking loudly. She spotted Kopzyck goofing around with Bingham and Latimer from downstairs. Kopzyck was turned out in a dark tailored suit with a smart tie. He must have gotten his hair cut too. His Captain America chin wagged up and down as he yucked it up with the two homicide detectives. Big smile on his face. Jesus, did he already get the job?

The Lieutenant came marching through the desks with files tucked under his arm and fresh coffee. Lara watched as Kopzyck straightened up and said hello. The Lieutenant asked if he was going to a wedding today and then marched on without waiting for an answer. Kopzyck's laugh was fake as he dipped back to his desk and became very busy.

The Lieutenant's footsteps boomed across the floor right up to her desk. "What are you doing?"

Lara motioned to the mess of papers cascading off her desk. What a stupid question, she thought. What she said was, "Nothing."

"I need to talk to you." The Lieutenant nodded in the direction of his office.

LIEUTENANT Vogel had worn contacts for sixteen years but he still had trouble putting the damn things in. He hunched over his desk, looking into an oval mirror and pulled open his eyelid. Lara sat opposite, watching him trying to pinch that tiny disk into his eye with those giant hands of his. It was not a pretty sight.

He blinked tears down his cheek and told her about Roberts being hurt and how the unit was down in numbers. Lara listened and watched him struggle with the lens. "How bad is Roberts's knee?"

"He'll live. But I'll have to bench him for the foreseeable future. Probably until retirement, which isn't too far away."

Lara nodded and made her face unreadable. She didn't think Vogel could see anything anyway, with the tears in his eyes, but a single thought rang through her ears. Don't blow this.

"So Homicide is short a man." He said. "You think you can do the job?"

"Absolutely."

"You know there's a catch, right?"

Her shoulders sank. Just a little. Isn't there always a catch?

"You'll have to ride with Gallagher for the probationary period. Still want the job?"

"Yes sir."

"I need a leash on that animal," he said. "He crosses a line, you report back to me. Understood?"

"You want me to babysit him?"

"No, just keep him in line. He'll hate you because you're straight but he'll mind his manners around you. Maybe some of your thoroughness will rub off on him, who knows."

"Okay." She wondered what 'straight' meant to the Lieutenant. Was she a geek or just not gay? Did it matter?

"He's down in the box. Go say hello."

Lara stood. "Should I put on the Kevlar first?"

THE shitbag looked a lot smaller without the bulky parka. His name was Raymond Declerk, lately of 1238 Holman Street. His mother's house. Five block west of that, Rae Dawn Munroe had been found in the back stairwell of her apartment, haemorrhaging badly. Her sometimes-boyfriend was the first person of interest but DeClerk could not be found. Rae Dawn had died in hospital and the assault charges were elevated to homicide. More charges were piled on after the incident in the alley and now Gallagher was letting him simmer in the box. Imagining the worst.

The best way to resolve a homicide is to let the suspect talk himself right into it. No Jedi mind tricks, no complicated piece of evidence. You let the guy talk and his own ignorance or arrogance will hang him. Gallagher had prepped DeClerk properly, letting him sweat it out overnight. But sometimes you get a rock and this son of a bitch would not budge.

"It's real simple, chief." Gallagher leaned back in his chair, DeClerk across the small table. "You wanna play retarded, I will clear my schedule to personally skullfuck you at every turn. I know where you live, what corners you work and more importantly, I know the people you answer to."

DeClerk looked at his feet and yawned. That's it.

"Or," Gallagher sat up, "you can share your feelings with us at this tragic turn of events for poor Rae Dawn."

"I dunno nothing about it." DeClerk shifted in his seat. "I need a Coke or some shit, man. I'm thirsty."

Gallagher leered at him. All teeth. "That's the spirit, chief." He got up, slid his chair to the wall and stood up on it. He took hold of the camera suspended from the ceiling and turned it to the wall. He smiled at DeClerk again.

DeClerk sat up. Looked scared. "The fuck you doing?"

Gallagher dropped off the chair. "I love a man who digs his own grave."

THE observation area outside of the interview rooms was actually just the hallway. Two hardbacked chairs and three monitor screens. All but one was live. Lara walked in and found Detective Bingham leaned against a cabinet watching the one monitor. He looked up.

"Whassup, Mendes?" Bingham smiled. Which could be dangerous. Adam Bingham had movie star good looks and a smile that was lethal. Rumor had it that his smile could atomize panties and a few women in Central Precinct could polygraph to that fact. Lara just felt awkward but everyone else seemed to melt around the guy, women and men both. Bingham had a respectable closure rate and Lara wondered how much his looks played into that. He flashed that smile and people just told him what he wanted to hear.

"Hi." She kept it short, looked at the monitor. "Is detective Gallagher in there?"

"That's his perp." Bingham nodded at the monitor labeled 'number three'. A pixelated black and white feed showed a man at the table and another man just out of camera range.

"What's the story on this guy?" Lara resumed her game face and took a seat.

Bingham ran through the notes he had, gave her the short version. He added that both the suspect and the victim had priors. Her rap sheet was almost as long as his.

Lara asked to see the paperwork and scanned through the details. She looked up at the screen again. "Let me guess. The boyfriend doesn't know anything about it."

Bingham feigned shock. "How did you know?"

"What is Gallagher doing?"

She pointed at the monitor, watching detective Gallagher thrust his mug into the lens and then turn the camera to the wall.

"Ah shit." Bingham reached for the door.

Lara stopped him. "I got it," she said.

A CHAIR sailed across the box and punched a hole in the crappy drywall. DeClerk lost his cool for a moment, remembering the beating he took from Gallagher in the alley. But he still denied everything and Gallagher was running out of luck. DeClerk had an alibi for his time when the beating of Rae Dawn occurred and he had a story for the bruise on his right hand. All of which Gallagher knew in his gut to be utter bullshit but gut was all he had at the moment.

A knock at the door. A woman with dark hair entered, holding a can of Orange Crush in her hand. Gallagher recognized her from the hallways but couldn't put a name to the face.

"You have a call." Lara left the door open. Nodded to the overturned chair. "Can you fix that?"

Gallagher tilted his head like she was from another planet. Whatever. He fixed the chair and then loosened his tie and slipped it from his neck. He turned to DeClerk and leered like a devil. "The nice lady here is gonna ask some more questions. When she's gone, do us all a favor. Use this." He dropped the loose tie in DeClerk's lap and left the room.

Lara sat down and slid the can across the table. DeClerk didn't touch it.

"You the good cop?" His eyes fixed with contempt. "Please."

Lara folded her hands together. "I knew your woman. Rae Dawn. I processed her for solicitation last May."

"Bullshit."

"The woman had a temper," she said. "She screamed and hollered the whole time. Demanding this and that, said she couldn't be treated like this. I'm guessing she did most of her screaming at you, didn't she? All that rage inside her? She took that out on you. Cutting you down every chance she got, blaming you for all her problems when what she needed to do was to take a hard look in the mirror."

DeClerk said nothing but his eyes betrayed him, casting about the room for something to fix upon. Anything at all.

Lara noted all of this and went on. "I don't know how you put up with her. You took care of her, provided for her. Did she appreciate everything you did for her?"

DeClerk melted into his seat. He grasped the can of soda and took a long slug.

OUTSIDE the box Gallagher watched as DeClerk leaned in and started waving his hands about. Telling the woman everything. He looked over at Bingham. "Do you believe this?"

"Check it out." Bingham pointed at the screen. "The dude's crying."

Gallagher groaned. "I'm gonna be sick.

Twenty minutes later, Lara escorted the suspect out and handed him off to a waiting uniform. Gallagher watched DeClerk being led away and then turned to Mendes.

"Nice job," he said. "Rachel?"

"Lara." She extended a hand. "Lara Mendes."

He shook her hand, holding it fast. "Why is Sex Assault barging into my interview?"

"I'm homicide now." She felt her hand crushed. She squeezed back. "Didn't the Lieutenant talk to you? We're working together."

His eyes narrowed. "The Lieutenant must be mixing his meds again."

Gallagher grabbed the nearest phone and punched an extension. Lara listened as he asked if the Lieutenant was fucking crazy. Gallagher held the phone away from his ear. She couldn't make out what was being said, it was all squawking, but clearly her new partner was being ripped a new one. An icy snowball rolled around her stomach.

Gallagher hung up and looked up at her. All he did was shrug. "I'm getting some coffee."

THE third floor kitchen looked like any other office kitchen. Dirty cups piled into the sink and coffee dripped all over the counter. A note on the fridge warned all comers that anyone who touches the roti inside will have their frigging hands chopped off. And, believe it or not, there was a box of donuts on the table.

Gallagher went right for the donuts. "When did you bust the victim?"

"I didn't." Lara checked the cupboard for a clean glass. There wasn't one.

"Then how'd you know all that stuff about her?"

"I saw her priors, took a guess. Men who assault their partners, the reason is almost always the same."

Gallagher flipped open the box but all that was left was a crummy plain donut. He crossed to the doorway and hollered out at the entire bullpen. "You assholes couldn't leave me one with sprinkles!"

No one looked up. Someone in the back hollered. "Shove it, Gallagher!"

He wet a finger to retrieve the loose sprinkles rolling around the bottom of the box. Looked at her. "What reason are we talking about?"

"Humiliation," she said. "Or their perceived sense of being humiliated."

"So you just pulled some voodoo on him?"

"No. I'm just trying to understand the person. It's about getting them to open up."

"Why?" He chased the last sprinkles round the box. "All they do is cry like they're the victim. Who wants to hear that?"

"Don't you want to know why someone does the things they do?"

"Hell no."

"Then what's the point of doing the job?"

He leaned back, taking a second assessment of her. "You're not one of them kids trying to make a difference, are you?"

Lara bit her tongue, watching this guy hunting sprinkles. She'd heard about Gallagher before, what an asshole he was, but she wasn't going to let him get to her. There was a bigger picture here. She held out her hand. "How about we start over here? I'm Lara."

He shook. "Lara, I want you to do me a favor."

Some nerve.

He went on. "Request another partner. Talk to the Lieutenant, tell him you can't work with an asshole like me. He'll understand."

She ended the handshake. "Done."

A uniformed officer leaned into the doorway. The name on his tag read Frid. "Gallagher? Call came in, ten fifty-four down on the river bank. Bingham said you're up."

"Bullshit. Bingham dodged the last one, he's up."

Frid shrugged, not wanting to get caught up in this. "I'm just telling you what he said."

"We'll take it," Lara said.

Gallagher scowled at her then he turned on Frid, snatching up the officer's tie. The uniform protested but Gallagher held him tight, scrutinizing the tie. "Are those sprinkles?"

5

THE BODY LAY IN THE WEEDS, a stone's throw from the river. A uniformed officer stood near it but kept her back to the remains. A second officer remained further up the bank, waving down the approaching car. The unmarked Crown Vic wheeled up and parked on the gravel spit. A second police cruiser sat idle on the gravel, two silhouettes seated in the backseat.

Gallagher and Mendes climbed out. Gallagher waved to the uniformed officer. "Who's in the car?" He nodded to the two occupants in the back of the blue and white.

"Two boys." The officer cocked his thumb downriver. "They found the body."

"Are they okay?" Lara asked.

"They're scared. Who likes sitting in a police car?"

"Sit on them there until we're ready to talk." Gallagher scanned the outlay. The river, the trees and the bridge overhead. "Where is it?"

The uniform motioned towards the water. "Down there."

Gallagher was already trampling through the wet grass. Lara followed his trail, knowing she'd be taking his cues for a while.

"Check your guts," the uniform called after them. "That's a nasty sight down there."

The body. White, female. That was about all that was discernible from the wreckage sprawled in the weeds of the riverbank. The belly had been torn open and ripped apart, the viscera pulled and scattered in the grass. The face was a mass of wet gristle and bone, turning purple in the sun. The left hand ruined and the right one simply missing, sheared off above the wrist. Parts of the thighs were gone.

Gallagher stopped eight feet shy of the body and simply stared at it, taking in the wreckage. Blowflies roiled up then settled back onto the remains. The victim was naked and from where he stood, he saw no rings or jewelry. No markers of any kind. He scanned the ground around him but saw no clothing, no purse, nothing. The weeds were trampled here and there but there was little blood. It had rained in the night and everything was wet. Gallagher shook his head at the mess before him. This was going to be bad.

Lara came up behind him, stepping where he stepped. She stopped cold when she saw the body. "Oh my God."

"For your first stiff," Gallagher said, "you picked a doozy, detective." He walked around the body, circling it slowly. "Work the edges carefully then circle your way in. Take it slow."

She didn't say anything. He looked up. "You all right, detective?"

"I can't even tell if that's a man or a woman."

"You need a minute?"

"I'm good." The way he looked at her, zero sympathy in his eyes. Testing her. "I'm just not sure what I'm looking at."

"Looks like she was run over by a lawn mower."

"It was dogs." The uniform standing nearby spoke up. Still with her back to the corpse on the ground."That's what the kid said." She chinned the cruiser up on the gravel. The two lumps in the backseat.

"No shit." Gallagher kept circling, kicking the weeds down, searching.

"Dogs did that?" Lara felt her stomach drop. Told herself to keep cool, but she blurted it out. "I hate dogs."

Gallagher saw her face turning ashen. "Don't you dare puke on my crime scene, detective. You gotta hurl, do it up on the pavement."

Lara gritted her teeth. "I said I'm fine."

He didn't believe her but he let it go. He snapped on the latex gloves and kept circling closer to the body, pressing aside the weeds with his foot. Give me something, he thought. Anything. Nothing was given and then he was standing over the remains. What he saw was the worst kind of luck you could draw. A body out in the raw elements with nothing to work from. No clothes and no ID. The body gone cold and washed in the rain. Zero chance of finding any hair or fibers. Not that it really mattered much. Gallagher couldn't remember the last time trace evidence ever led to a suspect. Still. Look at this mess. Give me a plain old drug murder in some shit-stained alley any day, I'll work it. But this? This was going to be hell to work and a bitch to close.

Lara kept her eyes down and methodically scoured the earth. Focusing on the ground gave her stomach a chance to settle. She'd hardened herself to blood and twisted limbs long ago, keeping up with the dark jokes every cop used to deal with the sight of broken and dying human beings. But these remains, that was a first. Her first day on Homicide Detail, being tested under the ape she got partnered up with and she gets that mess? Jesus. Never mind. Stay focused and work the scene harder than you ever worked a scene before.

She didn't see the second carcass until she was right on top of it. Bloated from the expanding gases and boiling with flies, it took a second to recognize it as a dog. Dead and reeking, its tongue lying in the grit.

That's when she puked. Lara doubled over and just let it rip. Game over.

ANOTHER Crown Vic arrived thirty minutes later, delivering detectives Latimer and Bingham to assist. Both men took one look at the scene and shook their heads in dismay, silently grateful they hadn't caught this call. They joined Detective Mendes in the ground search while Detective Gallagher hovered over the body. The meatwagon rolled up shortly after and the medical examiner waited on the gravel spur until the primary waved her in.

Gallagher straightened up, his legs numb from kneeling and his shoes soaked from the wet grass. He stepped away from the corpse and marched to where the secondary worked. "You got anything?"

Lara plucked a dented beer can from the mud with latexed fingers and popped it into a bag. "Nothing good", she said, holding up the can in the evidentiary bag. "Trash."

"Figures." He waved at the medical examiner to come on in. "Have you met the M.E.?"

Caroline Brunt had been with the Multnomah Coroner's Office for over a decade and had worked most of Gallagher's crime scenes. She was five foot nothing but freakishly strong and could haul a fat man onto a gurney easier than he could.

"Lara, this is Caroline. Champion body-bagger. Caroline, meet detective Lara Mendes. Super-cop in training."

They shook. Caroline spoke first. "Who did you piss off to get saddled with this creep?"

"I'm still trying to figure that out." Lara glanced back down the riverbank. "Just down there. Is there anything you need from us?"

"Just some room."

"There's a dog too."

Caroline looked at Gallagher. "Dog?"

"Over there. Can you have a look at it before the animal shelter collects it?"

Caroline nodded, then trod down the path. Gallagher looked up at the vehicles on the roadside. "Let's talk to the kids."

"WHO shot the dog?"

Owen Tilgard and Justin Brophey leaned against the cruiser, eyes on the ground. Not looking at the cops and not looking at each other. Owen couldn't believe they busted him. He called 911 and reported the body. His conscience clear, he didn't give it another thought.

Then a cruiser rolled up in front of his house and they hauled him away. It hadn't occurred to him that the cops would trace the call. They picked up Justin down the block and rolled in here. Justin hissed that he'd kill him when this was all over. And now this, this stanky cop barking at them like they'd done something wrong.

"He shot it," Justin said. Owen shot eyes at him but Justin didn't look back.

"This is what you two do for fun? Shoot dogs." Gallagher looked them over, a couple of brain-dead boys with nothing better to do than shoot up the riverbank. They find a body and just fucking leave it there. He wanted to knock their empty skulls together. He glanced over at Mendes, listening to these two idiots stutter, writing it all down in her spiral. She seemed impassive to it all. Aloof. Least she got that part right.

"How many dogs were there?" Lara looked up from her notes and zeroed in on the chubby kid. He phoned it in, he'd talk.

"I dunno. Lots."

"Have you ever seen these dogs before?"

Owen shook his head. Justin didn't say anything, just folded his arms like he needed to be somewhere else. Gallagher shoved him against the car. "The officer asked you a question, sparky. Speak up."

Shock then rage flashed in the kid's eyes. Gallagher smiled at him, pleased. "I ain't seen those dogs before. They were all mangy and shitty-looking."

"Then what?"

"We wanted to see what they were scrapping over," Owen said. "We went down and the dogs, they were..." His eyes rolled down the bank and he choked. So Justin finished for him.

"They were eating it."

GALLAGHER packed the boys back into the car and asked Latimer to take them to precinct and get their statements while he finished up here. Latimer groused but he always groused when Gallagher asked for something. Gallagher trudged down to Caroline and clocked Mendes working the grit again, giving the area a third pass. Least she's thorough.

"What's the verdict, Caroline? Suicide or old age?"

Caroline didn't look up from her clipboard. "You do know how to pick 'em. This is a beaut."

"You got nothing for me?" He feigned hurt.

"I've done all I can out here. I need to bring the body in."

"Sure. How soon can you ID her?"

"Don't wait up. Matching dental records takes a long time."

"Dental? Use the prints."

The medical examiner looked out over the rim of her glasses. "What prints? The left hand is mutilated and the right is missing altogether. All I have are teeth."

That was when someone yelled from the field. Bingo. Gallagher looked up. Who the hell yells out bingo? Twenty yards out stood his new partner, waving at him. Bingo.

LARA thought Gallagher was too rough on the boys and had told him so. You come down too hard on kids that age, they just shut you out. Gallagher guffawed, said he should've been harsher with those dipshits. Kids were so full of themselves, he said, that you gotta smack them just to wake them from the self-absorbed fogs they travel in. She asked if he had ever actually spent time with anyone under twenty. He just laughed then frigged off to talk to the M.E.

It wasn't worth getting mad about. She'd already humiliated herself by hurling on the crime scene and didn't need anymore bullshit from super-cop.

She went back to scouring the perimeter. The uniform they'd asked to help search the weeds was eager to help but not exactly diligent. Too easily distracted by his chirping cell. She took another pass at it, just to be sure.

That was when she spotted it, hidden under a tangle of matted reeds. Something dark and lumpy. She pushed the grass apart with a pen and looked down at the torn flesh. Severed at the elbow joint and mutilated into a lump of jellied blood. The missing arm, bloated and boiling with ants.

Lara sprang up and hollered out the first thing that crossed her mind. And immediately regretted it. Her first day in homicide detail hadn't gone bad enough, she had to shout out that? Jesus.

6

WORKING HOMICIDE WASN'T how she imagined it would be. One day in and Lara hated it.

She tossed her stuff onto the kitchen table and groaned when she saw the time glowing on the microwave. Stuffed into her bag was a file of current case reports and a thick protocol document for her new detail, all of which she had no time to read tonight. Not after this hellish day.

The bottle of wine in the fridge door poured only half a glass. She took it and the phone out to the deck off the kitchen. Her backyard was small. A failed vegetable garden and patio lights that had burned out long ago. Still, it was good enough to just sit back and listen to the crickets.

She smoothed her thumb over the number pads on the phone, wanting to call her sister. Marisol was a good listener, with a knack for teasing out the real problem underneath an earful of complaints. Lara wanted to vent about how bad her first day in Homicide had gone. She'd wanted this detail for so long only to get partnered with a rude ape and then humiliate herself by hurling all over the crime scene. Marisol would listen and say all the right things to her, shoring up her battered resolve to go back in the next morning with her head high and taking no prisoners. But her sister would be asleep by this time, exhausted after a day of chasing after her four-year old son. Lara smiled at the thought of her nephew. How big was he now? She hadn't seen him since Christmas.

Back inside the kitchen, inside the folder of homework was a first draft of a letter to Lieutenant Vogel. An official request to mentor with a new partner. She knew it would look bad to start her new detail this way but the problem here was Gallagher. Any other veteran homicide cop and she would be fine. She had planned to redraft it tonight but it would have to wait until morning. Which meant another early start to the day. Go to bed.

A noise skittered over the buzz of the crickets. A scratching sound coming from the far side of the yard. A plump raccoon waddled onto the top of the wood fence and looked at her. It slouched over and folded its creepy little hands together. Like it was surprised to see her and wanted her to leave. It was big and mangy and Lara hated raccoons. She shot to her feet like she would charge at it but the animal just scratched its belly and watched her.

Lara marched back into the house and slammed the door, as if emphasizing to the scavenger how displeased she was to see him. The raccoon clawed down the fence and waddled across the grass to her garbage bins.

THE jump into the Homicide unit had been fast, accelerated by the case dropped in her lap and Lara hadn't had time to move desks. Not a task she looked forward to as she wound through the fourth floor bullpen to her cubicle. She tried her best to keep her desk neat and orderly. Honest. It just never worked out that way. It overflowed with paperwork and files. The old school binders she kept for each case. She couldn't even see any personal stuff buried under all that riot.

"Hey, look who's back!"

Charlene Fabre came up behind and squeezed her elbow. Charlene was a detective in the Sex Assault Detail and, although they weren't partners, they shared a cubicle. "How's your first day?"

"Busy." Lara shuffled papers into binders and folders. "I'm there two minutes and we already got a body. Charlie, you wouldn't believe the condition of this poor woman. It was horrendous. I lost my lunch, totally embarrassed myself."

"Oh honey, that's awful."

"How about you? Miss me yet?"

"Do you know who's getting your desk? Reynard, the miserable SOB."

Lara winced. Reynard was a slow-eyed cretin who talked nonstop without ever actually saying anything useful.

"The man cornered me in the kitchen yesterday and prattled on for twenty minutes about property taxes. How am I going to endure that nonsense all day? I'll kill myself." Charlene wheeled her chair closer and lowered her voice. "Is it true they stuck you with Gallagher?"

"Yup."

"What is Vogel thinking sticking you with that gorilla? Like you don't have enough to do learning new detail."

"It isn't about me. The Lieutenant is punishing Gallagher, trying to reign him in. I just happen to be the next warm body."

Charlene patted her arm. "He gets out of line, you talk to Vogel straightaway. You don't need that man's foolishness."

A cell phone went off. Lara checked the ID. "Speak of the devil." She flipped it open and deadpanned, "Mendes".

"You know where the coroner's office is?" No hello, no how-are-you.

"It's on Knott, isn't it?"

"The M.E.'s got an initial report on the body. You wanna take part, I'll be there in twenty." He hung up. No goodbye.

She dropped the phone into her pocket, turned to Charlene. "I'll have to clean this up later. You okay with that?"

"Take your time. The sooner you clear out, the sooner Reynard moves in."

AN elevator ride down two levels, through a door and Lara was in the morgue. Two shroud covered gurneys were parked in the hallway. Something else she'd have to get used to in the new detail. She took a breath and went in to the morgue proper. Gallagher leaned against a stretcher, chatting away with Caroline like it was a tailgate party. He looked surprised that she showed up.

Caroline led them to the far end of the examining room. It was cold and it smelled awful. Lara tried to breathe through her mouth but that just made it worse, like tasting death on her tongue.

Caroline peeled back the sheet. The body of their vic laid out cold and exposed. The remains examined and cut, the flesh peeled back in layers. The severed arm that Lara had found lay reassembled below the raw right elbow.

"Female, Caucasian." Caroline read off the details from a clipboard. "Forty to fifty, fifty-five years old. And as you can see, she suffered an extraordinary amount of trauma. Most of the internal organs are missing, presumably devoured. So I didn't have a lot to work with."

Lara had her notebook out, scribbling down the pertinent details. Gallagher produced no notebook. He just started firing questions at Caroline.

"Can you ballpark the time of death?"

"Given the level of rigor, plus the fly larvae already embedded in the soft tissue, I'd say sometime within the last forty-eight hours."

Lara looked up from her notes. "Will you be able to narrow that down after the autopsy?"

"I hope so but with so much damage, I can't make any promises."

"Cause of death?"

"Tricky. You got multiple bite wounds to seventy-five percent of the body. Massive injuries to the head, neck and extremities. More here to the torso, followed by dismemberment. Difficult to determine a C.O.D." Caroline tilted the dead woman's chin, exposing the carnage at the throat. "For now, I'd say blood loss. The trauma here at the jugular and carotid. She bled out."

Gallagher stitched his brow. "So the dogs killed her?"

"It appears that way, but there's damage to the skull here." The medical examiner pointed to the jellied blood on the back of the skull. "Blunt force. It may have occurred during the attack."

"Or prior to?"

Caroline agreed. She righted the woman's head, returning the dead stare to the ceiling.

Lara shuddered. Just the idea of it, devoured by dogs. "Can you tell what kind of dogs attacked her? Or how many?"

"It's impossible to determine the breed of dog but I found the bite radius of at least four different dogs. These were big, I can tell you that. There's also— " Caroline broke off, her brow knotted up.

Gallagher leaned forward. "What is it?"

"This." Caroline pointed to a wound on the ribs. Gallagher just blinked at it, the torn flesh looked the same as all the rest. "This wound is much larger than the others."

Lara took a closer look but, like her partner, couldn't distinguish one wound from another. "Another bite mark?"

"Too big. Has to be something else. A dull weapon maybe?"

Gallagher broke in. "What if it is teeth?"

"Then you got one big animal on your hands."

The desk phone rang. Caroline excused herself to get it. Gallagher leaned over the face, the raw pull of exposed muscle and bone. The eyes cloudy and without warmth.

Lara wanted to sit, still finding her sea legs but there were no chairs. "Have you ever seen anything like this?"

"I've seen people mauled by their own dogs. Assholes bit up at dog-fights. But this, eaten up the way she is? This is a first."

Caroline came back with a sheet of paper. "I got her prints. The thumb was too damaged but the index and middle fingers were clean."

"Thanks. You check under the nails?"

"Scraped and sent to the lab. I'll let you know what we find."

BACK to precinct and up to homicide, where Gallagher shared cubicle space with Detective Roberts. He fed the prints into the system. Lara took Roberts's empty chair and used his desktop to write the initial report. Gallagher finished up, looked at her. "Don't get too comfortable in that chair," he said. Then he left without another word.

Lara scanned through her notes, sorting it all out before typing anything. Knocking out a good report was tricky, sifting pages of hurried notes and crafting it into a succinct summation of a crime. Be concise but most of all be brief. People hated reading anything, most of all your superiors, and they resented you for putting it on their desk. Anything over two pages and you can expect an email instructing your dumb ass to get to the point and leave the writing to fucking Shakespeare.

There were two photos on Roberts's desk, both of his wife and three kids (two boys, one girl). A Father's Day card made from orange construction paper and pinned to the cubicle wall. Two cartoons clipped from the Oregonian, neither of them funny. A favorite coffee mug and a metal spur paperweight, a souvenir from a trip to Arizona. A working detective's desk, nothing more.

Both desks butted up in the cramped space. Gallagher's desk was clean and without clutter. Paperwork filed and binders squared up neatly to the wall. There were no photos, no unfunny cartoons nor tacky souvenirs. The desk looked unused, like something out of a catalogue.

"You finished yet?" Gallagher lumbered back, spitting pink sprinkles from the donut he was chewing.

"Almost."

"Wrap it up, huh. Leave the writing to Vonnegut."

"You like Vonnegut?"

"Hey." He sat up straight, seeing what lit up on his screen. "We got a hit."

The database returned a match on the prints. A harshly lit DMV photograph of a woman. Pale and drawn, she looked to be in her late forties. Gallagher gleaned the pertinent details. "Elizabeth Riley, age forty-two. No criminal record, no occupation. Nothing."

"Then why is she in the system?"

"Who knows." Gallagher jotted down a few notes.

"There's an address. We can start there."

"I'll do that," he said. "Round up a few uniforms and canvass the area where the body was found."

"We should both check her place. Two eyes and all that."

"No, we split the work. No sense getting cozy." He rose. "You file that request yet?"

"I'm writing it up."

"Good." He headed for the door.

7

THE DECEASED WOMAN'S APARTMENT was up on the 8800 block of North Edison, where it crossed Baltimore. Elizabeth Riley lived in a dumpy low rise with a battered intercom box and two yellowed stovetops stacked outside the front entrance. The Super was an uncooperative prick in moldy flip-flops who bitched until Gallagher mentioned the sour tang of weed drifting out of his basement burrow. The prick got the keys and lead Gallagher up to a door on the second floor.

Gallagher waited while the guy squinted at the labels on each key. "You ever see a boyfriend hanging around? Any friends or family"

"I dunno anything about these people." He separated a key, tried it. "How soon can I clear her shit outta here?"

"You know she's dead, right?"

The guy shrugged. "And now I got an empty unit that needs to be rented."

Gallagher crowded the man, stepping on his flip-flops. "How about I plaster that door with police tape until you fucking die?"

The lock popped. The Super pushed the door open then slunk away. Gallagher stepped inside and scanned round the small room. What a shithole.

He tossed the entire place within the hour and came up with nothing. No personal info, no private phone book, not even a laptop. Any identification she possessed, she must have had on her. Meaning it was lost. He flopped down onto the couch. What had he missed?

His cell rang. The caller ID read Cheryl. He grimaced. "Cheryl, what's up?"

"You need to come get her." The voice on the other end was sharp.

"I'm picking her up Sunday."

"I'm bumping you up. When can you get here?"

Stick to the damn routine, woman. That's what he wanted to say. "What happened?"

"I don't have time to go into it right now. How soon can you be here?"

"I'm on the clock, Cheryl."

"John..."

"Two hours." She groused. He hung up, stretched his feet onto the coffee table. Did he have time for a ten-minute nap? Tilted his wrist to see the watch face. Yup.

LARA pulled the victim's photo and details into a police flyer and printed copies. She found a uniformed officer named Lee, bored with deskwork. He agreed to help her with the canvassing, anything to get out of the precinct.

There wasn't a lot to canvass, considering where the body was found. An auto body shop, a warehouse and a small marina south of the bridge but no one there remembered seeing the woman. North of the bridge was a strip club called The Devil's Backside. The bar staff were less than helpful and the daytime drinkers downright hostile. Lara stepped out of the bar, shielding her eyes from the sun after the gloomy interior of the bar.

Officer Lee smoothed a flyer against a post and staple-gunned it into place. Looked her way. "Where to now, detective?"

"Next dive up the road. Start all over."

They climbed back into the car. She keyed the ignition, said, "Thanks for giving me a hand with this."

"No problem." He squared up another handful of flyers. "Shouldn't your partner be doing this with you?"

"You'd think."

CHERYL lived out near Tabor Park in a pretty colonial with blue trim and a front garden of native plants. Gallagher wheeled into the driveway, bopped the horn once and watched the windows for movement.

He drummed his fingers on the wheel, waiting. Cheryl was going to make him ring the bell, he knew it. He has to drop everything and rush over here but she's gonna make him wait? He hated this, this stupid brinkmanship that just came naturally with shared parenting.

Hell with it. He climbed out of the truck, having forfeited his pride a long time ago. The front door opened just as he strode up the stone pathway. His daughter stepped outside.

Amy Gallagher was sixteen years old. She looked a lot like her mom but you could still see a little of her old man in there. There, in the angry lines stitching up her forehead as she dragged a lumpy hockey bag behind her.

Gallagher took the bag from her and tossed it into the back. Amy hauled her backpack across her knees and Gallagher reversed back out the driveway. The front door closed without a glimpse of Cheryl.

Gallagher turned out of the neighborhood and glanced at his daughter. He knew by the set of her mouth and the crossed arms that she wasn't going to speak first. More brinkmanship. He simply didn't have the energy for it anymore, so he spoke up. "You want to tell me what happened or do I gotta ease into it with small talk?"

Amy watched the street, houses blurring past through the rain-spackled window. "Neither," she said. Trying to abort the chitchat with her tone.

"Okay."

Silence filled up the cab and rain dotted the windshield again.

He caved. "You hungry?"

"Sorta." She finally looked at him, grateful for the change in topic. "I-Hop?"

He smiled. Shrugged up an affirmative and took the next left.

RASPBERRY pancakes with whip cream. Eggs, toast and bacon. They sat near the window and he asked about school. She said it was fine. The school could have burnt to the ground in an apocalyptic fire and her answer would have been the same. Fine.

"How's basketball?" Amy played small forward.

Amy swirled a hunk of pancake in the syrup. "I got a game coming up."

"I know. You working the drills like we practiced?"

"Yeah. Sorta. I got pummeled last game by this bigass dyke."

"You gotta work on your Spidey-sense. Keep your eye on the action but be aware of the bruisers looking to take your head off." He mopped up the egg yolk with his toast. "So what were you and mom fighting about?"

"Nothing," she said. "Everything."

"That narrows it down."

"She's always riding me about homework and stuff. Like I don't have enough stress right now. You know what she's like."

"Yeah." He pushed his plate away. "But we both know that you goof off if someone isn't on you. Right?"

"Whatever."

Whatever. He wished he could take a pair of scissors and cut that word from her vocabulary forever. Gallagher had to remind himself to mind his temper every time he heard it. He leaned in and squared up her eyes. Meaning business. "What else? Come on, out with it."

"I dunno. It's Greg too. He's such a drip."

Greg was Cheryl's boyfriend. He was a drip, but he couldn't officially agree with his kid on that one. Play nice. Cheryl seemed happy with him. "What about him?"

"He's always on mom's side. About everything."

"He has to be. That's how it works." He patted her hand. "Listen, I know mom can be tough but she's not wrong. It just comes out wrong sometimes. Go easy on her, huh?"

The word 'whatever' was ready to spill from her lips but Amy checked herself. Instead she slurped her straw and switched gears. "I saw in the paper that that Gunwold guy got sentenced to twenty-five years. Good job."

Gunwold was a braindead waste who shot holes into his friend and his friend's woman over a bullshit amount of money. Gallagher worked the case hard and came down on the little bastard like a ton of bricks. That was three years ago, the sentencing came down last week.

"I didn't have anything to do with his sentencing."

"But that was your case. Cheers."

They got back in the truck and the starter squealed. It did that when it rained. Amy buckled up. "What are you working on now?"

The kid was always asking about work, wanting to know the gruesome details and petty motives. He used to take pride in that. How many kids are actually interested in what their old man does for a living? He even thought his daughter was interested in law enforcement, the apple rolling not too far from the tree, but that wasn't the case. She liked sharing the gory details with her friends. Like celebrity gossip, it was fun to speculate. A pack of Nancy Drews solving cases through hearsay and a teenager's understanding of psychology.

There were only two kinds of murders he told her about now, of which both had moved out of his influence on their path to righteous justice or complete farce. Cases that had finally gone to trial or those that the DA claimed he couldn't convict and thus dismissed. Sensitive cases too, involving a child, he kept mum about. But that never stopped the kid from trying. Amy read the crime section religiously, trying to guess which new murders her dad was working. It was a game.

"Nothing much," he said and they rode quiet all the way home. After the divorce, Gallagher had settled for the typical dad schedule of weekends and holidays. His work schedule was too erratic for anything else. How he hated it, slowly eroding from father to distant relative with his own kid. So when Amy turned thirteen, they changed up the schedule. Two weeks at mom's and two weeks at dad's. Amy was a responsible kid and Gallagher knew she'd be fine if he came home late. His partner, his boss, hell the whole detail knew that when it was his two weeks with his daughter, he had to be home by dinner time. The other guys ragged him about it but never got in his way. Half of them were already divorced and of the ones still married, half of those were hurtling blind towards divorce court too.

Crossing Fremont Street, Amy said, "I got some movies for us to watch. Borrowed them off Stella's dad. He's got, like, every western ever made."

"Have I met him?"

"Twice." She pulled a handful of DVDs from her backpack. "I got the kind you like too. Violence, crude language and nudity."

Gallagher silently thanked God his daughter had moved past her phase of watching musicals. If he had to sit through Grease one more time, he was gonna put a bullet through his head.

REGGIE pulled back the curtain and looked outside. His was a small room inside a boarding house and he had been here for two months. Reggie wasn't his real name, it was just the one he told people here. He was happy with the boarding house. It suited his needs. He figured he'd be safe here for a few months at least unless something came up.

Something came up.

A news item on the radio, half heard down in the common room. He told the other guys to shut up but he'd already missed it. He gave Perkins a dollar to go to the corner and get a newspaper for him. Reggie took it up to his room and locked the door. The news item said very little. A woman's body found near the river, the poor condition of her remains. The name was being withheld until family could be notified. Good luck with that, he thought.

Reggie would have to move. He was already hiding from the law, as were half the men in here. The rooming house was a good place for that but it wouldn't be enough now. Something more than the cops was looking for him and his stink was all over this place. It wouldn't be long before it tracked him here.

Reggie felt his throat tickle and swallowed, trying to stifle the cough. Didn't work. His cheeks blew out in a coughing jag that left him winded and blind. Reggie was a sick man and the task of diving even further underground might kill him.

8

LARA MENDES DROVE TO PRECINCT early to get a jump on the day. She packed a hastily made lunch into the fridge in the kitchen and watched the shift change. The graveyard shift was logging off and looking drained, shooting the shit with the detectives stumbling in for the day shift. The night shift was hell on the body but everybody did their rotation with a minimal amount of bellyaching and cursing. The transition was the worst, switching from days to nights and then back again. It left you foggy for days and Lara hated it. She said hello to the night crew and got ribbed a good deal about being the latest cherry on the crew. Detective Latimer, whom she initially pegged to be an asshole, was chatty and friendly in his exhaustion. Bingham, the impossibly good-looking one, was grouchy and withdrawn.

Gallagher was a no-show, his desk unoccupied, but she'd expected that. What she hadn't expected was to find Robertson's desk cleared of all personal items and his cabinets cleared of everything but the open cases. Her own box of personal stuff, the one she'd left abandoned on the floor, was sitting square on the now emptied and spotless desktop.

A post-it note clung to the box, scrawled in Lieutenant Vogel's peculiar script. Settle in, get to work.

Yes sir.

She organized her things but left the personal stuff in the box. She wanted to update the case file on the Riley woman but had little to add to it. No word from the M.E., the toxicology and trace reports still pending. The results of yesterday's canvassing could be summed up in one word; nada. She called up the Missing Persons file to see if anyone had reported Elizabeth Riley's disappearance but nothing materialized there. She drummed her nails on the desk about how to proceed next.

Shortly after ten, a call came in about a shooting out at Northeast 40th and Sandy. Rowe and Varadero picked it up, signed a car out of the garage and left. Things settled back down and Lara glared at Gallagher's empty chair. She tried the number she had for him but his cell was unavailable. How the hell could he have his phone off on a Wednesday morning?

She thought about the attack on Riley that ended her life. The idea of being devoured by dogs churned her guts. She hated dogs, always had, and the notion of dying that way went beyond revolting. But it led to an idea, something. Drawing up two windows, she searched through incident reports and 911 calls with the same query. Dog attacks. There was a man on SE Franklin, mauled by his own pit bull. A woman on Quimby bitten by her neighbor's Rottweiler. Two men severely injured by dogs at a suspected dog-fighting pit up in No Po. Nothing unusual stood out in the reports, all incidents involving one or two dogs and nothing approaching the ferocity of the attack on the Riley woman. She kept digging, working through the current year and deep into the previous year. She ate her lunch over her keyboard, still digging, but found nothing.

She gave up, rubbed her eyes and tried her partner's number again. It rang this time. Click. "Gallagher."

"Hey, it's Detective Mendes." The partner you abandoned, remember? "You coming into work today?"

"I am working. What's up?"

"I've worked every dead-end I can think of," she said. "Did you find anything at the victim's apartment?"

"Zip. No personal phone book, no computer, practically no mail. No names of friends or family. I don't think she'd been living at that shithole very long."

"Did you get all the other tenants? Someone must have known her."

"Nobody knows her. That's the usual response when a cop knocks on your door but these braindeads were being honest. This woman kept to herself."

"Let's canvass her neighborhood. Do every door within a five block radius."

"Recruit another uniform to give you a hand. Let me know what you find."

Lara looked at the phone like it smelled bad. "No. You come help. You're the primary, remember?"

"I'm busy. Keep me posted."

The guy just hung up. Lara tossed the phone back and ground her teeth. Screw this. She swiveled back to the keyboard and drew up a fresh document on department letterhead. She addressed it to Lieutenant Vogel, keyed down a few lines and wrote out an official request for a new partner.

NO uniformed officers were available so Lara hit the streets alone with a stack of fresh police flyers and knocked her knuckles raw. Working her way out in a circle from the dead woman's apartment block, Lara disturbed every door to find out no one knew the woman in the picture. She got lucky at the corner Kwiki-Mart where the guy behind the counter recognized the face on the police flyer. The deceased woman smoked Marlboro Lights, bought two packs every time she was in. That's it, the extent of the clerk's knowledge. Wow, Lara told herself on the way out. What a significant break in the case.

Sweet Hearts was a shitty bar four blocks from the vic's shitty apartment complex. Dimly lit with two TV screens and four daytime drinkers. Lara went to the bar and roused the woman working the taps from the paperback she was reading. Sliding the flyer across the bar, she went into the same preamble about the woman in the photograph. The bartender surprised Lara by admitting she knew her. When Lara told her the woman was deceased, the bartender dropped the flyer like it was contaminated. "She's dead?"

Lara rummaged up her notepad and a pen. The barkeep told her how the woman, Elizabeth Riley, came in almost every afternoon and always left before the place got busy with the happy hour crowd. She never said much. She came in, nursed a couple of glasses of draft and went home. Sometimes she'd curse at the TV or scratch away at lottery cards. Twice, the bartender remembered, she had complained about her ex-husband.

Lara latched onto that tiny piece of information. Elizabeth Riley was divorced?

The bartender had little to offer beyond that. The woman had grumbled about the divorce and how she had been screwed over by her ex but that was all. No names or details, just surly curses and then the woman would sink back into silence, muttering into her glass.

Lara slid her card across the bar and asked the woman to call if she remembered anything else. She posted the flyer on a wall near the restrooms and left.

LIKE before, a background check on Elizabeth Riley turned up nothing. There was no record of marriage or divorce. In fact, apart from the driver's license, there was no record of Elizabeth Riley at all. No social insurance number, no employment, no health records. How was that even possible?

The rest of the day was spent on the phone, being transferred from department to department, trying to get answers. She got nowhere. She remained on hold through the shift change and finally gave up when the city departments closed down for the day.

Detective James LaBayer buzzed her desk on his way home, asked if she was making out all right. LaBayer was a veteran homicide man with one of the best career closure rates in the detail. He had an easy smile and a warmth about him that made everyone want to be his friend. Even the bad guys.

His day had been kept busy with a stabbing up in North Portland. Some poor bastard got punctured twenty-two times in a dispute over drug money. LaBayer and his partner simply followed the blood drops down the alley and into an empty loading dock. The suspect was hunkered down lighting a bowl with blood still on his hands.

"That's what you call a dunker. Easy close." LaBayer looked over the paperwork on her desk. He knew the details of her case, the mutilated remains. Everyone knew, it was that gruesome. "Now, what you got, Mendes," he said, "is a stone cold whodunit."

"Can't argue with you," Lara smiled at him. "It's a dead weight that won't budge."

"There ought to be a rule about drawing your first homicide. I'm not saying every newbie should be handed a dunker but nobody deserves to pull a horrorshow like this the first jump out of the gate."

Lara loved LaBayer. He was like the favorite uncle in this weird family of cops. When he asked how she was getting along with her partner, she lied and said everything was fine. LaBayer knew Gallagher and knew she was lying but he didn't call her on it. Complaining about one's partner was unseemly and a sure way to bring scorn from every other body on the shop floor. She had seen Kopzyck do it just after starting in Sex Assault and the haranguing he'd gotten for it was cruel and relentless.

LaBayer knew she wouldn't make the same mistake but left the door open a little. "Gallagher can be a real pill. You want to talk, just drop by. Alright?"

Lara packed up her things wishing she had been partnered up with LaBayer instead of Mister Personality. On the drive home she thought of amending the request she'd drafted for a new partner, asking specifically to be partnered up with Detective James LaBayer. So what if he already had a partner? Maybe the Lieutenant would see the wisdom in switching the line-up. She'd sleep on it.

Driving back into work the next morning, Lara decided to do just that. It could backfire on her but any fallout from that couldn't be any worse than her situation now. Her plan to redraft the request was backburnered by a jigsaw piece waiting at her desk. A phone message from a city clerk she'd talked to yesterday. He had an answer to why Elizabeth Riley had no official history prior to June of 2008. The woman had changed her name and somewhere along the chain of paperwork, the records to her previous name had been lost. Misplaced, misfiled and chewed up in the creaky data files of an outdated system. Sorry, the clerk said. Click.

9

DECLERK WALKED. GALLAGHER SPIT when he heard the news, deciding then and there to just kill the motherfucker.

After he blubbered out his sob story to Lara Mendes, DeClerk got smart and lawyered up. No more questions. The lawyer made him recant and claim it was made under duress. The D.A. screamed at Gallagher over the phone, declaring it to be a shit case with shit evidence. Gallagher told him he was a pussy and promised to break his legs with a hammer next time he saw him. It was all bluster, Gallagher knew how skittish juries were. Skittish and stupid. To convince a jury of the shitbag's peers, you had to catch the bastard with a smoking gun and extract a full confession. Anything less, no matter how compelling, just would not sway those twelve bodies in the box. Add to that the insistence on DNA and fiber analysis they all wanted to hear. The pretty TV cops put away a creep a week with nothing more than a single pubic hair, these people in the jury box want to see the same here.

Raymond DeClerk was back on the streets, limping around in his parka and probably beating another woman senseless at this very moment. So to hell with it. Steal a gun out of the evidence room and blow a hole in the brain dead son of a bitch. Toss the piece in the Willamette and go home. Sleep the sleep of the righteous.

That was the plan at least. Instead, Gallagher spent the day haunting DeClerk. Watching him openly on the street and following him into stores. Eye-fucking him every time until Parka Man got the sweats and ran home to his mother's house.

Two hours sitting in the Cherokee watching the door but DeClerk didn't come out again. He went home and threw a pork loin on the barbecue while Amy made salad. They watched Pale Rider and munched popcorn. Amy spent half the movie texting her friends.

Sipping coffee the next morning, Gallagher went over the DeClerk case in his head. Trying to uncover something he'd missed, some thin wedge he could split open and crucify the prick. Nothing came. Even on the drive to work, bumpering up on the Burnside bridge to the westside, nothing came to him. A sickening truth flapped into his guts and nested for the winter. The Rae Dawn Munroe homicide would remain unsolved. An open case poisoning Gallagher's desk until it was archived in the cold room.

Turning a corner into his cubicle he damn near dropped the coffee in his hand. "What the hell is this?"

Robertson's desk was awash in loose paper and unorganized files. Photos of the Elizabeth Riley crime scene were pinned to the cubicle wall, along with the police flyer. Lara Mendes was busy hanging up a large city map. "Morning," she muttered through pushpins clenched in her teeth. "Nice of you join us today, detective."

"Look at this mess." Gallagher gathered up the stray paper that had migrated onto his pristine desk.

"Yeah, sorry. It kind of got away from me."

"No shit." He retrieved the paperwork waiting in his in-tray. Memos, policy changes, staff announcements. He tossed it wholesale into the recycling bin and turned his eyes to the rudimentary evidence board she had created. "What's all this?"

"Where have you been?" An edge to her tone.

"Went fishing. You gonna tell me what you got or do I gotta guess?"

"Couple of developments." Lara smoothed the edge. Still pissed but eager to share what she'd learned so far. "Our victim may as well be a Jane Doe. Two years ago, she legally changed her name to Elizabeth Riley. Unfortunately, her old identity got lost somewhere in the process."

"Brilliant."

"I chewed out a couple of department heads over it. They promised to look harder but I'm pretty sure they just wanted to get off the phone. I did, however, find a bartender who remembered our vic. According to her, Riley was divorced and bitter over it."

"Who's the ex-husband?" Gallagher sat on the edge of her desk, crumpling paper.

"Again, the records were lost and the bartender doesn't remember Riley ever mentioning his name."

"Too bad. We need to talk to him. Even if this isn't a homicide, we need him."

"It is a homicide. The ME report confirmed it."

"Where's the report?"

"Under your ass."

He straightened and rifled through the mess for the report. An envelope fell to the floor. He picked it up and looked at it. Sealed but unmarked. "What's this?"

"Request for a new partner."

"Good" He took a pushpin and fixed the envelope to the wall. Skimmed through the ME report, flipping pages quickly. An eyebrow went up. "Semen?"

"Yeah. They're trying to strain the DNA from it."

"Anything else in here?" His eyes went back to the report.

"Blood under the fingernails. The DNA will take a while but Caroline identified the blood types. It's in there."

"Type O blood, also canine blood and… what?"

"Yet to be determined," she said. "Blood sample that's neither human nor dog. She's working on it."

Gallagher scratched his chin, mulling it over. "So she's attacked, possibly raped. She fights the guy off, gets meat under her fingernails."

"But she's still alive when the dogs go at her," Lara outlined the rest. "She fights them off, getting dog blood under her nails."

"So the dogs actually killed her, not her attacker."

"Possibly."

Gallagher looked over the photos on the wall, then down to her desk. Sitting atop loose paper was a yellow legal pad scribbled with notes. Books lying open, pages dog-eared for bookmarks. "What is all this stuff?"

Lara shrugged. "Desperation. I'm trying to puzzle out our attacker."

He glanced over her notes. "A psych profile? Don't waste your time."

"There's the semen, right? Whether he paid for it or raped her, he attacks her when he's done. That speaks volumes. It suggests someone who hates women."

"It's guesswork. Where does it get you?"

She looked at him. Was he being funny? "It's an insight into our perp."

"It's flashy and the Lieutenant will love it but does it actually help us find the guy? No. Put your time elsewhere."

"Why be so narrow minded?" She lifted her hands, palms up. "We have nothing."

"We have a ton of leads on the tip line." He counted off the fingers of his left hand. "Two callers claim they did it and three more swear their neighbor did it. And you and I have to follow up every one of those concerned citizens."

Lara leaned back into the wall and crossed her arms. Going through the calls from the tip line was a tedious, hateful process. Like shoveling shit from a sitting position.

Gallagher smiled, loving nothing more than bursting expectations. "I got one dude who says he's the devil himself and he wants to tell us why did it." He fished a quarter from his pocket. "Wanna flip for it?"

THEY suffered through the messages on the tip line, each caller crazier than the last. Lara endured it, grinding her molars until her jaws ached. Half of the callers sounded drunk or strung out. What was wrong with these people? She understood having a beef with a neighbor or someone at work, but to call up a police info line and accuse them of murdering someone? She rubbed the bridge of her nose and went on to the next message. Three days into her inaugural homicide investigation and this was their only lead. These paranoid shut-ins with nothing better to do than watch the news and call Crime Stoppers hoping to make fifty bucks to rat out their serial killer, baby-kidnapping, dog kicking neighbors.

Gallagher grinned through it all, knowing full well she hated every minute of it. When they had screened every excruciating nutbar message, he divided up the callers between them. Now she had to actually talk to these people. Looking through the list, she realized he had given her the number for the guy who claimed to be the devil.

"Satan?" She held up the page to him. "Seriously? Can't you take this guy?"

"You got a problem talking to Mister Satan?"

"I'm Catholic." She couldn't think of anything else.

"All the more reason." He just laughed. A sinister, grating chuckle like some vaudeville diablo.

THE dogs came out at night, running as a pack along the banks of the river, through the empty industrial yards and over the loamy ground of the hillside. The alpha led them up the riverbank and onto the crushed stone of the railway line. Following the tracks into the city, they traveled unseen, unheard.

The wolf made forays off the tracks and onto the dark streets, nose in the air, filtering the stench of the city for one particular stink among the many. The dogs grew restless and bored. Fights broke out, one mangy animal challenging another over its place in the pack order. When the sky turned grey in the predawn hours, the pack trotted back up the rail line to the river, retreating to their den to sleep and wait.

RAIN pelted the streets into a soggy mire, an unending drizzle that crept into everyone's bones. The police flyers flapped in the wind and melted in the downpour, the photo of the dead woman shredding into a grey sludge down the creosote poles.

Gallagher watched the rain rivulet down the window, working his way through the tipline but each caller turned out to be flake. Lonely or bored or just wanting attention. Something to break up the drone of the day.

When he had time, he kept his vigil outside of Raymond DeClerk's mother's house. He'd park right out front and watch the front windows. A curtain would fold back and he knew DeClerk saw him out here. The shitbag stayed inside and sent his mom limping out to the Kwiki-Mart for smokes. Small comfort though. The case had dissolved to nothing and there was nothing left to do. Add to that the stone-cold Riley homicide and Gallagher now had two open cases on his desk, ruining his run of six consecutive closures.

His phone went off. Lieutenant Vogel wanted an update on this "dead woman and dog file" and he wanted it now. Gallagher groaned but wasn't in a position to piss off the big man any further. Said he was on his way.

He took one last look at the house and then turned the ignition.

LIEUTENANT Vogel propped an elbow on the cubicle wall, dwarfing everything around him. His mouth soured, unhappy with what he was hearing.

Lara avoided her boss's eyes. A school kid with unfinished homework. Gallagher slouched in his chair, nonchalant as he explained how their case turned to shit in their hands.

"So you got nothing." Lieutenant Vogel remained unfazed. Foremost among the cops in Homicide Detail, he was a magnet for bad news.

"We searched the area, canvassed the neighborhood and followed up every wingnut on the tip line." Gallagher shrugged in surrender. "Nothing."

"We're still waiting on DNA." Lara spoke up, unwilling to let it be a complete disaster. "We might get a hit when it's put into the system."

"Yeah and I might win the lottery," Vogel said. "You've gone three, four days? Any chance of solving this is evaporating fast."

Gallagher stretched out his legs. "Yup."

The Lieutenant looked over the chaos of Lara's workspace. "Do you always keep such a clean house, Mendes?"

"Sorry." Turning red. "I'm trying to build a profile on our perp."

"Really?" Vogel perked up at that, glancing over her evidence board. When he spoke, he spoke to her but squared his eyes on her partner. "Now that shows initiative."

Gallagher beamed at his Lieutenant, as if proud of his own lack of initiative. It was his personal mission to drive Vogel batshit until the big man popped a blood vessel and keeled over. "Too bad it stalled out too. But there was one interesting development." Gallagher shot to his feet and plucked the unmarked envelope off the wall. Her official request for a new partner. He crunched it into Lara's palm and folded her fingers around it. He smiled at her. "Detective?"

Vogel straightened, hopeful for any fragile snowflake of good news.

"It needs work." Lara opened a drawer, tossed the envelope in and shut the drawer. She watched Gallagher's grin drop from his face. Vogel simply looked sad.

The desk phone chimed. Lara picked it up.

Lieutenant Vogel chin-wagged towards the aisle, waving at Gallagher to follow. They went to the kitchen where Vogel searched for a clean glass. "How's detective Mendes working out?"

"She's all right."

"Just all right?"

"She's good. Thorough, persistent." Gallagher rifled through the fridge, other cop's lunches. Found a banana with the name "Bingham" written on the skin in Sharpie. "But there's a personality conflict. I'm no good mentoring these kids."

Vogel searched cupboard after cupboard but there was never clean glassware. "Make do."

Gallagher went on, a wad of banana bulging his cheek. "You know who's good at this? LaBayer. He loves teaching. He and Mendes would get along great."

"LaBayer's busy. Deal with what you got. Is there any water in there?"

Gallagher fished out a bottle of water, also marked "Bingham", and tossed it to his boss. The big man said thanks and left.

Gallagher looked out the window. The rain had stopped. He didn't hear Lara come in behind him.

"The animal shelter called," she said. "They finished with the dog."

"The carcass near the body?"

"The same." Lara jangled a set of keys. "I'm heading up there. Are you coming?"

"Sure. Hold this."

He handed her the half-eaten banana and left the kitchen, passing Latimer and Bingham on their way in. Bingham looked at her.

"Are you eating my lunch?"

10

TRAFFIC HAD STALLED UP THE HIGHWAY so Lara shot over to Martin Luther King and headed north. Gallagher sat shotgun. Neither spoke, listening to the dispatcher call out the make and model of a stolen car.

"We had an agreement." Gallagher broke the ice.

Lara swerved around a cube van. Said nothing.

He went on. "You were going to request another partner. Remember? We agreed."

"Not with a case going cold. It will look like I'm giving up."

"What, you worried about your wunderkind status?"

She gritted her teeth. "Why don't you ask for a new partner?"

"Missing the point, chief. I don't want a partner."

"Right." Lara took the Lombard exit. "You're the cowboy."

BARKING dogs. Just the sound of it and Lara wanted to turn around and walk back out the door. When they pulled up to the Multnomah County Animal Shelter, Gallagher said he knew the head guy, Pablo somebody or other. The woman at the front desk waved them through and Gallagher was already opening the door to the kennels.

It was loud in the lobby but inside the kennel, it was deafening. A long galley of pens running both sides of a big space where the noise bounced off the cinderblock walls. Each pen had a metal grate door, snouts poking through the mesh. German Shepherds barked and paced their pens. A Dachshund and two labs coiled up, sleeping through the racket. A pit bull, chin on the floor, watching everything. A Dalmatian limped round its pen in never-ending circles, unable to lie or sit.

Lara winced at the crack of each bark, loathing every minute of it. Her revulsion of dogs was deep, maybe irrational, but there it was just the same. And the smell wasn't helping matters, dog urine and disinfectant.

A man in a stained lab coat knelt before a cage at the far end of the hall. Tall, black, with dreadlocks trailing down the back of his lab coat. Beside him stood a teenage girl, a volunteer, listening intently to his instructions.

"Pablo!" Gallagher hailed the guy but his voice was lost in the din. He walked over and waved when the man looked up. Pablo straightened up, said something to the volunteer then met Gallagher halfway.

"Hey G." Pablo shook the detective's hand. "How's business?"

"Booming." Gallagher yelled back. "How do you work in this noise?"

Pablo pulled a spongy tube from his ear. "These. The kind musicians use." He chin-wagged at something behind Gallagher. "Hey, is she okay?"

Lara stayed near the double doors. Ramrod straight, trying to keep her cool around all of these crazed dogs.

Gallagher grinned. "She's more of a cat person. Is there somewhere else we can talk?"

They went back out to the lobby, where the air was cooler and considerably less rank. Lara shook off the goose-flesh, hating herself for being paralyzed like that. How could anyone work in all that chaos?

"Do you want to see it?" Pablo turned to both of them.

"The carcass? No. Just gimme the details."

Pablo stepped past Gallagher, extending his hand to Lara. "I'm Pablo, by the way. You working with this ill-mannered lout?"

"Unfortunately," she said. Charmed. "Detective Mendes. Did you perform the autopsy on the animal?"

"No, Stella did. She's the expert in that department. But I have her report." Pablo handed her a copy. "This was a Staffordshire Boxer mix. Male, about three years old."

"What's that in dog years?" Lara didn't know from dogs. "Still a pup?"

"More like a teenager. Aggressive, with a hell of a chomp. We checked the stomach contents and found human tissue. But if you need the DNA profile, you'll have to send it to the lab yourself." Pablo shrugged. "We just don't have the budget for that kind of stuff."

"Was there anything wrong with this dog?" Gallagher asked. "Did it have rabies or something?"

"No. No distemper either. There was no ID chip, so it was possibly a stray."

"Have you ever seen anything like this?" Lara looked up from the report. "A pack of dogs killing and eating someone?"

"I've seen dogs and cats chew on their owners after death. You know, trapped in an apartment with their dead owners and starving. But this, dogs stalking and devouring a person? Never. That's something wild animals do. Wolves and coyotes, you know?"

The doors swung open and the teenage volunteer came out leading a shorthaired terrier. Pablo excused himself and went to help return the dog to a mom and daughter. Gallagher watched the family coo over the animal.

Lara stepped away, eyes drawn to a wall decorated with flyers for missing pets. A Collie named Rocky and a cat named Mephisto. Photos and contact information. Some flyers offered rewards, others simply bargaining on the kindness of strangers. Typed up neatly or scrawled in marker, each bill pleading for their pets to come home. Hundreds of them, running the length of the wall.

Lara read one after another, noting the sadness in some pleas, the perfunctory in others. Something nagged in her head about it all. Where were all these dogs and cats now? Were they dead in a ditch somewhere or shivering and dehydrated far from home? Were they taken in by someone kind or snatched up as bait for a dog-fighting pit? "Gallagher? Take a look at this."

He crossed the floor. Ran his eyes over the lost pets. Daisy, Muffin, Oswald, Killer, Freddy. "Did you lose your cat?"

"Look at all these animals," she said. "What if we're wrong about the dogs that mutilated the vic? We just assumed they were strays. What if they actually belonged to someone?"

"The perp?"

"He used them to cover his tracks. Eat the evidence."

Gallagher scanned through the snapshots of lost dogs. He turned and hollered at his friend. "Pablo? You get complaints here, yeah? People calling about their neighbor's dogs and whatever?"

Pablo came up, wiping his hands on a rag. "All the time."

"Any complaints about an asshole with a lot of dogs? Big ones. I mean, anything out of the ordinary?"

"We get calls about pit fights, breeding pens. Offhand, I can't think of anything unusual."

Lara brightened at the prospect of a lead. Any lead. "Do you log those calls?"

Pablo stuffed the rag into a back pocket. "We have to."

"Can we see them?"

PABLO led them to his office and called up the complaint log on a lethargic desktop. The calls were logged as they came in; date, time, location and the name and number of the caller. Not everyone offered their name. Following those details were the nature of the complaint, notes on any call-back and whether the complaint was investigated. If investigated, the name of the humane officer was listed along with their report.

The log went back six months. And it was huge. Some days they logged as many as twenty calls a day, other days just a few. The log was chronological, with no way to narrow the search by animal type or location. No way to make it a quick job.

"Christ." Gallagher peered over Lara's shoulder. "We're gonna be here all day."

He's already looking for an excuse to leave, she thought. "I can do this if you need to be somewhere. But you'll have to pick me up later if you take the car."

"We got nothing else to push, let's do this." He pulled up a chair. "You go through the list, I'll start calling anybody you red-flag."

They were actually going to work together? She stopped and looked right at him. It caught him off guard. "What?"

She went to work, plowing threw the catalogue of complaints. He made two calls into precinct then put his phone away. Watched Mendes scroll down the call log but he couldn't sit still. He ducked out.

Back in the kennels, walking the row of cages. A Pinscher barked at him and a Collie slept. The crazed Dalmatian kept circling its pen. A long-eared Bluetick hound thumped its tail on the floor as he passed by. Gallagher kneeled down and the hound licked his fingers through the cage. He had wanted a dog for a long time but the timing was never right. Getting one when Amy was younger seemed a bad idea for a struggling single parent and now that she was older, neither of them were home enough to look after one properly. The poor dog would die of loneliness or boredom. But maybe a dog like this would be better. An older dog who wouldn't tear the place apart the way a rambunctious puppy would.

The teenage volunteer was sweeping out a pen. He hollered at her. "Hey! What's the story on this old hound? Is he looking for a home?"

"No," she said. "Samson got lucky. We found his owners. They're picking him up today. Isn't that great?"

When he got back to the little office, Mendes was gone. The computer abandoned. A pad of paper lay next to the mouse, scribbled with notes. He skimmed through it. Names and addresses, a few scattered question marks.

"Hey" Lara swung back into the room, uncapping a bottle of water.

"I thought you ran out on me."

"I needed some air. The smell in here."

"What is it with you and dogs anyway?"

"I just don't like them. Never have."

He looked at her. "You keep yourself buttoned up tight, don't you?"

"What do you want, a sob story?"

"God no." He wagged the notepad at her. "You find anything?"

"You thought our tip line was bad? You wouldn't believe the nonsense that comes into this place. People call in to complain about dog crap on the sidewalk. Not once in a while, I mean nonstop. There must be a dozen calls about that alone every day." She wagged her chin in disbelief. "And here I am, complaining about the complainers. It's contagious."

He eased up a little. The kid made a funny, maybe she wasn't all bad. "So what'd you find?"

"A couple of possibles popped up, may be worth a call back. Then this showed up." She circled an entry at the bottom of the notepad. "A complaint about a pack of dogs running wild up near the industrial yards."

"Not that far from our crime scene."

"A coincidence, maybe. But then I found this." She flipped the page and circled another entry. "Two days earlier, someone called in about a vagrant squatting in that area. And the squatter has a bunch of mangy pit bulls with him."

He took the pad from her. "Did Pablo send someone out to check it out?"

"Twice. No sign of the vagrant or the dogs."

Gallagher straightened at that. "What's the address?"

II

NORTH TERMINAL ROAD WINDS a path through industrial yards and scrub oak. Squat buildings and pot-holed gravel lots hemmed in by chain link fence. Broken pavement thudded under their tires as they drove past empty structures and ghost industries. The ground hollowed out and poisoned.

Lara slowed as they rumbled past a yard of sea crates. Gallagher rode shotgun, scanning the road. A few trucks passed them, then one car. No pedestrians.

"What are we looking for?"

"Dunno. Dogs running loose. A squatter's camp." He eye-balled his side of the road. Flat topped bunkers of cinderblock, a Quonset hut. "Slow down."

Lara coasted to a crawl and lowered her window.

"There."

She pulled to the shoulder and leaned in to see what he was pointing at. A dog slunk out from the shadow of a tree and trotted across the road and vanished into shade again.

"See where he goes."

She rolled forward into a gravel lot, the tires sloshing through potholes. The dog stepped into the sunlight again, ambling lazily through a patch of weeds. It stopped when it heard the car. Turned its head to them, tongue swinging. Gallagher couldn't make out the breed from here. It was ugly, big. The dog went on, moving northeast until it vanished into another shadow.

Lara kept a slow momentum, careful not to spook the animal. They rolled under the shade trees but the dog was gone. Just the empty road, not even a road. "We lost it."

"Keep going. Let's see what's back here."

Bleeding out from behind a stand of pines stood a small bungalow. Old and unused, the paint peeling and the porch listing badly. The windows were crossed with duct tape, a cartoonish appearance of dead eyes.

Lara studied the house. "Cute."

Movement on the porch. A dog rose up out of nothing. Not the dog they trailed but some other dog. Some other bastard breed. The dog watched the car, mouth closed. It padded down the steps and stood in the crabgrass. Hair rising up its back.

"He looks friendly." Gallagher popped his door handle.

Lara stopped him. "He looks rabid. Let's call animal control. They can take care of it."

"And what, sit here for an hour while they mosey on over?" He pushed the door open and stepped out. His right palm balancing over the butt of the service issue on his belt. When he straightened up, the dog was gone. "Where'd he go?"

"Took off behind the house."

Gallagher closed the door and crossed the yard.

Lara stayed under the wheel. Shit. The last thing she wanted was more dogs. Especially these big, ugly mothers here. But the cowboy stood at the bottom porch step, looking back her way. She bit down and got out.

They clomped up the porch, stretching over the third step which had rotted clean through. Gallagher banged on the door. "Police! Open the door, please!"

No answer, no noise. Lara peered into the window. Dark.

Noise spun their heads round in unison. The dogs were back, the one they'd followed and the one risen from its vigil on the porch. A third dog was with them, this one a pure pit bull. The dogs trotted back and forth across the yard, sniffing the air. One barked, then they all barked. Guttural snaps at intruders on their territory. The dogs paced, knocking into one another, but did not advance.

"Bold fuckers, aren't they?" Gallagher watched them from his vantage.

Lara unsnapped the holster. She fought back the urge to unsheathe and just start shooting.

"Oh look," said Gallagher, turning back to the entrance. "The door's open." He punched his elbow through the small plate window. The glass snapped and he bashed out the remaining shards, knocking the frame free of glass.

"Whoa," she said."We don't have a warrant."

"What warrant? The door just happened to be open, so we took a look." He reached through the frame and groped for the lock.

"Stop. We're not cutting corners—"

A roar from inside cut her off. Gallagher snapped his arm back. A snout shot through the window frame, teeth catching his sleeve. The dog inside the house shook its head savagely. Would not let go. Gallagher yanked his gun and cracked it hard across the nose until the dog let go.

Nails skittering across the floor, the dog was gone. Gallagher looked at his torn sleeve, checked his arm. No blood.

"Son of a bitch."

"Are you alright?" She took his arm. "Let me see."

"He didn't break the skin." He peered through the broken frame. Nothing moved within. He reached back inside, turned the lock and withdrew quickly. Pushed the door open.

"Gallagher, we need to do this right or not at all."

"You want to stay out here with them?" He chin-cocked the dogs pacing the front yard and went through. The dogs barked. She stepped over the threshold.

It was dark. Curtains drawn, the windows yellow squares in the gloom. The air was stale and ripe with animal smells. A foyer that opened onto a living room on the left, a kitchen on the right. A hallway with doors, then stairs to the basement.

Gallagher swept the living room. A torn up sofa, its padding bleeding out. Trash over the scuffed floors, more of it on the coffee table. Cartons of rotting takeout and crushed beer cans. A hockey stick propped up in the corner. Flies buzzed the room, dotting the window. The TV was on, flickering pale light over the filth. Grainy porn played onscreen. Three naked men, grunting in Russian, held a woman down on a bed.

"This is rank." She covered her nose.

"Ten bucks says there's severed heads in the icebox." He tried the lightswitch but the overhead stayed dark. Burnt or disconnected. "We need a flashlight."

"Gloves too." She looked back to the front door. "In the car."

"Stay here."

A racket rose from the back of the house. Thuds. Skittering claws. Barking. Dogs roared up the back steps and charged into the narrow hallway. Three, maybe four vicious looking animals. Jaws popping.

Lara drew her weapon. More goddamn dogs.

Gallagher snatched up the hockey stick and charged, hollering and swinging the stick like some crazy person. "Get outta here! GET!"

The dogs backpedalled, confused and cowed. Gallagher smacked the nearest hard across the snout. It scrambled for the back, the other two skittered through an open door. He pulled the door shut, trapping the dogs inside a bedroom. A clattering sound further down as the others sailed through the backdoor.

Lara swung the barrel down and held her breath. Muffled barking from the closed room but that was all. Her hand was shaky from gripping the gun so tight.

"Those mutts come back," he said, "just start shooting."

He went out the door, came back with two Maglites and latex gloves. They searched the house.

She cleared the kitchen, finding more trash and flies. Bowls of dog food on the floor, kibble scattered across the linoleum. She couldn't step anywhere without crunching it underfoot. She sifted through the trash on the small table but found nothing useful. The dusty cupboards held a few dishes, a can of wasp killer. The fridge last. She gripped the chrome handle and scenes from a dozen horror movies flickered through her imagination. What one finds in the refrigerator.

The interior bulb was burnt out. It stank but all it held was rancid leftovers and cloudy jars. Two cans of Pabst, still in the plastic ring.

Gallagher checked the room off the hallway. Wire hangers on the floor, dust. A crucifix on the wall, hung over a bed that was no longer there. He skipped the room where he had trapped the crazy dogs. They scratched at the wood, noses snorting the crack under the door.

He played the flashlight over the dark bathroom. The sink and backsplash were filthy with some dark stain. He touched it. Black and brittle, it flaked away under his finger-tip.

They reconnoitered at the back stairwell. "No heads in the icebox," she said. "You owe me ten."

"Maybe he's got a meat freezer in the basement."

She tried the wall switch. Nothing. Wooden steps scaled down into the darkness.

The stairs creaked, a groove worn into the wood. Their beams didn't travel far, tubes of dust in the air. Lara swung her light up. Pipes and wires exposed between the joists. Her first thought was asbestos.

They moved apart, splitting the search. The walls were damp, beads of moisture on the cinderblock. Broken furniture crowded the floor space, a maze of chair spindles and chipped cabinets.

Lara wound through the junk, working towards the front of the house. A card table and chair nestled under the cob-webbed window. On the table, a cracked lamp and a note-book. Cheap school supply with a flimsy black cover. A pen folded inside. She prodded the notebook open to where the pen held. Scribbled notes, cramped and difficult to decipher. She turned the pages. More fevered script, the dense blocks of text separated by a symbol; a star inside a circle. There was a name for this symbol but it escaped her. Lara blinked, understanding what it was.

The cheap little notebook was a journal.

GALLAGHER scoured the south half of the cellar. Junk and little else. Then his light caught the chains. Heavy gauge link, suspended from the ceiling and trailing down about waist high. Two lengths of it, each chain ending in an iron cuff. Not slim like police bracelets but wide and thick, fastened together with a simple cotter pin.

More chain on the floor, coiled up and kicked under his feet. Attached to something at the end. He lifted the chain and threw his light over a girth of tooled leather and metal chink. Some kind of harness or restraint.

"Chains and leather, huh?" He let it fall to the floor. "How original."

The throw of light played into the deeper corners. An oil stained workbench hugged the wall, tools scattered overtop. Clamps and awls, cast iron tongs and a benchvise. The whole stinking cellar felt like some kind of medieval torture chamber.

Air blew in through the broken basement window, the breeze riffling pictures tacked to the wall. Pages torn from wank mags. Dull-eyed women cupping overflowing boobs. Scattered among these were pages from a children's book of bible stories. Soft focus illustrations of Mary and Jesus. John with the lambs and Daniel petting lions. The cheeseball sacred and the pedestrian profane.

Gallagher leaned and spit onto the concrete. "Well, well, well. Aren't we complicated."

A slash of red picked up in the light. His first thought was blood but it was too shiny. Just paint. Pulling back, the slash became an arced line of graffiti. It was big, a red circle some four feet in diameter. Within the ring, a crude star with five points. The pain splashed on thick and careless, running rivulets down the cinderblock. It tripped a memory, something on a record cover when he was a kid. Black Sabbath, Alice Cooper, stuff like that.

Lara's voice called out from the far side of the basement. He squeezed past the upright tables and bed frames until he found her sitting at the little card table under the window. Reading something.

"Look at this." She held the notebook up for him to see. He shrugged, all Greek to him. "It's a journal," she said.

"Like a diary? Who are we looking for, a twelve year old girl?"

"Look at this," she said, impatient for him to understand. "Most of this is illegible but I could read bits here and there. This guy, whoever he is, he describes an affliction he can't control. One he's powerless to stop. He refers to it as a curse."

Suspended over the table was a crate nailed into the wall, a hackjob shelf. Filed onto it were more of the same cheap notebooks. He took one down, flipped through it. "There's more here."

"Six in all." She glanced up from the pages, her brow creased. "This curse he describes? He fights it off and pushes it down, trying to control it. But it builds and builds until he can't fight it anymore. He explodes."

Antennae unfolded from Gallagher's brain. "Then what?"

"He blacks out. Wakes up covered in blood. Then he's sick with shame and self-loathing."

"Get outta here." This had to be bullshit. Dunkers like this don't exist. And they sure as hell don't just drop in your lap.

"Look closer." She laid the notebook on the table and turned the pages. "There are no dates anywhere but let's assume that each block of text separated by this weird symbol is an entry. Let's also assume an entry a day. When was Elizabeth Riley killed? Best estimate."

"Seven to twelve days ago. Maybe more."

She turned to the last entry and flipped backwards, counting down the entries. "The last blackout period he describes was nine entries ago. Nine days, maybe ten if he takes Sundays off."

Lara straightened her back. Eat that. Gallagher riffled the pages, counting the entries himself. Impressed as hell at what she'd found but damned if he would let her see that. You gotta keep the young guns in line, otherwise they run giddy and trip over their six-shooters.

"Okay," he allowed.

"Okay?" She spit it back at him. Was he completely dense? "Don't you get it? This is smoking gun territory, Gallagher. Look at it!"

"Put it back."

"What?"

"How did you find this?"

She closed the notebook and squared it up on the table. "Like this."

He wrapped his hand round her bicep. "Time to do it your way." He beckoned towards the stairs. "We get a warrant and seal this place off."

12

THE SKY WAS DARK WHEN THEY CAME out of the decrepit little house. More rain coming. Of the dogs there was no sign.

"Can we call ahead, get things moving?" Lara dug for the car keys. "Maybe LaBayer can write up the warrant and have it ready to go."

"Yeah. Except one of us needs to stay here and seal off the site. Keep an eye open if this guy comes back."

Lara stopped cold. No way did she want to stay here alone. "Who goes, who stays?"

He crossed the yard to the car. "Depends which judge we're going after for a signature. You friendly with any of them?"

No response. He turned, saw her staring past him. "Mendes?"

"Behind you." She pointed. "Up the road."

A man stood in the distance.

Fifteen, maybe twenty yards up the dirt path. Little more than a silhouette in this light. Tall and bearded, his face hidden under the hood of his tattered raincoat. A dog stood at attention at his knees, as still as the man. It was big. Gallagher guessed it to be a Husky. The man watched them. He didn't move.

Gallagher moved away from the car and into the road, facing the stranger. Like a scene in a Western, two hombres staring each other down. He half expected the man to reach for his six-guns.

"Easy." Lara's voice was quiet. "Don't spook him."

The man moved. Turned and marched away with long strides. The dog at his heels.

Gallagher went after him. "Hey!"

The man broke into a run. Disappeared into a stand of trees. Gallagher hollered back to Lara. "Get the car!"

Gallagher sprinted after him, turned into the trees. Through a ditch and up the other side. A gravel lot of puddles and pot-holes. Two low buildings and a fence. No sign of the creep.

A clang. Gallagher zeroed in on the noise. The man squeezed through a seam in the chain-link, holding it open for the dog to jump through. Fast motherfucker.

LARA slammed the car into gear and took off, spitting gravel behind her. She gunned it past the trees and further down where the fence opened onto a lot.

She caught a blur of Gallagher hoofing it across the gravel and spun towards him. The car bounced hard over the pot-holes, forcing her to slow down. She didn't see anything, no movement, no man—

There. Bounding from behind a shed, the man and the dog. Both hurtling fast into the open. She gunned the engine, steering right at him.

The spooky man changed direction and ran right at her. Charging the car in a game of chicken. Jesus. She was going to splatter the crazy bastard. She braked.

The man leaped and stomped up over the hood. Dented the roof and rolled down the trunk. A blur in the rearview mirror. The man sprawled to the ground, rolled to his feet and kept running.

She cranked the wheel hard but Gallagher shot out of nowhere and slammed over the hood. He snarled at her, then bolted away.

Gallagher lost sight of the man when he hit the car but he kept running. Lungs blowing hard. It was raining now. He wiped his eyes. Where the hell did he go?

A blur in his periphery. A sooty building to his left, the door banging closed. That way.

The inside was dark and musty-smelling. Windows a story above his head brought some light into the space but not much. Adjusting to the gloom, Gallagher could make out some heavy machinery. A track of conveyor trestle twisting through the air. The polished steel rollers still gleamed in the available light. Dust roiled the air, kicked up from the floor. Gallagher leaned over, hands on his knees. He listened for movement but all he heard were his own lungs sucking air.

He slid his weapon from the holster and kept it trained on the floor. He hollered into the darkness. "Police! Show yourself!"

Silence. He ducked under the conveyor trestle, past workbenches. Dust motes pixied in the shafts of light, sucking into his lungs. He spat and called out again. "Hit the floor, asshole, and call out! Before I accidentally blow your head off!"

Not a peep. Fine. We'll talk after I blow a hole through your heart. Where the hell was Mendes?

Skittering to his left. He swung the gun up. The dog came at him. Barking and snapping. Gallagher drew a bead on it but the Husky kept its distance. The barking rang off all the metal, deafening him.

Something made him look up.

The man was flying. No, not flying. Dropping from above.

The creep's full weight slammed him to the floor. Knocked the wind from his lungs. Couldn't breathe or even think. The gun knocked from his hand. He watched, almost amused, as it spun across the floor.

He was being hit. The son of a bitch was pummeling him. Gallagher sucked oxygen and rolled, bucked. The creep came back for more. He kicked out like a mule and popped the man's knee. The bastard crumpled and Gallagher groped for the gun. Where is the fucking gun?

A freight train knocked him over. They rolled, tangled. Gallagher kneed, punched, elbowed and gouged. Fuck the gun, he'd rip the bastard's eyes out with his bare hands.

An elbow smashed his nose. Blind pain. He felt himself hoisted up and thrown. His skull rang off a machine press. White pixies in his eyes. Shit. Don't pass out. Don't pass out.

Course hands locked round his throat, crushing his windpipe. The spook leaned in close, grunting obscenely. Long stringy hair, spittle threading into the foul beard. The eyes tweaked. A scar on his brow, a cross carved between the eyes. Words chopped out between the teeth.

"You fucking pigs. Always get in the way."

The man was strong. Younger too. Gallagher couldn't hit back, couldn't get free.

Pop. Pop. Gunshots. Mendes.

Lara charged, gun up. Saw Gallagher flat on his back, the suspect chocking him to death. She yelled at him to stop, then she fired. Two rounds to get his attention. It was the first time Lara Mendes had ever discharged her weapon on duty.

"Get on the ground! Now!" She drew a bead on the assailant's chest.

He bolted. Faster than she could follow, he was just gone. Swallowed up in the machinery. She sprinted after him, ducking under cables. A glimpse, the man scrambling up a trestle. He leaped into space and sailed clean through a broken window.

She climbed up after him, slipping on the greasy metal. Her hands found the window frame and hauled herself up. A vista of rail cars and sea crates in a vast yard. No movement, no tell-tale dust cloud. The man was simply gone.

She found Gallagher sitting on the floor, one hand folded over the back of his head. Lara knelt down next to him. "You okay?"

"Yeah. Just dizzy."

She took his arm to help him up, saw the blood on his fingers. She turned his head, saw more blood clotting his hair. "That looks bad," she said.

"Just help me up."

She pivoted backwards and pulled him to his feet. He straightened up then teetered forward. She propped him upright.

"Shit," he said. His eyes rolled over white and he timbered down onto her. They both went down. She smacked his cheek, called his name. No response, officer down.

EMERGENCY lights strobed the face of the dead building, red then blue over the mottled brickwork. Two prowl cars and an ambulance parked outside the entrance.

Paramedics wheeled the stretcher out and loaded Gallagher into the bus. All they could tell detective Mendes was that he was concussed with a lacerated scalp. She waited until the ambulance was away before turning to the uniformed officers waiting on her.

Lara led two of the uniforms back to the decrepit bungalow at the end of the lane. She told them about the dogs trapped inside the house and warned there were others in the area. They searched the house again. The dogs locked in the bedroom went berserk, barking crazily behind the thin wooden door. One uniform, a kid in his twenties, shied away from the door as it jostled and banged in its frame. "If that busts open," he said, "you all better duck cause I'm just gonna start shooting."

The other chided him for being so willing to kill a poor dog. Did he hate animals? The young man loved animals as long as they were kittens or bunnies and such. Rabid street dogs he had no time for.

When the premises were cleared, detective Mendes closed up the front and back doors to contain the dogs should the bedroom door fail. She called precinct and spoke to detective Bingham, asked him to send out the crime scene techs. He took the information, offered his help. She thanked him for that. It was a small place but there was a lot of crap to sift through.

The uniforms waited on her. The one who didn't care for dogs asked what she wanted to do next.

"Seal off the property. One car here at the house, park the other up at the road. Stop anyone who turns in. Get their name and details." Lara walked back to her car, a plastic evidence bag tucked under her arm. The officer followed. “Call the animal shelter, get them down here. Tell them we got two big dogs in the house and more strays in the area. I'll be back soon.”

“Where you going? Isn't this your crime scene?”

“It's the tech's scene now. I'll be at the hospital.” She climbed under the wheel, tossed the evidence bag onto the passenger seat. Inside was a cheap black notebook.

13

IN A BUSY EMERGENCY ROOM, EVEN a cop has a hard time getting a straight answer. Lara had to reach over the counter to find out where Gallagher was. Up to the third floor, east wing. Follow the green lines.

She found the room, looked in the window. Gallagher sat on the bed, shoulders slouched forward. A doctor was in the room, speaking to him but Gallagher didn't seem to be listening. Quel shocker.

There was a third person in the room, a girl in her teens. Lara put her age at sixteen, maybe seventeen years. Hair falling down her face, arms folded. Gallagher put a hand on her shoulder but the girl shrugged it off and flopped into the chair. The doctor kept talking. Gallagher's eyes went back to the floor. He looked defeated. Ashamed maybe.

Who was this girl?

Lara pilfered a pair of latex gloves from an untended cart and found a chair. She slipped the notebook from the plastic bag. The handwriting was frenzied, the paper grooved from the pen strokes. Hard to decipher the words but the first entry was an obscenity spewed rant against someone who had wronged him. It was a laundry list of torments planned to make the person suffer but the target of the rage was never mentioned by name. She found sketches scattered throughout. Dogs or maybe wolves. Nude women in supine poses. Skulls. A house bordered by trees. Then more pages of cramped writing. No dates. The entries, if that's what they were, separated by the crude star inside a circle.

Lara fanned through the pages, hoping the suspect had scrawled his John Henry somewhere in the book. Nothing. A face flipped by. She thumbed back through the pages, found a man's face taking up the entire page. Long hair, beard, the eyes shaded under the brow. A cross-shaped scar marred the skin between the eyes. Was this a self-portrait? Damn. The creepy dude provided his own police sketch.

She tucked her feet under her and got comfortable. Flipping back to the beginning of the notebook, Lara settled in to decipher the cramped gibberish.

THE click of the door brought Lara's eyes from the page. The girl in Gallagher's room stepped into the hallway, her eyes tired and puffy. Is this who she spoke to on the phone when she called Gallagher's house? Lara put the book aside and stood. "Is he okay?"

Amy looked at the woman sitting in the hallway. Shrugged. "Doctor says so," she said. "Not that it really matters to Dad. He doesn't much like doctors."

"You're Amy," Lara said. The name on Gallagher's emergency contact was a daughter, not a spouse like she had assumed. "I must have frightened you when I called. I'm sorry."

"Yeah. Kinda freaked me out. But no, I'm glad you did." Amy rubbed her eyes, smoothing the puffiness away. "None of Dad's other partners ever called when he got hurt. I'd never know till it was all over. So. Thanks."

Lara swiped a pack of tissues from the cart, handed it to the girl. "Do you need a lift home? I can get someone to drive you."

"I'm okay. My friend's waiting for me. She has a car." Amy turned to go then stopped. "What's your name?"

"I'm Detective Mendes."

"No. Your first name."

"Lara."

"Thanks, Lara." Amy gave a little wave and went down the hall, backtracking the green line on the floor.

Lara watched her go. Nice girl. How could she be Gallagher's kid?

GALLAGHER fumbled the buttons on his shirt, still woozy. Why do doctors always make you strip for anything?

The knock he took was to the head but still they insisted he remove all his clothes. Why? Probably so they could pilfer every damn cent from his pockets.

When the door opened he thought it was Amy, forgetting something like she always did. Mendes entered instead, a white box tucked under her arm. "How are you feeling?"

"Who the hell told my daughter I was here?" He knew it had to be her but he needed to bark at someone.

"My mistake," Lara said. "I saw her name in your emergency contact. I just assumed it was your wife. Sorry"

Gallagher slung the tie round his neck, measured the length. Still pissed.

"She's a sweet kid." Lara put the box on the bedside table.

"You know why she's a sweet kid? Because she doesn't get calls about her old man winding up in the hospital." He scooped up his keys, dropped them into a pocket. "You need to file that request. We made a break in the case so it won't look like you're giving up."

"Are you kidding me? This is just getting good."

He growled. "Mendes."

"I got a warrant on the way," she said. "Not that we need it now. We got PC up the ying-yang with this guy. Maybe you should go home, rest up."

He scalded her with a look. "What's in the box?"

"Get dressed. I'm parked out front." Detective Mendes left the room.

Gallagher looked at the box on the table. He flipped the lid open. Donuts. Every one of them covered in sprinkles.

TEETH popped and chomped, trying to bite Pablo, bite anything. Two loops of rope choking its neck, the Staffordshire twisted and jerked against the restraints. Pablo and another man kept the snapping dog at bay with restraint poles noosed round the animal's neck. Both men strained against the animal's ferocity, pushing the Staffordshire to the truck marked ANIMAL SHELTER. Pablo dropped his pole, leaving the other man to hold the dog still, while he grabbed the tail and hoisted the animal into the cage. They slackened the cord, slid the loop off the dog and locked the cage.

"I told ya we should of used the tranq," said the other man, out of breath.

"Lot of fight left in these hounds." Pablo nodded at the first dog they removed from the premises, already caged in the truck. "Look at them."

"Is that your buddy?"

The unmarked car trundled past the CSU truck to a spot on the weed blown yard. Gallagher climbed out and waved to Pablo. The shelter director looked at the bandage on the detective's forehead. "What happened to you?"

"Dog bit me." Gallagher checked the dogs caged inside the truck. "These the two in the house, yeah? You find any others?"

"There was one sniffing around when we pulled in," said Pablo. "But it took off. We'll take a spin around, see if we can find him."

Gallagher thanked him and went on up to the house. Lara gave the penned dogs a wide berth and ducked under the police tape.

Portable lamps trucked in from the CSU vehicle lit up every dingy corner. A crime scene technician sifted garbage on the floor while another popped photographs. Two uniforms stood in the kitchen clutching cold cups of coffee.

Lara stepped over the cables running along the floor. "Forensics are still bagging stuff. I held off on the APB, you got a better look at him than I did."

"What's the story on this dump?"

"Condemned. Our boy's squatting."

Gallagher picked through the litter on the kitchen table. "Any luck finding a name?"

"Maybe. Come see."

The basement steps still creaked but there was nothing spooky about the place now, with floodlights pushing every shadow to the corners. Gallagher followed Lara to the little card table under the window. A shoe box sat on top. She upended it on the table. Credit cards and driver's licenses spilled out.

"I found these all over the house. The guy likes his aliases."

"Any of these belong to our boy?"

"You tell me." Lara fanned the licenses across the formica. A police lineup of DMV photos. "Can you pick him out?"

He scrutinized each one. "He's not in here."

"Okay." Lara pulled one of the notebooks off the crate shelf and flipped it open to a page she had dog-eared. "How about this?"

Gallagher studied the drawing. The hair, beard and that cross-shaped scar, all rendered neatly in pencil. "That's the creep. Quite the Picasso." He leafed through the rest of the notebook, skimming over the fevered handwriting. "You find a name in any of these?"

"Nada," Lara said. "But the techs lifted a lot of good prints. Fingers crossed, this guy's in the system."

"I can't read this chicken scratch. Is it even English?"

"You're not going to believe what I found in here." She took the notebook back. "At least the parts I can decipher. I told you how he describes this affliction he has? Sometimes he refers to it like a disease, a chronic ailment he tries to manage. Other times he calls it a curse."

"Right. He gets all pent up and boom. Someone's dead." Already dismissing it, Gallagher turned to the graffiti on the basement wall. "Sounds like he's laying the groundwork for an insanity plea."

"It gets better. Way better."

"Yeah," he said. Barely paying attention.

"This affliction he describes? His curse? He's given it a name." Lara balked, unsure of even how to pronounce it right. She blurted it out. "Lycanthropy."

"Like-a-what?"

"Lycanthropy. The guy thinks he's a werewolf."

That stopped him cold and he turned his eyes to her. Parsing what the hell she just said. The word just hung there in the air between them.

"Great." He finally shrugged, like he came across this every day. "Now he's the dog-catcher's problem."

Not the reaction she was looking for. Lara pulled down the rest of the notebooks and shoved them into his hands. "There are six of these journals. Most of what I've deciphered describes the same thing over and over. Pushing it down, fighting it until it overwhelms him. He comes out of it racked with remorse. Suicidal over his guilt. This guy has killed before. God knows how many times."

The dismissive turn of mouth dropped away. He flipped through the top notebook. "You find any names or dates? Locations?"

"Nothing solid to go on. So far anyway." She crossed the floor to where a chain dangled from the joists overhead. "But I found out what these are for."

Lara trailed up the end of a chain, held up the iron cuff. "My first guess was this stuff was some S and M gear, but it's not. They're his restraints. He chains himself up when he feels the urge come over him."

THE Siberian sniffed the perimeter of the rooftop, padding through puddles in the warped tar. It found a dry spot, circled twice and bedded down. Chin to the ground, waiting.

The man sat on the roof's edge, one leg dangling over. His eyes were hidden behind mirrored sunglasses, teeth clenched in the whiskers of his beard. From his perch he could see his home. What used to be his home. Now it was ringed with police vehicles with their stupid flashing lights. He watched the pigs come and go, tearing apart his home. He cocked his head and spit. After a while, he turned away and crossed the tar roof to the exit.

The Siberian rose and fell in line behind him.

THE premises search turned up nothing else to identify the squatter. No other identification, no correspondence nor bills. There was no landline and no cell phone to go on. Nothing with a name on it.

The CSU techs came back with a number of fingerprints. All of these were sorted and fed into the system, fingers crossed that something would match up. DNA swabs were taken from the beer cans and utensils and sent to lab. With any luck, it would match one of the myriad profiles found on the victim. But that would take time, their job joining a backlog of samples waiting against a logjam of other investigations waiting to move forward.

Lara stuck her nose in the pages of the notebooks and didn't come up for air. She studied the crazed writing for any tangibles like locations or names. She scrutinized every sketch, the renderings of wolves and naked women. The drawings of the house seemed important. Always the same house but rendered from different perspectives. Significant but with no context, useless to her.

She found seven self-portraits peppered throughout the notebooks. She photocopied each one and pinned them to her evidence board. With no dates, she hazarded a guess to their chronological order, based solely on the increasingly sordid look of the subject. Lines etched deeper into the face, the hair longer and the beard progressively more foul.

Gallagher stayed with the premises, canvassing every business around the site of the little broken down house. He tramped into the trees, searching for anything. He dropped to his knees twice, winded and frail but waved off the concern of the uniforms and resumed the search. It took a direct call from the Lieutenant himself before Gallagher went home to rest up.

Detective Mendes called early the next morning while Gallagher was making breakfast. They got a hit on the prints and the system just spit out a name.

14

IVAN PRALL.

Lara's screen popped open a partial list of priors. No photograph available. She turned to her evidence board, which by now resembled an art project stapled up by some deranged child. She tore one of the photocopied self-portraits from the wall and handed it to Gallagher. "Ivan Prall. No fixed address, no known relatives."

"What the hell kinda name is that?" He nodded to her screen. "What do you got?"

"Not a lot," she said. "Both parents deceased. The father beat his mother to death, then hung himself inside the county jail. At age ten, Prall enters the system, gets shuffled through a number of foster homes."

"Where was this? Here in town?" Gallagher took his chair, stretched out his legs.

"Damascus." Lara toggled down the screen. "Later on he lands in a foster home here in Portland and gets into trouble. Theft, arson, assault. Two years in a juvenile detention center, then he's released to a halfway house for troubled kids.

"Prall flees the halfway house, missing for a couple days and then shows up in a hospital ER with wounds from—" Lara leaned into the monitor to read the details. "An unspecified animal attack, probably a dog."

"Sad story. Then what?"

"Nothing. He disappears from the hospital and he's never seen again."

"When did he disappear?"

"Six years ago." Lara tapped a pen on her knee. "Where's he been all this time?"

"Living off the grid. What about this halfway house? Somebody there must remember him."

"I checked. " Lara read from her notes. "The place was shut down over a year ago. The guy who ran it was charged with abusing the kids in his care. All the records were sealed."

"Who worked the case?"

"Doesn't say."

"Find out, talk to them." Gallagher stood. "I'll check in later."

She tossed one of the black notebooks at him. "Hold on, cowboy. We got six of these to decipher. Pull up a chair."

"It's insane gibberish. There's no specifics to these attacks he describes. Nothing to work from."

"Where are you going?"

"I know a few paranoids who live off the grid. Maybe they know our boy."

He left. Lara swiveled her chair around and got to work.

"IT was a horrrorshow."

This was detective Roy Hammond, sitting across a checkered two-top in a diner off Quimby Street. He pushed the chair back to make room for the basketball swishing inside his shirt. He and Lara ordered coffee and discussed the weather until it arrived.

Mendes had spent the morning digging up the files about their suspect's last known address, the Gethsemane House of Transition and Redemption. She found the name of the investigating officer within in the Child Abuse Team, a primary partner of the Sex Assault Detail. Detective Roy Hammond had handled that charge but was now working in Fraud Detail, a lateral career move for a man of his age but he had to get out of CAT. He did not want to see anymore of the horrorshow or the tragedy it wreaked.

Having put it behind him, Hammond didn't want to talk but Lara persisted. And here he was, stirring two sugars into his coffee while Lara left hers black and let the detective talk.

"The Gethsemane House was supposed to transition kids out of juvie and back home. If they had one." Hammond slurped his cup. "But this place, it just fucked them up worse."

Lara stayed quiet. Hammond's distaste for his former detail was clear by the grimace on his face. How many ruined kids had this guy seen? She kept her questions in check, letting him come around to it. He was doing her a favor after all.

"One of the former residents came forward, spilled the beans about how he was abused as a kid there. We investigated and shut the horrorshow down."

"Who was the abuser?"

"Ronald Kovacks. He'd been at it for years. Really did a number on these kids. We nailed him on four convictions but there was more. A lot more."

"None of the other victims wanted to press charges." Lara guessed.

"In a nutshell. Kovacks and his wife ran the place like a bible camp. He really indoctrinated the kids in his care. Even fifteen years later, these people deny anything happened to them."

"What about the wife? She was never charged."

Hammond shrugged. "We didn't have enough on her. She knew what was going on but kept herself pickled most of the time. So we focused on him."

Lara took out a pen. "What was her name?"

"Betty? No, Bethany Kovacks. See, these two started out as foster parents. They got money from the state to provide for the boys in their care. Then they realized they could get more money if they turned their place into a halfway house.

More kids that way, plus they got money from the city in addition to the funds from the state level."

"Where's Kovacks now?"

"Disappeared. The wife puts up the bail. He goes home and promptly fucks off. Dunno what happened to her. She lost the house, everything. She signed a complete statement against him and then she disappeared too."

Lara unfolded a piece of paper, smoothing it down on the table. The self portrait, photocopied from the black notebook. "What about this man? He was one of the residents about six years ago. His name's Ivan Prall."

Hammond studied the picture. "Don't recognize him. You think he's another abuse victim?"

"Could be. He's wanted for homicide."

Hammond studied the sketch again but nothing more rang his memory. "Sorry."

"Where would I find the records from the Gethsemane House?"

"Stored away somewhere. I'll call my old partner, she still works CAT."

There was little else to move on. The conversation drifted back to the mundane, both trading gripes about the job. Lara got the bill and thanked him for his time.

"You're working with Gallagher on this, right?" He held the door as they left the diner.

"Yup."

"Keep your spidey-senses tingling. The man's hard on partners."

THE kitchen was dark, save for the bulb under the hood fan. Music filtered down from Amy's room. Gallagher had long given up trying to understand his daughter's taste in music, just as she withered painfully at his. He left his keys in the bowl and pulled the holster from his belt, remembering a time when they both sang along to the Tammy Wynette disc in the truck. Those moments, he thought 'Wow, my kid's cool'. Then Amy turned twelve and declared his music stupid.

He thumbed the release and the magazine slid into his palm. He made sure the chamber was empty. The gun, clip and holster went into a cupboard over the fridge. Routine habit.

Last night's chicken was in the fridge. Easy enough to make a sandwich. Instead he got a glass and poured a lethal length of Bushmills. Put his feet up. The scotch warmed his gut but teased out a dull ache along his shoulders.

"Tough day at the office?" Amy padded barefoot into the kitchen, carrying dirty dishes from her room. All of it clanging as it went into the sink.

"Why are you still up?" He flexed his fingers, warding off the swelling.

Amy took hold of his hand and looked at the raw knuckles. "You should ice that."

"How was school today?"

"Everything was beautiful and nothing hurt." Amy had read that in a book for English class and the sarcasm of it stayed with her.

He took his hand back. "Go to bed."

"You gotta watch out for this stuff, dad. Remember Grandmama's arthritis?"

His mom, Amy's grandmother. Her hands gnarled with it. She adored Amy and spoiled her rotten every chance she got. It was mutual, Amy doting on her grandmother, helping out when her hands curled up into knotty stumps. Gallagher thought about it whenever his knuckles went stiff.

"Do you know how obnoxious it is to be scolded by your own kid?"

"Get some ice," she said. "I'll find the Advil."

A new picture hung from a pin on the evidence board. A medieval woodcut of a young girl being devoured by a werewolf, the figures stiff and doll-like. Lara had found it in a library book. Something about the picture, the simple lines, the expression on the woman's face, appealed to her. She couldn't say why, it just did. There were other pin-ups like this, not evidence but reference points and visual cues. Anything to get her brain stirring, to string together some insight into what she was dealing with.

The last two days had been spent searching the system for any suspicious deaths involving dogs or remains that had been interfered with by dogs. Starting within the city, then expanding out to the surrounding towns and then the state. A few results had trickled in. Nothing conclusive, nothing even classed as a homicide. A body found by hikers outside of Longview, the remains partially devoured and scattered by animals. COD unknown. A similar incident across the state lines near Shelton, Washington. Badly decomposed remains found near a creek, the pieces scattered by animals. In both instances, the bodies remained unidentified, their deaths unresolved. Intriguing but there was nothing to string them together, nothing to tie in with the death of Elizabeth Riley.

"Where's Gallagher?"

Someone looming up behind her. She looked up to see Lieutenant Vogel, big as a mountain.

"God knows. He doesn't answer his phone."

"That's because he knows it's you." The Lieutenant opened his cell and dialed. Lara watched him drum his fingers on the chair and then bark into the phone. "Where the hell are you? What? No. Stop talking. Stay put."

Vogel ended the call, turned back to her. "He's down at the amusement park. Oaks Bottom."

She spun her jacket off the chair, scooped a notepad off the desk.

"Hold on." He blocked her way. "What's he been up to? Have you seen him pull any stunts?"

"Stunts?"

"Has he been cutting corners? Abusing suspects, bullying witnesses or otherwise treating procedure like dog shit on his shoes?"

Are you kidding me? In the short time they had worked together, Lara had watched Gallagher threaten and cajole half a dozen people so far. He broke procedure the way he breathed, made up his own stupid rules on the fly. She looked her boss straight in the eye. "No."

Vogel was silent. Staring down at her, sniffing out a lie. A tinge of disappointment in his eyes. Was he regretting his decision to make her homicide? An eternity, then he turned away. "What are you waiting for? Go catch him before he takes off again."

She marched quickly for the door. Lara had always considered her mother, being both Mexican and Catholic, to be the master of the guilt trip. She realized now the woman had nothing on Lieutenant Vogel. The man was a ninja master of refracted guilt. She wondered if she had time to stop at the nearest church and light a candle to the Guadalupe. Probably not.

OAKS Bottom, a rank marsh of black oaks and reeds, and a long time ago someone had built an amusement park at the butt end of it. The smell of popcorn and corn dogs had settled into the trees and the asphalt, a greasy haze of fun hanging like a mist.

Gallagher had been here as a kid and came back when he was a dad. Lifting Amy into kiddie rocket ride or blowing twenty bucks on the ring toss to win a stuffed froggy that spilled its stuffing two days later. He hadn't been back since the summer Amy was ten. Amy still came to the park but only with her friends now, not her old man. Another door slamming shut on his connection with a daughter eager to grow up. No more Tilt-A-Whirls.

The smell finally got to him. The last two hours spent hunkered behind the wheel in the parking lot, playing a hunch. Waiting for the owner of one of the food stands to come back to his vehicle. Gallagher neglected to pack a lunch and his stomach curled in on itself. The greasy smell of onion rings was too much.

The lot was half full of cars. No one had come or gone in the last twenty minutes. He made a dash for the nearest stall and came back with two cheeseburgers and spicy fries. The paper in the tray already translucent with grease before he got back into the Cherokee.

Detective Mendes sat in the passenger bucket.

"Thanks for returning my calls, pardner," she said.

He settled the tray onto the dashboard. "What do ya want, Mendes? I'm on the clock."

Her eyes swept the amusement park and came back to the tray steaming up the windshield. "Doing what exactly?"

He unwrapped a cheeseburger. "You want some spicy fries? Best in town."

Lara leaned back in the seat, watching the Ferris wheel circle over the fair grounds. Why didn't she send in that request when she had a chance?

"Unclench, chief. You're wound up too tight. Eat something." He held out the tray. She took a fry. "So what do ya got?"

"I found five deaths where the remains were partially consumed by animals, possibly dogs. One in Oregon, two in Washington state and two more across the border in B.C." She licked her fingers, reached for another. "All of them inconclusive because of decomposition, cause of death undetermined."

"You think it's him?"

"There's no consistency to it," she said. "The deceased are both male and female. Two were in their twenties, the last one was a man in his fifties. But if it is him, it shows his movement over the last year and a half."

"That's more than we had yesterday." Gallagher's eyes looked past her, scanning over the parking lot. Watching people return to their cars. "Just don't fall in love with it. You might have to dump it all later on."

She tucked into the fries again, last time. Promise. "I went through his journals again, the parts that I can decipher. And the thing is, this guy knows he's got a problem but he can't stop it. Weirder still, he's remorseful. Ashamed even."

"That's the Catholic in him. Did you see all those Jesus pictures in the basement?" He wiped the mustard from the corner of his mouth. "The guy's a looney-tune, Mendes. Don't waste your time crawling into his head."

"Dismissing him as crazy is too easy." Lara caught the disappointment in Gallagher's eyes when he realized half his fries were gone. Oops. "He knows right from wrong. He's even tried to cure himself."

"Dude thinks he's the wolfman. That's as crazy as they come."

She shook her head. "No. He's misdiagnosed his own psychosis. Instead of seeing the real problem, he believes he's a wolf. It actually makes a weird kind of sense."

Crumbs flew from his teeth. "How does that make any sense?"

"Prall was abused at this halfway house, like all the others. What happens to these kids when they grow up?"

He shrugged. "Tough lives. Drugs, suicide, downward spirals. Some of them become abusers themselves."

"Right. Once subjected to it, the affliction or pathology or whatever it is, is passed on. The werewolf myth works the same way. If you're bitten by one, you become a wolf too."

Gallagher knocked the idea around. "That's real interesting and everything but, again, it doesn't help us with the practical."

"Well what do you have? You're scarfing burgers at an amusement park."

"Me? I'm just trying to find a crazy dude who likes dogs—" He sat up suddenly, wiped his hands on his jeans and reached for the ignition. "I gotta go."

Lara followed his eyes across the parking lot. A rotund man waddled through the cars and unlocked the door to a Land Rover. The S-20 type, forest green with a tan interior. The man huffed in, the Rover tilting under his weight. The brake lights lit up.

"See you at the office." Gallagher started the truck, waiting for her to get out.

Lara pulled the seatbelt round. "You're not ditching me again."

"You're not gonna like this, Mendes."

The Land Rover backed out of the spot and rolled to the exit.

"Just go. Before you lose the guy."

15

THE ROVER TURNED SOUTH on SE Seventeenth and merged onto the Milwaukee Expressway. Traffic wasn't bad yet, allowing Gallagher to lay back four car lengths behind the Rover.

The takeout tray slid across the dashboard. Lara caught it, tucked it away under the seat. "So who is this guy?"

"Eugene Shockton," Gallagher said. "Douchebag I busted years ago. He's got a concession booth at the park and a lunch counter in No-Po. A coin laundry too."

"And how is he a douchebag?"

"Eugene likes to gamble. He got himself in hawk to some bad people a while ago. Now he launders money for them through his businesses."

Lara kept her eyes on the Rover. "Was he involved in a homicide?"

"No. I busted him back working Robbery Detail. Eugene's got his mitts in a lot of things. Sometimes if I'm stuck, Eugene's a good guy to talk to."

"Your informant." She lost sight of the Rover and leaned her head against the glass to see around the ass end of traffic.

"A reluctant one. But he responds well to pain."

"So why are we following him? Just ask him if he knows anything about Ivan Prall."

"I'm not interested in what Eugene knows. It's his hobbies that interest me."

A blur of green up ahead, Lara's eyes tracked the Rover as it weaved to an exit ramp. "He's getting off the expressway."

Gallagher took the exit but there were no cars between them and the Rover now. He slowed, letting out the distance between them. A minivan rode up their tail, honking. Gallagher touched the brake, forcing the infuriated driver to pass and roar up behind the chase car.

The Rover veered into an industrial strip, trawling past a carpet cleaner and a Japanese food importer. Gallagher swung into a parking slot and killed the engine. They watched the green truck roll behind the strip to a squat bunker of yellow brick.

"What is this place?" Lara scanned the other vehicles lined alongside, blocking the rollup doors. Eugene

Shockton weeble-wobbled from his vehicle to a side door. "A gambling house?"

"Sort of." Gallagher crooked an arm over the wheel. "Eugene loves to gamble large. He plays the ponies, the cockfights. Whatever you got, he'll lay a wager on it. But his true love? Right yonder"

He waved at a pickup rolling through the strip towards the bunker. Built into the box was a kennel top with small grated windows. Behind the mesh were dogs, their noses pressed to the cage window.

"Dog fighting?"

"Our perp likes dogs, right? Maybe he tests his mutts in the ring." He reached behind the seat and dragged up a black hoodie. Tossed it into her lap. "Put that on."

She shook dust from it. "This smells."

"They're aren't a lot of women at these things. Put it on, pull up the hood." He grinned at her then climbed out. "Told ya you wouldn't like it."

She made no move to follow or even open her door. More dogs? Gallagher looked back, took her measure and strode towards the bunker. He didn't look back.

Shit.

THE wedge of sunlight thinned until the door clanged shut behind them. Lara barely made out Gallagher, quickly paying the brute manning the door and pulling her along after him. The doorman looked her up and down but said nothing. A riot of noise then; dogs barking, people hollering overtop the heavy-bottomed beat thrumming the floor. The corridor opened into a warehouse space, bodies milling about in the dark. Lights fingered up from somewhere in the center.

Lara kept her head down, eyes peering out under the dip of the hood. Too-tough black guys with masks of stone. Cracker whites with ballcaps reversed on their greasy heads. Chinese in suits and cigarettes. Some with jailhouse tattoos and others with soft, manicured hands. Everyone peeling off twenties and laying down. Bikers, bankers and candlestick makers.

The dogs brayed and barked, shut up behind grates or chained to poles. All of them alert and tensed. Teeth filed down to razors by their flabby owners, muscles pumped with steroids. The newbies patted their dog's flanks, trying hard to look bored. The pros scrawled their dog's names onto fight cards. These men batted their animals in the snout to aggravate them, key them up to the fight. Many held kits. Scalpels and needles to stitch up their prize fighters after each bout. Hypodermics topped with pentobarbital to euthanize the losers too ripped up to save.

Lara squeezed through the bodies towards the lights at the center. Up on her toes to peek over shoulders at the main event. Straw bails, packed three twines high, formed the arena where two dogs were killing each other. A Staffordshire bit down hard, its teeth ripping the snout from a Rottweiler mix. The Rotty whimpered as the Staffordshire sawed its head back and forth, peeling the face off the lost dog. The dog owners hollered foul from the hay bales and the gap-toothed referee leaned his hands on his knees but no one moved to stop the bloodshed. The Rottweiler's legs gave out and it dropped to the strawdust but the other dog didn't let up, given over to its mindless frenzy.

Lara turned away, unable to stomach anymore. God Almighty, is this what happened to Elizabeth Riley? Was she alive when she endured that? Without thinking she genuflected, something she hadn't done in a very long time.

A man stepped over the hay bales, boxing the ears of the referee and chasing him from the ring. Clad in a leather butcher's apron that glistened with blood, no shirt beneath it. Thick arms inked to the wrists. He tried to haul the victor off but the Staffordshire would not relent. The butcher man snatched an ear in one hand and stabbed his fingers into the dog's anus with the other hand. The animal released and he hurled it into the bails.

The Rottweiler lay wheezing in its own blood. It raised its head to its master, the snout all but sheered from the bone. It wagged its tail twice and lay back down. Someone threw a blanket over it. The owner carried his dog from the pit and laid it down near a wall. This man had no hypodermic to end the animal's suffering nor could he buy one from another contender, having lost so much money already. He didn't know what to do. The dog wheezed at his feet, unable to even whimper.

In the pit, the man in the butcher's apron threw sawdust over the blood on the floor. The men leaning over the bails drank and settled their bets and wagered anew, calling out for the next bout.

"Are you fuckers ready for the next fight?" Butcher man turned round inside the pit, addressing all. "Entering the ring we have three time champion Popeye! Bitch killer of Multnomah county!" Two more dogs were walked into the pit and positioned opposite each end of the ring. The onlookers cheered and cajoled and thumped each other like apes.

Lara backpedalled from the horror, felt a hand grip her elbow. Gallagher asked if she was okay but she didn't answer.

"Wipe it from your eyes, Mendes. Stay on point. We sweep the room and look for Prall. If he isn't here, we'll call this in and stop it. Okay?"

"Agreed." She looked over the crowd, their backs to them. "Where's your friend? If he spots you, we're sunk."

"He's probably leaning over the pit. Any luck, he'll fall in and get bit."

The noise from the pit grew louder, the butcher man bellowing over the crack of the barking. The onlookers pressed in, jostling for a better view. Gallagher nodded at the crowd arcing round the pit. "Circle around, eyes peeled for Prall."

He went east, she west. Ducking through the flailing hands and spit-laced cries. Lara peered out from under the hoodie, searching every face. Lager sloshed from a can and spilled down her shoulder. A heel crunched her toes. Keep moving.

The butcher man whistled to start the bout. The men holding the pit bulls let them slip. The dogs collided, each snapping for the other's throat. A roar went through the crowd.

Lara was elbowed and jostled but kept moving, scanning every face. She caught sight of Gallagher on the other side, then a stray arm caught her in the ribs. She fought the urge to club the bastard over the head in return. The task at hand, she muttered to herself.

Gallagher was waving crazily, drawing her gaze due north. She spotted him.

A tall man at the far end of the crowd, his hood pulled up over his head. Mirrored sunglasses hid his eyes but his scraggly beard stuck out. Ivan Prall.

Don't run. Too far away, too many people. Lara pushed forward, looking to flag her partner. Gallagher found her eyes and she signaled to him. Gallagher spotted her target.

The man turned and slipped for the exit sign.

She bolted, shoving assholes out of her way. She heard Gallagher bellowing for the man to stop. He ran for the door but got sidelined hard into the bricks. Gallagher jack-hammered his face before yanking the hood back.

It wasn't Ivan Prall. Just some loser in a filthy beard. He struck Gallagher's chin, rabbit punches. Gallagher laughed like some crazed banshee and pummeled the man mercilessly, as if blaming him for not being their suspect. He kept hitting him, even as he crumpled to the floor and begged Gallagher to stop.

Eugene Shockton looked up at the ruckus and clocked detective John Gallagher beating the bejesus out of some poor bastard. He screamed. "COPS!"

Everybody ran.

Lara was swept back in the rush for the exit. Shouldered this way and elbowed that way, tripped up and kicked down. Someone yelled “bitch”. A boot stomped her knee and the man leered down at her, called her a bitch again. Lara struck hard, an uppercut to the groin. A blur of running legs all round her, pumping for the doors. Where the hell was Gallagher?

The man in the butcher's apron marched upstream through the refugees clutching an enormous shillelagh in both hands. He arced it overhead and brought the mallet down cold on Gallagher's back. Gallagher flopped onto the hooded man, the air punched out of his lungs. The butcher man swung again, like a contender at a fairground trying to ring a bell. Gallagher rolled out of the way and the shillelagh broke two ribs of the hooded man.

Onto his back, kicking the butcher's knee. The big man timbered slantways to the floor but didn't let go of the Irish bludgeon. Gallagher pulled his weapon and cracked the man's temple with it. He didn't see the biker coming up behind him but he felt the boot to his ribs. The biker's boot lifted again, eager to trample the cop again but found a gun barrel in his face.

“Get off him.” Lara aimed the Glock dead on the biker's face, keeping the butcher man in her periphery. She'd had enough. Everything had gone to hell so fast.

The biker called a bluff. “Go fuck yourself.” Lara shoved the barrel up his nose and the man shut up after that. She looked to Gallagher, saw his knee pinned over the butcher's throat.

The room had cleared. Three dogs remained chained to a post, abandoned by their owners. A wet twenty dollar bill pasted to the floor. Gallagher watched Mendes cuff the biker. When she looked up at him again, he laughed. Like they had just stumbled off a roller coaster car together.

Her hands were shaking. "This is a mess," she said.

"Think of the overtime." He straightened his tie but it remained mangled. "How do I look?"

"Like a guy who got his guts kicked in."

"Perfect."

She took hold of his tie, tugged it straight and smoothed it flat.

Her face up close. She had freckles, faint and not many. He'd never noticed that before. His grin went lopsided, forced.

Lara stepped back, self-conscious. "We better call this in," she said.

16

MOPPING UP OPERATIONS ATE THE rest of the day. The butcher and the biker were charged with assaulting police officers, a charge that would stick better than running a dog-fighting ring or animal cruelty. Both men had prior arrests and each knew how to carry themselves in the box. Gallagher and Mendes took turns questioning each man about their suspect. They were shown the self-portrait sketch, asked about any violent characters who owned a lot of dogs. Hints were dropped that their charges would be reduced if they knew anything about the man named Ivan Prall. The biker tried to play out some useless information but in the end neither man knew anything.

By the evening shift change, detective Mendes and detective Gallagher were still at their desks writing up incident reports and the charges against the two men. No new information was added to the investigation into the Riley homicide or the suspect Ivan Prall.

They went down to the break room for coffee. Gallagher pilfered an apple from the fridge. When they came back, a black and white photo had materialized on the evidence board. The wolfman. Lon Chaney Junior made up in yak hair and rubber fangs. Scrawled in Sharpie at the bottom of the picture were words: Have you seen this man?

"Cute." Lara crumpled it into a ball and pitched it out over the bullpen of cubicles. It came sailing back a moment later, over the cubicles and bouncing onto Bingham's desk. The homicide detectives returned to their keyboards, hoping to finish up before sundown.

"Hi Lara."

Amy stood at the cubicle entrance, giving a little wave. "Hey Dad."

"Hello Amy." Lara smiled back. She hadn't seen Amy smile when they had met her in the hospital. Understandable. She had a beautiful smile. All girls do really, Lara thought. "How are you?"

"Alright." Amy dropped into her dad's chair, poked through the papers on his desk. Gallagher was flummoxed but he masked it with sternness. "What are you doing here?"

Amy shrugged. "I tried to make a curry for tonight. It didn't go well."

"So use the phone. You know I don't want you coming down here."

"I know." Amy's roving eye found the evidence board. Her jaw gaped at the crime scene photos. The remains of the dead woman. "Oh my God, is that real?"

Gallagher crossed to block the worst of the photos. "Alright. Let's go. Out of here."

"But it was my turn to cook. I messed up."

Lara shifted in her chair, suddenly stuck in the middle of a family squabble.

Gallagher took his daughter by the shoulders and turned her towards the exit. "Just call next time. I'll pick up something on the way home."

"Or," she held up a finger, "there's that Indian place you always rave about. The one near here."

He sighed through his nose, the way he did to show his frustration. That meant no. Even Lara saw that coming, so she interrupted. "Go on. I'll finish this up."

His eyebrow shot up. Why was she being nice? "You sure?"

"Yeah. Go on."

"Why don't you come with us, Lara?" Amy asked.

"Honey," he said, having none of it. "Detective Mendes has better things to do."

"I do have work to finish." Lara was right in her initial assessment. She was a sweet kid. "But thanks."

"Aw, come on. Get your stuff." Amy couldn't be bothered with either of their nonsense. She was hungry. "Paperwork can wait, dinner can't."

Amy marched for the elevator. Lara looked at Gallagher but he simply shrugged. What are you gonna do?

THE Blue Ganesha was a closet sized eatery three blocks from central precinct. The decor was frugal. Mismatched chairs and a chipped statue of the blue elephant deity. Indian pop music squelching out over bad speakers. But the food? Outstanding.

The three of them squeezed into a table near the window, one uneven leg stabilized under a wad of matchbooks. The waiter brought a coke and two Kingfishers.

"So?" Amy tilted her head to the straw. "Anyone get hurt today?"

Lara felt Gallagher's stare. "Just another day at the office."

"You're working the dead prostitute case, right?"

"Amy," Gallagher scolded.

"What?" Amy rolled her eyes, then leaned into Lara. "He never talks about work."

"That's probably a good idea. Ruin your appetite," Lara said. "What about you? You play basketball, right?"

She nodded. Gallagher beamed, said "We got a game tomorrow night. You ready?"

"Always." Amy turned back to Mendes. "How long have you worked homicide, Lara?"

"Not long. Your dad's showing me the ropes." Lara caught him wincing at the remark. Good.

The waiter brought a basket of papadams and Amy tucked into it. “Is it true the prostitute was eaten by dogs?”

“Stop already,” Gallagher ordered. The kid just didn't listen.

“Do you have a boyfriend Amy?”

“No,” he answered for her. “No boyfriends until she's seventeen.”

Amy shared a look with Lara. Dad was clearly clueless. She pointed a shard of papadam at Lara. “What about you? You got a boyfriend?”

Gallagher cringed. Why was his kid so nosy? He blamed her mother. Lara didn't seem to mind. “No,” she said. “Too busy for that stuff right now.”

“Enough already.” Gallagher got to his feet. “Everybody to the buffet. Before dad has a conniption fit.”

Lara didn't need to be told twice. She was starving and the long buffet table was right in front of them. Gallagher was already trowelling food onto a plate.

Amy hung back, taking a pull off dad's Kingfisher when no one was looking. Her eyes stayed on Lara, watching her every move. An odd glimmer of apprehension on her pretty face.

“SO Dad’s got the guy in cuffs but he's late for the game. So what does he do? He brings the perp with him and sits in the front bleacher.”

Amy was telling the story. The table was lousy with plates and small bowls. The wicker basket rested on the windowsill.

"Do you have to tell this story?" Gallagher reached for his beer but it was empty.

Amy ignored him. "This guy, he's higher than a kite. Starts yelling stuff to us on the court, rude stuff. Dad clocks him in the head to shut him up. All the other parents are looking, shocked. They can see the cuffs on the guy's wrist. I turned beet red. Blew the game I was so embarrassed."

Gallagher's face reddened. "I didn't want to miss the game."

"Aw, that's cute." Lara laughed, leaning forward on the table.

"That's not how the Lieutenant saw it."

"How did you get away with that?" Lara asked. "Vogel must have had a fit."

"I have compromising photos of the Lieutenant with a Shetland pony." He winked at her.

Amy caught that. It was a nanosecond, that little wink, but she caught it. She caught everything. Everyone was loosened up, relaxed under a full belly. Amy liked Lara, thought it was cool that she was a homicide detective. All the other cops in dad's unit were men. They were nice, cracking jokes and acting the goofy uncle around her but Lara seemed different, a certain frankness about her that Amy responded to. But then there was that look between Lara and dad. What was that about?

Gallagher took up his plate. "If you're finished embarrassing me, I'm going back for seconds."

"You mean thirds," Amy said.

"Go to your room."

He lumbered back to the buffet table. Amy huddled in towards Mendes. Girl talk. "So how come you're single?"

Lara leaned back from the question, unaccustomed to a teenager's tactlessness. "I broke up with someone not too long ago. So. I'm just not looking right now."

"You're really pretty," Amy said. "You must have guys buzzing around you all the time."

"No. Not really."

"You know Dad's single. But he's kinda clueless when it comes to women."

Disquiet spilled over the table. Lara pushed her plate back. "Amy, you're not playing matchmaker, are you? Because, well..."

"I'm not. The opposite actually."

Where was this going? Lara couldn't tell. So she listened. Amy filled in the silence. "Cops hook up all the time. Especially partners. Sort of a job hazard. But it always ends badly."

"It happens," Lara said. "But not to everybody."

"I saw the way he looked at you. You're pretty, you're smart. And worse, you're considerate."

"You're watching out for your dad." Lara relaxed, understanding what the girl was trying to say. It was kind of endearing.

"It's happened before. That's how he and mom met."

"Your mom is a police officer?"

"She was. But that ended badly. For everybody."

Lara tilted her head. "You're warning me away. Right?"

"Yeah. I guess so. Just think it through."

Gallagher came back with another plate and felt the chill. He looked at Amy, looked at Lara. "Who died?"

NIGHT shift at the Multnomah County Animal Shelter. Reuben Bendwater worked security alongside one other staff member on the front desk from six till midnight. Staffing these two positions was a tough but necessary dent in the shelter's budget. All manner of people brought animals in once the sun went down. Sometimes there was trouble. Reuben's job was to keep the crazies at bay.

Rueben made his rounds through the basement level. He didn't mind the cold room where the carcasses were kept but the crematory room always gave him the creeps. Like everyone at the shelter, Rueben was an animal lover and this room was both macabre and sad.

Upstairs in the kennel the dogs were quiet, even the feral ones brought in last week. One was a Belgian Malamute mix and the other a bull mastiff with a tan hide and black mask. Rueben had tried to befriend these dogs as he did all the new arrivals but these animals were skittish and aggressive. Sometimes street dogs went that way, nothing you could do. The feral strays did not sleep but they were quiet, chins on the floor. Their eyes watched everything.

Down the row of pens to a cage near the double swing doors. A droopy eyed hound stood up and wagged its tail. Rueben slipped a strip of beef jerky from his shirt pocket and fed it to the dog. He knew he shouldn't but it was just a small piece and the hound was old. No one adopted old dogs.

He scratched the hound's ears. "Here you go, buddy."

Every dog woke at the same moment. On their feet and pacing their cage. Ears up. All barking in an ear-cracking cacophony. Scratching at the grates. The feral dogs stood, tails up, the only animals not barking.

Rueben jolted as if stung. The racket echoed off the painted cinderblock, amplified until the security guard covered his ears. He shouted and shushed but the dogs would not quiet. They barked and yowled and clawed their pens.

Something wrong materialized inside the kennel, down near the rear exit.

A man rose up out of the shadows, out of nothing, at the far end. All stringy hair and beard. A vagrant in a tattered jacket and bare chest. He squatted before the cages holding the latest arrivals, speaking softly to the feral dogs.

"Hey!" Reuben strode forward, his left hand finding the baton. "Get away from there!"

Homeless dudes and crackheads were no stranger to the shelter, wandering in after finding an unlocked door. They usually bolted when Reuben hollered at them. Not this guy, he didn't even look up. Instead, he slid back the bolt and opened the cage door.

"Hey! Stop!" The guy must be fucking crazy. "That dog will bite, asshole!"

That big bull mastiff lumbered out of the cage, licked the man's hand and swung its squared head towards Reuben.

Reuben stopped, boots skidding on the linoleum.

The mastiff charged, nails clicking the floor. Reuben ran for the doors. Instinct pumping his legs. This is crazy.

It slammed into his back, pitching him to the floor. Its jaws clamped his calf and the great dog whipped its head back and forth in violent jerks.

Reuben rolled, kicking out like he was on fire. It wouldn't let go. Something loomed into his field of vision, upside down. The stranger kneeling over him. His grime encrusted hands ripped Reuben by the hair and bounced his skull off the floor. More teeth punctured his groin, the second feral ripping into him.

The other dogs barked and spun in their cages.

PABLO slung his bag over his shoulder, heading out the door. He stopped to go over a few things with Jenny at the front desk. Details that probably could wait but he couldn't help himself, car keys jangling in hand. What's another minute?

Then the clamor from the other side of the swing doors. The dogs going nuts like he had never heard before. Jenny shot out of her chair.

He pushed through the kennel doors with Jenny on his heels. Every dog was loose, running crazily. The door to each pen stood wide open.

Reuben Bendwater lay on the floor.

Pablo waded through the bounding dogs and the animals buckled into his knees. The security guard's face was a rictus of blood, the cheek torn loose in a wet flap. More blood seeped dark over his crotch and bloomed into a widening pool on the tiles. Reuben convulsed, going into shock.

Jenny sprinted back to the lobby to dial 911.

Pablo didn't know what to do. He folded the torn flesh back onto Reuben's face and told him to hang on. He looked up and saw someone else inside the kennel. The dogs raced back and forth, blurring his sightline but he saw it. A figure striding through the crazed dogs, slamming the release bar on the rear door. Two dogs trotted at his heels, the feral canines collected at the crime scene.

The man led the two dogs out to the alley and disappeared behind the shutting door.

17

THE DOGS RAN CRAZY ALONG THE river bank, tumbling together and nipping at each other's ruff. The mastiff and the Malamute ran flat out, tongues flapping loose. The frustration and energy pent up inside the cages now pumped their legs through the weeds and they ran ahead of the others in a deranged glee. When the other caught up, the pack doubled back to find the man.

He scolded them to close ranks and stay away from the lights. They crossed one road and then another, slipping from shadow to shadow. Silent as cats. Off the asphalt road onto a service road of packed gravel to a driveway choked with raspberry bushes. Down a rutted track of mud that bent and curved until they saw the house.

Hidden behind the swaying branches of a weeping willow, a three story clapboard with a porch wrapping the front and north side. The ground floor windows boarded over with plywood, the upper windows dark. The dogs bounded through the blackberry bushes growing wild on every side, lifting their legs to mark territory.

Ivan Prall slipped the duffel bag from his shoulder and looked up at the house. It looked smaller now and the elements had battered it senseless. Paint peeled from the clapboard in curls. The porch sagged this way, every angle tilted out of plumb.

No plywood blocked the backdoor but it was locked. He kicked it in and the dogs bottlenecked the doorframe to get inside. The place smelled of damp rot and earth. Kids had been here, leaving behind their empty bottles and graffiti on the walls.

He dragged the duffel through the mouse droppings to the front of the house, the dogs banging his knees as they raced from room to room. The front room was big, originally a parlor, and some little moonlight fingered its way through the bare windows. The Rottweiler sniffed a corner and lifted a leg to spray. Prall booted the animal away, scolding it.

A folding chair lay flat on the floor. He snapped it open and sat. Rummaged through the bag until he found the bottle of Jack. It spilled into his beard and he wiped it away with the back of his hand. More spray paint marred the walls in this room, the misspelled dirty words of juvenile boys. The knife unfolded with a snap and Ivan Prall carved into the old sheetrock, cutting through the painted glyphs of penises and breasts. The pentagram he carved was crude but it was big and it sanctified the room.

He went back to the chair and took up the bottle. In a while he would go upstairs, to where the horrors had taken place and he would consecrate those rooms too.

THE monster on the television screen roared. Grainy 1970's Technicolor. A stuntman geared up in a hairy monster costume. Ears flopping crazily, the rubber mask unnatural and stiff. The scene was dark, masking the poor production values and slim budget.

Lara sat on the couch, her feet tucked under her. On her lap was one of the black notebooks, a pen and notepad in her hand. Deciphering more of the illegible handwriting. Doing her homework in front of the idiot box, a habit formed in childhood. Flipping over to the news, she found this old monster movie and let it run. Italian, badly dubbed into English, the plot centered on a priest who had been mauled by a werewolf. Struggling to hide his curse, the priest administered mass during the day and transformed into a beast at night, slaughtering his own parishioners.

The climax unspooled and Lara put aside her work altogether. A young nun, secretly enamored of the cursed priest, had uncovered his secret and was now running for her life through a medieval graveyard. She had armed herself with a crossbow, the bolts blessed and sprinkled with holy water, hoping to end the priest's suffering. Hiding among the graves, she struggled to notch another bolt into the heavy weapon but didn't have the strength. The monster tracked her scent through the churchyard, stalking closer and closer. The monster sprang just as she locked her last bolt and fired. The blessed missile pierced the werewolf's heart and it thrashed in the leaves. With tears streaming, the young nun took up a torch and set the monster ablaze. The frame pulled back into a widening shot of the flames amongst the tombstones and the credits crawled up the screen.

Her cell buzzed, floating across the coffee table. The desk sergeant. There was an incident at the animal shelter and detective Gallagher was already on scene. How soon could she be there?

DETECTIVE Mendes badged her way past the uniforms, saw Pablo sitting with detective Rowe. Rowe waved hello and cocked a thumb towards the kennel area. More dogs.

Again the smell of urine and disinfectant. The dogs had been corralled back into the pens and they stood watching but still agitated.

Gallagher kneeled over a body on the floor, hands sheathed in latex as he peeled back a bloodied flap of shirt from the ribcage. Blood grouted the yellow ceramic tiles. Beyond that the floor was smeared with wide swathes of blood, telling of a violent assault. A plastic ID tag swam in the red stuff. Lara knelt down and read the name without touching it. Reuben Bendwater, security.

Gallagher nodded hello. "What do you think, chief? Heart attack or stroke? My first guess was spontaneous human explosion but I may have to revise that theory."

Lara swept the body up and down. The wounds not dissimilar to her first homicide. "What happened?"

"Break and enter," Gallagher said. "Security guard must have surprised the guy, got his skull crushed for his troubles."

"But he's ripped up. Those wounds look like the ones on the Riley woman."

"Yup." Gallagher hollered to the uniform near the door. "Ask Pablo to come in here."

The director returned but kept his eyes from the wreckage at their feet.

"Pablo," Gallagher said, "tell detective Mendes what you told me."

Pablo folded his arms. "I was on my way out when I heard the dogs go crazy. All of them, barking like the place was on fire. I ran back and the dogs were all out of their pens. And there's this guy. The son of a bitch sets all the dogs loose and just walks out the door with two of them at his heel. Like it was nothing."

Lara looked up. "He stole some dogs?"

"Two. The ones from your crime scene. I ran after him but I tripped over… well". Pablo's eyes finally fell to the body. He turned away, one hand over his mouth, the other held up in surrender. "I'm sorry. I can't."

"That's okay." Lara waved at the uniform to lead him out. "Thank you, Pablo." She watched him stagger out then spun back to Gallagher. "He came back for his dogs?"

"Ballsy fuck just waltzes in, kills this poor guy and takes his dogs." Gallagher wanted to spit but choked it back to avoid contaminating the scene. "He's laughing at us."

"This isn't about us. He didn't do this to show off."

"Then why? Why risk this?"

"He came for his wolf pack."

He gritted his teeth. "What?"

"These animals aren't his pets," she said. "They're his pack. His family."

"Don't start with the wolfman shit. Please."

"Then why risk coming here? Think like him for a second, Gallagher. He's a wolf. The pack leader. But he's a wolf without his pack. So he busts in to get them back."

A dog barked through the mesh. Lara looked over the pens, found the eyes of dogs staring back at her. "I should have seen this coming."

"You can't anticipate a psycho, Mendes."

"Yeah, you can. If you're willing to crawl inside his head."

The swing doors breezed open and the CSU techs entered. The one with the camera began shuttering pictures right away.

Gallagher looked at Mendes. "Show me," he said. "Soon as we're done here, show me."

THERE wasn't a lot to be gained at the crime scene. No workable prints were taken from the kennel, neither the cage nor the exit door. The shelter had no security video and the initial canvass of the area turned up nothing. Pablo had only gotten a glimpse of the suspect's back.

Four hours and two coffee runs later, they went back to precinct, leaving the CSU crew to do their work. Gallagher grumbled the whole way back. It wasn't even their case, the call having come in on Rowe's shift, but because of the connection with the stolen dogs, detectives Mendes and Gallagher would share the file. That meant three open cases on his desk.

"Alright detective," he said when they found their desks. "The floor is yours."

Lara looked over the riot of photos and notes on her evidence board, groping for a starting point. "Age ten," she dove in, "Ivan Prall witnesses his father beat his mother to death in a drunken rage. The father goes to jail. With no other family around, the boy is moved into the foster system and shuffled through a number of homes. He gets into trouble as a teen, winds up in juvie jail for two years. After that he's placed in the Gethsemane halfway house where he's abused by the owner, Ronald Kovacks. He runs away and is found three days later on the side of a highway, wounded in some kind of animal attack."

"Yeah." Gallagher knew this part. "The doctor said it was probably a dog, not a wolf."

"Bear with me. Prall is ordered back to the halfway house as soon as he's fit to be moved. But he slips the hospital and disappears." Lara tapped a finger against her lips, gathering the notes in her head. "Clearly he didn't want to go back to the abuse that waited for him at the hands of this Kovacks guy. But now he's alone, scrambling to survive with absolutely nothing. God knows how he did it. No friends, no family and surviving what he did. No way to process what he's been through. Alone and on the run, his only companions are these stray dogs. They become his family. Prall develops this werewolf fantasy to cope with the abuse he suffered. And the violent rages he experiences."

Gallagher frowned, unmoved. "That's a lot of speculation."

"I'm extrapolating from what I've deciphered in his notebooks. But just run with it for now. During this period, there are suspicious deaths similar to ours where the body is mutilated by stray dogs. All of the deceased were engaged in what we call a "high risk lifestyle". Three prostitutes, two female and one male. The fourth and fifth were homeless women."

"But we can't connect any of those."

"Not yet. But look at the locations of the crime scenes." She pointed to five yellow pushpins dotting her map. "One here in Oregon, two in Washington state and two across the border in Canada. In that order too.

"Moving north up the coast, away from Portland. The last death occurs six weeks ago in British Colombia. And then, out of the blue, here." Her finger swung back to a red pushpin in the city of Portland. "He's travelling straight north, not just out of the state but out of the country. Probably headed for the B.C. interior. But Prall stops and beelines back to Portland. Why?"

Gallagher snorted up the obvious. "Because he's fucking crazy."

Lara pulled two newspapers from the chaos of her workspace and handed them over. Gallagher scrutinized the small articles circled in highlighter. Not front page material, the headlines buried in the backpages. *HALFWAY HOUSE OF HORRORS, STAFF CHARGED WITH ABUSE.*

He shrugged. "The Gethsemane house bust. What about it?"

"Look at the date."

He checked the date in the header, little more than a month ago. "The halfway house was busted over a year ago. Why is it only being reported now?"

"The DA has been trying to track down every former resident of the halfway house before going public with it. And since it involved minors, the judge ordered a publication ban on it. The ban finally lifted a month ago. Then the headlines appeared."

"A month ago? The same time Prall stops moving north and comes back here."

"He saw the news," she said. "That's what brought him back."

His shook his head. "Why? He sure as shit didn't come back to press charges."

She took a guess. "Revenge."

Gallagher skimmed the article, looking for a name. "Where are these people from the halfway house? This Kolchak guy?"

"Kovacks. Ronald A. He skipped bail, disappeared. You know Hammond? He lead the halfway house investigation. He thinks Kovacks is still in town, but gone to ground."

"Good luck finding him." Gallagher stretched, popping his spine. He handed the newspapers back to her. "It's late. Go home, get some sleep."

Lara looked at her watch. "Wow, a whole four hours before our shift starts."

"Better than none at all, detective." He strode for the exit, fishing keys out of a pocket. He stopped and turned back. "Hey, Mendes."

She tossed the papers down and looked up. "Yeah?"

"Nice work," he said, halfway through the exit door.

FOUR hours was nothing. Lara had just closed her eyes when the alarm hit. Her morning coffee did nothing to blow the fog from her head nor did the double long espresso snagged before hitting the office.

Gallagher phoned in, asked her to man the desk. He had a court date he'd forgotten about. An investigation from last spring had finally rolled its way into the court and he had to testify. Lara sympathized. Wandering the halls of the courthouse waiting to give your piece was a tedious circle of hell endured by cops of every stripe. Rank and experience held no sway here, all were grist milled to dust.

She wished him luck.

The clock ticked towards noon and detective Rowe's report on the animal shelter homicide still hadn't landed in her in-tray or email. She had to hunt it down. For some reason, it had gone to the Lieutenant first. Why, she didn't know but she wasn't comfortable with it. Was it an error or something else?

Lara went through it, starting with the initial incident report from the responding uniform, the witness statement from Pablo and Rowe's write-up. There was nothing she didn't already know. She needed to talk to Pablo, hear firsthand his account of the incident but it was too soon. The poor guy was such a mess last night. She started reading Rowe's report a second time when the desk phone rang. She scooped it up, said "Mendes."

"Hey, it's detective Hammond. Remember me?"

"Two sugars, no cream. How's business, detective?"

"Brisk." His voice thin down the line. "Course, it depends which side of the fence you're on. The bad guys are raking it in."

She smiled at that. "You thinking about switching sides?"

"Shit, I wouldn't mind tooling around in a big Escalade, nothing to do all day but smoke weed. I wonder what kinda 401 K plan they got?"

She wondered if detective Hammond had called simply to chitchat. Fine by her, the workday slowly going nowhere. Detective Hammond got to the point.

"Listen," he said, "I've been following up on the Kovacks case like you asked. Finally pried loose some answers about the wife, the one who disappeared. Turns out she changed her name."

Lara sat up, snatched up a pen. "What name is that?"

"You sitting down? Her maiden name; Riley. Elizabeth Riley. Your homicide victim."

When Lara didn't say anything, Hammond laughed, wishing he could see her face. “You still there, Mendes?”

“Are you sure?”

“Positive,” he laughed. “Merry Christmas, detective.”

Lara put the receiver down and sat very still. She looked down at her notepad, the doodles scrawled out while Hammond chitchatted. Before he dropped his bomb on her. She had doodled five pointed stars inside circles. Just like the ones scribbled in Prall's notebooks. Pentagrams.

18

GALLAGHER WAS ASLEEP IN THE Cherokee, snores bouncing around inside the cab, oblivious to his own racket. What woke him up was the Mazda parked next to him. Its alarm went off for no reason and Gallagher jerked awake. Pain spiked up his neck, a pinched nerve or strained muscle. He blinked stupidly through the windshield. Still in the parking garage.

His day had started off bad and slid downhill from there. Two hours of sleep before the alarm chimed. He got up so tired he felt drunk. The morning routine was slow-motion, his brains numb and hands clumsy. Hollering at Amy to get up, checking his schedule. The court date. He'd forgotten all about it. The day hadn't even started and it was already shot to hell.

Then it was a rush to get Amy up and off to school. Her normal morning state was little better than that of a shuffling zombie, deaf to his prompting to get moving. Irritated, he barked at her to snap out of it and get her lazy ass to school.

Uncool, dad, uncool. Amy was silent on the drive to school. He apologized but she wouldn't have any of it. He told himself he'd fix it over dinner. They'd have to eat early tonight, Amy had a basketball game.

Court dates were the worst. And being grilled by some piece of shit defense lawyer wasn't the tough part. It was the waiting that killed you. Something always went wrong, something always got delayed. Your day was shot, that was it. Raised Catholic, Gallagher still believed in Hell. It will be this, he knew. Haunting a hallway, waiting for something that will never happen.

The case was shit too. A drug killing last May, Gallagher kneeling over the body of a nineteen year old kid named Tovar, face down in a puddle. Grilling the victim's girlfriend, he learned that Tovar owed money to some braindead named Delaney. He even pried loose a couple of witnesses who saw Delaney talking to the victim earlier that night. They had shell casings at the scene, nine millimeter. Common as dirt but they had no weapon on Delaney. A few other details but it was all small stuff. The lawyer from the DA office tried to bully the accused to plea deal but Delaney refused and forced it to trial. Now it was showtime and Gallagher knew they were sunk but there was no way to turn the train around now. So he waited.

The call came after three. Gallagher endured a grilling from a wide-eared defense lawyer determined to make him look like a brainless jackass. Gallagher bristled but kept his face stone no matter what the little shit said. You had to keep your cool. The minute you got angry, you were dead because juries read anger as guilt or denial. Even from a cop.

He climbed back into his truck in the parking garage, exhausted. Testifying is a workout without the work. Adrenaline juices up your heart but all you do is sit there. Five minutes, he told himself. A five minute nap, then the drive home.

The Mazda's alarm zapped him awake. Pie-eyed, drooling at the dashboard clock. Five twenty. Jesus Christ. He keyed the ignition and squealed the tires down the garage ramp.

Amy's basketball game was at six-thirty. He needed to have dinner on the table by five on a game night. Now the poor kid was going to go play ball on an empty stomach. Plus he still needed to smooth things over for barking at her this morning.

"You are the world's worst fucking dad," he spit. "Put that on a frigging T-shirt and wear it."

He dug for his phone. If she hadn't eaten already, he'd call Pizzzadelic and they could pick it up on the way, eat in the truck. The cell screen was dark. He'd turned it off before going into the box and had forgotten to turn it back on. Dumbass. He thumbed it on, waited for the stupid thing to boot up. Nine messages. Two from home, three from the office and four from Mendes's cell. He dialed home, the rest would have to wait.

AFTER leaving the second message, Amy got her gear and threw dinner together. Gyro sandwiches using last night's pork loin, a green salad. She caught the phone on the first ring and made his to go. He ate it on the way, steering with his knees.

He apologized for barking at her this morning, said being tired was no excuse. She admitted she hated mornings too and they left it at that. They rolled into the parking lot and Amy bolted for the gym.

He squeezed onto the second bleacher between the other parents. He said hello to the few people he knew and waved at the parents whose names he'd forgotten. All of them couples, moms and dads watching their daughters go up against the visiting team. And here he was, the single parent. An object of pity, a reminder to children of what happens in broken homes. Gallagher loved watching Amy's games, basketball and soccer and all the way back to T-ball, but he never felt comfortable around other parents. Judgment hung in the air, the stacking up of social status and comparable incomes. It was exhausting.

Shoes squealed on the hardwood. The ball was thrown back into play and Amy rushed to position. The visiting team was big, almost all of them looming a foot over Amy. They charged in fast and Amy lunged up to block a shot, got knocked to the floor. The whistle blew and two of Amy's team helped her up. She shook it off and limped back to position.

Gallagher shot to his feet and barked at the ref to open his goddamn eyes. Amy waved him off, her hand gesture signaling two meanings: I'm fine and please don't embarrass me. He sat back down and glared at the offending player with the same death-rays he reserved for shitbags on the street. He couldn't help it.

His phone buzzed. He put it to his ear. "Gallagher."

"Are you okay?" Lara's voice over the line. "I couldn't get through."

"Technical problems." He watched the ball go back into play. "What's up?"

"Our victim, Elizabeth Riley? She knew Ivan Prall."

"How do you know that?"

"Because she used to be Bethany Kovacks," she said. "Married to Ronald Kovacks. They ran the halfway house where Prall was abused. She filed divorced papers, changed her name."

"Damn," he said. His attention split between the call and the game. "She's the one whose records disappeared."

"Say that again. I can't hear you."

"You were right," he spoke up. "Prall came back for a reason."

"I want to take a look at that halfway house. How soon can you be there?"

"I can't. We'll do it tomorrow. First thing."

"Where are you?" She strained to hear him through the background racket. "I can barely hear you."

"Amy's basketball game."

"Oh. Well, wish her luck."

There was a pause over the line. Gallagher covered his other ear to block out the noise around him. "What?"

"I'll fill you in tomorrow," she said.

"Don't be a cowboy, Mendes," he shouted into the phone. "Wait until tomorrow, we'll both go."

"Cowboy? Is that supposed to be funny?"

"You know what I mean."

"Have fun." She hung up.

Gallagher dropped the cell into his pocket, turned his attention to the game. He checked the scoreboard. The visitors scored again and he'd missed it entirely. Amy leapt for the ball and took another hit from the same girl who hammered her earlier. Amy took the hit and stayed on her feet. Atta girl.

He fidgeted on the bleacher, one thought nagging him. She wouldn't do anything stupid, would she? Stupid was his department. Mendes played it safe.

Right?

TUCKED inside a dog-eared file folder was a photograph of the Gethsemane Halfway House. The files from the investigation into Ronald Kovacks were still tied up in the evidentiary chain but Hammond had sent over some copies he'd made for his own use. Lara hadn't found anything useful in it but remembered seeing a photo of the house. She dug it out and studied the picture. A big clapboard house, sturdy but badly used up. Nothing special.

Still, this was where their suspect had been placed after a stint in juvie and subsequently abused by the man who ran the place. Ivan Prall had returned to Portland, tracked down the woman who used to run the place and killed her. His dogs devoured the body in an attempt to conceal evidence. Something had happened inside this house that sent their suspect into the wilderness, into the company of stray dogs and solitude.

The house looked familiar. Where had she seen it before? She laid the photo aside and pulled out the notebooks taken from the suspect's squat. She flipped through the pencil sketches. In the third notebook, she found a drawing of a house with a porch wrapping two sides, flanked by willows. The Gethsemane house.

The artist was a fair draftsman, the perspective true and the scale accurate. She went back to Hammond's file and found the address. A road she didn't recognize, somewhere north of an industrial park near the river. She printed off a Google map and circled the road in red ink for a quick reference tomorrow morning.

Detective Rowe buzzed by her desk, late on the shift change. He said hello, she said goodnight.

THE rain had slowed to a light mist that hazed the lights on the streets. Lara hit the tail end of rush hour but shot past the turnoff for home. She just wanted to see the place, that's all. What could one look hurt?

She swung west over Columbia and then up North Portland Road over the slough where the road thinned between the lake and the golf course. Into a gravel lot where the driveway was supposed to be. She missed it the first time, overgrown with weeds as it was. Slow over the rutted driveway, the path twisting through the dogwood trees and then the house appeared. The headlights played over the facade. A signboard creaked in the breeze, hung from a chain on the porch roof. She tilted her head to read the words. GETHSEMANE HOUSE - Center for transition and redemption.

Lara wanted a closer look. She cut the engine but left the headlamps on. The steps rang hollow under her feet, the floorboards of the veranda uneven and creaky. The front door was boarded up with plywood, as were all the first floor windows.

"Okay," she said to no one. Herself. "You've had a look. Go home."

Back to the car. She popped the trunk and found the long handled Maglite. She dug around the mess and pulled out a prybar. The trunk banged shut and she stopped, rethinking what she was about to do. This wasn't like her. This is how Gallagher did things. Just bust in, trample procedure and justify it all later. For Christ's sakes, Lara Estela. Go home.

The prybar sunk cleanly under the plywood. She pried the nails up and hauled back the plywood, shredding the edges. The front door was unlocked but stuck tight in its frame. It popped open under her shoulder.

The flashlight cut a borehole through the darkness. A roomy foyer with a small desk, then on towards a common area. An office on her right. The air was ripe with mould and wet carpet. Graffiti on the walls and empty jugs of Colt 45 dead on the floor. The fate of any property left abandoned too long. Down the hallway to a large kitchen. A table but no chairs, more trash on the green tiled floor. Everything desiccated and forgotten.

Back to the hallway and the staircase to the second floor. The lightbeam rolled up the steps before her, vanishing into a black hole at the top. She stopped on a step and listened. A noise? She realized her heart was pounding. This is crazy. She did not want to run into any vagrant squatter in the dark. Her nerves so keyed up, she'd blow his head off first before asking any questions.

She hollered out. "This is detective Mendes of the Portland Police! Announce yourself now! I am armed!"

Her voice was swallowed up. The house ticked and creaked around her. Crickets in the yard. She went up.

The hallway flanked by a handrail, doors on her right. She pushed open the first one, throwing the light inside. Metal bunks stripped of bedding and two mismatched dressers. A footlocker. She moved on, opening the rest of the doors. A bathroom and then another room with empty bunks. The window was broken and the breeze fluttered a rotting web of curtain.

That left the room at the end. No door, the hall opening into another common room at the front of the house. It was roomy and bare. A single armchair near the bay window. A mound of clothes piled near it, another empty bottle rolled to the baseboard. She trailed her light over it.

This wasn't just more random trash. The clothes spilled from a duffel bag, a bedroll next to it. Beer cans, drained and crushed. Something crunched under her heel and the Maglite found kibble scattered on the floor. More dog feed spilled from a bag in the corner.

A single thought rang in her head. He's here. Lara backed up and the light arced over the wall. Carved into the old plaster was another pentagram.

19

THEY WERE LOSING, TRAILING THE visitors by fourteen points. Seven minutes left in the quarter. Amy's knee throbbed, her limp becoming more pronounced. The coach benched her and she turned around to find her dad. He looked worried.

Gallagher hollered down, asked if she was okay. She gave him a thumbs-up but her face was flushed and she didn't smile. That's okay, he told himself. She's focused on the game. She needed to be, the visiting team was handing them their asses on a plate. He gave back an enthusiastic thumbs up. You can still turn this around. Miracles happen.

His phone went off and he ignored the first five rings before looking at the display. He thumbed the button and cupped his palm over his other ear. "Mendes?"

"He's here." Her voice was shrill, all wrong.

"What?"

"I'm at the halfway house. I wanted to see it." Her voice choked, gulping air. "He's here."

"You went alone? I said we'd go tomorrow—"

"Shut up." She cut him off. "His things are here. He's camped out in this house."

She broke in. Gallagher couldn't believe it. Mendes was such a straight arrow. "Get out of there. Call the precinct, get some uniforms out there right now."

"Oh shit." Her voice crackled, fading in and out of reception. He jammed his palm harder into his free ear.

"Mendes? I can't hear you!"

The line crackled back to life. "He's here! Oh shit. He's— "

"Lara?"

The line went dead. He lost her.

Gallagher hit the return-call. He gripped the elbow of the woman next to him. Her daughter was on the team, a friend of Amy's. The woman startled but he blurted past her protests, saying he had an emergency and would she please drive Amy home. The woman agreed, seeing the urgency in his face. Gallagher hustled down the row, knocking into the other parents.

The coach hurled Amy back onto the floor and she took her position just as the ball was thrown. She glanced up just in time to see her dad race for the exit. Where was he going?

Boom. She got knocked again, landing ass first on the hardwood.

LARA debated who to call when she saw the pentagram on the wall. Gallagher or backup? She'd broken in without a warrant so Gallagher it was. He had a knack for justifying rash actions after the fact.

He had just picked up when noise broke from outside. She swept aside the tattered drape in the window and looked down. Dogs trotted back and forth over the driveway, skulking around her car. One marked its scent on a wheel, another lunged up and stood square on the hood. These were Prall's dogs. The animals bolted for the house, disappearing from her eyeline under the eaves.

Frost etched up her backbone. Not the dogs. The phone went silent, the screen winking out like a snuffed candle. Her fingers had white-knuckled around it, inadvertently killing the connection.

Something else moved down in the yard. Ivan Prall lumbered out of the shadows. He looked down at the car then swiveled his head up and looked right up at her.

She ran for the stairs but everything seemed wrong. Her feet were numb, like dead clubs at the end of her ankles. Clumsy and slow, she staggered through the corridor to the stairs. The dogs were already inside the house. They surged forward at a dead run and hit the landing. Bounding up the steps. Gnashing teeth and foaming maws.

She backpedalled along the wall. Pulled her weapon.

The dogs tore up the stairs, one leaping over the other to get at her. She swung the gun up and fired. One dog yowled but didn't drop. The forerunner balked at the sound of gunfire but the rest pitched forward. Too many, too fast.

Lara fell backwards into a room and kicked the door, slamming it into the frame. The dogs thundered into it. The door jostled as the animals slammed against it. Lara shoved back with both heels.

The flashlight rolled an arc over the floorboards. She dug in and leveled the Glock in both hands. Her guts told her to fire straight through the door but the old door might splinter apart, letting them in. Did she have enough rounds to put down all of the dogs? No.

The phone. Where was the phone? It was in her hand but all she held now was the gun. She must have dropped it. Out there.

"Oh God."

The cell phone lay on the floor in the corridor. It spun around, kicked about by the crazed dogs. A hand reached down, batted the animals away and picked it up. Ivan Prall flipped it open and then snapped it in two.

GALLAGHER tore into traffic, swerving crazily between lanes. Cars honked, one driver thrusting a hand out the window to give him the finger. The dashboard beeped nonstop for him to put on his seatbelt.

He hit the speed dial. Her phone rang three times then went dead. He tried again but this time it didn't even ring.

He called dispatch and barked at someone to get the address for the Gethsemane Halfway House. He spelled it for her. The dispatcher came back with an address and he repeated the number to himself. He briefed dispatch on the emergency, any unit in the vicinity to respond to that address.

He hung up and tried Mendes's number again. Nothing. He gunned the engine harder and lay on the horn for everyone to get the hell out of the way.

THE dogs ceased ramming the door, stopped barking. No sound at all from the other side. She dropped her feet from the door and rolled to her knees. Nothing happened.

Lara held her breath to listen. Wind rattled the window but that was all. She gripped the knob, said a prayer and flung the door back, ready to blow the hell out of the first thing that moved. Nothing did. The corridor was empty.

She retrieved the Maglite and threw the beam down the hallway. Her phone lay on the floor, snapped off at the hinge. Moving forward to the landing, the lightbeam rippled down each step to the bottom. Nothing to see. No noise at all.

The car was in the yard, the keys in her pocket. She had let off one round, still a full clip if she needed it. Move.

Down the stairs, each step creaking louder than the last. More darkness at the bottom of the stairs, the hallway empty. Ten paces to the door and she'd be outside, then a dead run to the car.

Counting strides, she crossed through the front room towards the door. She heard the dogs before she saw them. Panting in the dark. A dozen eyes twinkling in the dark, blocking her path. None of them moved nor did they bark. Waiting for something to happen.

"You. You busted up my den."

Her heart failed. The voice behind her. She swung round until both the beam and the gun barrel found him.

Ivan Prall stood in the doorway, watching her. His teeth shone through the foul beard, eyes thatched under stringy hair. Shirtless beneath a tattered green raincoat. Two dogs at his feet, one a crossbreed pit and the other a pale-eyed Husky.

Lara lost and then found her voice. "Get on the ground. On the ground!"

The dogs barked, reacting to the threat. Lara felt them close in behind her. Revulsion inched bile up her throat, made her knees quake.

Prall didn't move. "The cousins don't like guns."

She notched the barrel from his torso up to his face. "Call off the dogs. Do it now."

"I got shit to do, sister. Go hunt somebody else."

He didn't move, didn't react to having a gun aimed at his head. Lara gritted her teeth. One eye on him, one on the damn dogs. Not enough guns to go around. Try something else. "Prall," she scaled back the tone. "Listen to me. You're sick. You need help. I can help you. But first you have to call off the dogs."

"You know, don't you?" His nostrils flared, sniffing the air. Smelling her. He stepped forward. "You know about the wolf."

"I swear to God," she hissed. "I will blow your brains out. Call off the dogs!"

"You scared, little piggy. I can smell it on you."

His teeth grinned in the light, wet and stained. Another step closer. "You ain't gonna shoot. Don't got it in you."

Lara swung the barrel down, drew a dead aim at the pit bull and shot the animal through the head. It flopped back, blood spattering the other animal. Prall went crazy.

"YOU FUCKING PIG!"

And then it all went to hell. The dogs lunged at her back. She spun and fired and fired and fired.

God knows what she hit, not a single animal fell. The dogs scrambled away and then circled back. Teeth popping, eager to kill.

Lara fought back the raw urge to blast out the entire magazine. She steadied and drew a bead on the nearest animal, an enormous mastiff, but the dogs turned and ran. Bolting away like rats across the floorboards. Slipping into the dark.

She wheeled the gun back to Prall but the corridor stood empty. The dead pit bull on the floor, its legs kicking as it died.

A noise, unnatural and out of place. Low, guttural. Something moved in the dark. The air pressure in the room dropped. She swung the light round to find it.

Teeth flashed in the beam. Big and sharp. The snout enormous and terrible like some prehistoric thing.

It slammed into her midsection, folding her in two like paper. Her back hit the floor. Lara screamed.

She pulled the trigger. Bang. Bang. Bang. The thing backed off. She blasted another round but it was gone.

Heels dug in, propelling herself away from the damn thing. Her stomach withered against the pain. One hand instinctively clutching her belly, coming back hot and wet. She was bleeding. How bad? Jesus, how bad?

She had lost the flashlight. It rolled across the floor-boards, spinning its beam round and round the room. It strobed past the thing. It was enormous, its dark hackles crested into razor points along its back. Muzzle low to the ground. A wolf and yet not a wolf. A monster dredged up from primeval memories and the grimmest of fairy tales.

Lara raised the weapon but her arm was numb, the gun a dead weight in her hand. She fired, it went stray. The mon-ster sidled forward and grunted, a vile sound like nothing she'd ever heard before.

It launched at her. She fired. Jaws clamped her arm, jerked her back and forth like a rag. She clubbed at it. The monster let go of her arm and dug for her guts, pushing her clear across the floor.

Don't pass out. That was all she thought. Don't pass out. Don't die.

GALLAGHER had dinged two bumpers and picked up one police cruiser speeding on his tail with full lights and siren. Whether this was the backup he called for or a uni-form chasing a reckless driver he couldn't tell. It didn't mat-ter.

The Cherokee fishtailed as it hit the gravel road, tires spitting stones at the police vehicle behind it. Gallagher stomped the accelerator, looking for the house. It rose out of the trees, Mendes's car out front. Dogs swarmed over the tilting porch, eyes swinging up to the rambling vehicles. They bolted away at the racket of the sirens.

Gallagher sprinted for the door, hollering her name. No response. Something moved inside, crashing and thudding.

He charged in, gun out. A flashlight on the floor. Framed in the cone of light, Mendes. Something big pinning her down, hovering obscenely over her. Too big to be a fucking dog, more like a bear. He aimed and fired.

It spun and loped away. He fired and fired but it was long gone. Whatever the hell it was.

He dropped to Mendes, called her name again. Mendes didn't move, did not respond. A wet gurgle bubbled from her throat. There was blood and a lot of it. He couldn't tell where it came from. He didn't know what to do. He gripped her hand.

"Hang on, Lara. You're gonna be all right. Just hang on."

He didn't know what else to say so he just kept repeating it.

The uniform huffed into the house. Gallagher screamed at him to call an ambulance. Officer down.

20

DETECTIVE LARA MENDES WAS jostled hard on the stretcher as the paramedics scrambled into emergency. Gallagher was stopped by a nurse who told him to stay back and let the doctors do their job. He watched the gurney disappear behind a set of double doors and someone stuck a clipboard of forms in his hand. Said the best way to help her now was to provide them with her information. The officer who had chased him into the house stayed with him now, prodding Gallagher to a chair. His name was DiMatteo and when they waited for the ambulance to come, officer DiMatteo had had the presence of mind to pull Mendes's bag from her car. The officer sifted through the bag and pulled up a wallet of credit cards and

ID, placed it in Gallagher's hands and turned to the exit. The detective watched the officer leave, making a mental note of the kid's name. He'd look him up in the roll and thank him later.

He rooted for his phone and called home. Amy was fine but a little freaked seeing him book from the gym so fast. He apologized, said it was an emergency but did not mention Mendes's name. He told her everything was fine but he'd be late and hung up. Looking down at the forms, he realized he hadn't even asked if they'd won the game.

Some of the information he had to leave blank. He simply didn't know and couldn't find anymore info in her bag. He should call somebody, a boyfriend or family. He leaned back in the chair, realizing he didn't know anything at all about Lara Mendes.

The cell came back out and he called into precinct, told the desk to patch him through to whoever was working night shift homicide. He got Varadero, who immediately assaulted him with questions about the Bendwater file. The security guard at the animal shelter. Gallagher told him to shut up and briefed him on the assault on Mendes. He asked Varadero to look up her personal info and find her emergency contact info.

He listened to Varadero bitch about sharing info as he pulled up the profile. "Got it," said Varadero. "Marisol Sparks."

"Marisol?" Gallagher dug into Mendes's bag for a pen. "What's the relation?"

"Sister. You want the number?"

He wrote it down, thanked Varadero and put the phone away. A sister? Lara had mentioned once that she had family down south but that was all. He dug though the wallet and slipped out a photo webbed with creases. Lara with her arm around a dark haired woman at a backyard barbecue. A boy of about four or five with his head sandwiched between them. He could see the resemblance between Lara and her sister Marisol but could not tell which one was older, which one the younger.

He looked at the phone number Varadero had given him for the sister. A New Mexico prefix. He looked at his watch. What time was it in Albuquerque? No sense calling the woman up in the middle of the night with no clue as to her sister's condition. He'd call tomorrow when he knew more.

Why had she never mentioned a sister? Maybe she had and he just wasn't listening. Gee, how unlike him. He'd been hard on her, bullying her into requesting another partner but Mendes hadn't caved. She stuck it out, took the punishment and look where it got her. He had put another partner in the hospital. Great fucking work, Detective Gallagher.

The forms went back to the nurse and he asked about Mendes's condition. The nurse couldn't tell him, the doctors were still with her. She promised to let him know as soon as she heard anything.

So he waited, slumped in a chair and looking around at the other people waiting. He went through the course of events, mentally drafting his incident report, but he kept stumbling on one image. The thing that was attacking her.

He had no more than a glimpse of it but it was huge. More like a grizzly than a dog. What the hell was it?

People came and went, the injured and the concerned. He grew tired of figuring out what he had seen and what would go down in his incident report. It was a dog. Just a big flipping dog.

THE dogs ran and ran, a full quarter mile before slowing down or even looking back. Every animal feverish after the sprint, tongues lolling from their chops. The wolf paced and trotted, striking out at the lesser animals. These dogs whined and squatted submission. The others hung their tails low. The pack lead was unappeasable, furious at having been run out of another den. The bitch leaned into the alpha, offering her rump. The only female left in the pack now. The wolf sunk its teeth into her scruff and chased her off. The pack backed away and kept their heads down.

All except the Pincer. An immature male that had joined them three nights ago. It was young and ignorant of hierarchy. The Pincer kept its tail up and crossed broadside before the lead. An affront by a pup who confused agitation with bravado.

The alpha stopped cold at the mutt's boldness. The pack sklathed away, sensing what was coming.

The wolf struck without a sound and without warning. Its hellish jaws snapped the Pincer's snout bone into splinters and the animal shrieked. The wolf released and dug into its neck, teeth puncturing to the spine. It rent the dog's throat violently, almost shearing the animal's head from its neck. Blood geysered out to steam on the cold ground. The wolf tore at it until its hide was slick with offal. Then it loped for the trees, a mist of blood clinging to it, and the others chased after it.

IT was two hours before someone came out to talk to him. The doctor, a woman who looked no older than his daughter, stated that Mendes had suffered trauma to her abdomen and left arm and right leg. The puncture wounds were severe and there was some blood loss and the small finger on the left hand was broken. The doctor asked what had happened. Gallagher said his partner had been attacked by dogs. The doctor didn't know what to make of that, having treated dog bites before. She said they would monitor Mendes for twenty-four hours before treating her for rabies. He asked if that was necessary but she thought it better to err on the side of caution.

Gallagher winced at the thought of twenty needles injected straight into the navel, asked if that was wise given the wounds to Mendes's abdomen.

“Oh, we don't do that anymore,” the doctor said. “Rabies treatment is much easier now. We'll monitor her for infection from the dog bites. The real risk now is sepsis.”

“When will she wake up?”

“Hard to say really. She might sleep straight through until tomorrow or she could wake within the hour.”

“Can I see her?”

LARA Mendes looked dead. A loose hospital gown had been fitted on, folded up just below the chest. Below that her torso was bandaged up. Her left arm was wrapped and elevated. She was so pale. Her eyes closed, mouth slightly parted. Gallagher reached out and touched her cheek. Her skin was cool and damp. He wanted to say something, anything, but nothing came.

A figure filled the doorway. Gallagher turned to see the Lieutenant standing there. Vogel waved at him to step out of the room. Gallagher sighed. Time to pay the piper.

They stood in the corridor, looking through the window at Mendes as Gallagher gave his boss a brief rundown of the events. The Lieutenant listened, arms folded. Unimpressed to say the least. "That's it?"

Gallagher shrugged. "She was following a lead. Ran right into the son of a bitch."

"Mendes?" Vogel wasn't buying any of it. "Mendes acts alone and breaks into this place with no warrant? That's your MO, not hers."

"She's a quick study."

"Don't get cute, Gallagher. You put another cop in a sick bed."

"I wasn't even there."

"You should have been."

Gallagher worked his jaw but held his tongue. No choice but to eat it.

Vogel scratched his chin. "The doctor say how long she'll need to recover?"

"They don't know."

"Okay. I want Bingham and Latimer to step in. You bring them up to speed on this."

"No." Gallagher's jaw worked overtime. "No fucking way. Sir."

"Be practical, John. You're down a detective."

"She'll get better. And when she does, we will nail this asshole to the wall."

Vogel's eyes drifted back to Mendes. "Did you call her family?"

"They're out of state. I'm gonna wait until I know more. No need for them to hop on a plane for nothing."

"Someone should be here when she wakes up."

"Someone will," Gallagher said.

Vogel exhaled through his nose. "You got three days. If Mendes doesn't pull out of this, the file goes to Bingham." He walked away, calling back over his shoulder. "Find a bed, John. Get some sleep."

HE left his number with the hospital staff and asked them to call immediately if there was any change in her condition. Gallagher drove to work and went up to the Sex Assault unit. He spoke to the night shift Sergeant about Mendes, asked what friends she had in her old unit. He found Charlene Farbre, told her about Mendes and said he needed volunteers to stay with her. He'd work out a shift. Charlene agreed without hesitation, piling work into a tote bag. She'd go now, she could work from the hospital room but she had to leave at three. Charlene jotted down the names of a few other people who could help and then left.

Gallagher made a few calls from his desk and then piled up some work to take home. He looked at the notebooks teetering on Mendes's desk. Prall's journals. He took three of them and headed for the parking garage.

AMY WAS hurting. Her left leg was bruised blue and her elbow ached like it was busted. She pounded the alarm off and blinked at the time. Late. Dad's bark usually woke her before the alarm but not this morning. The house was quiet and still.

She padded downstairs to an empty kitchen. No coffee brewing in the pot. Dad was on the sofa, snoring into a dented cushion. Paperwork and photographs piled up on the coffee table. A cheap looking notebook lay open on his chest.

"Dad." Amy shook his shoulder. Gentle at first, then not so gentle.

His eyes blinked at her in a stupefied glaze like he didn't recognize her. He tilted into a sitting position, letting the notebook fall to the floor. "I'm up. What time is it?"

"Late." Amy looked at the mess of work. "Did you pull an all-nighter?"

"Sorta." He staggered to the kitchen and fumbled with the coffeemaker. "Hey, how'd the game go last night?"

"What happened to Lara?" Amy leaned against the counter but the formica edge bit into her bruised hip. "Is she okay?"

"What? Amy..." He looked over and gave her his patented disapproving-dad glare. Gallagher kept a police radio in his office. Amy had a bad habit of tuning it in and listening when she was bored. Or worried. "What have I told you about listening to the police ban?"

"How bad is she?"

"She's gonna be okay," he said.

"The dispatcher said she was mauled by dogs. Like that woman, the dead prostitute."

He poured water into the coffee maker, set the pot on the burner and looked at her. "That's police business, honey. Now go get ready for school. I'll make breakfast."

She slid off the stool. He noticed her limp. "Hey, are you hurt?"

"Just sore."

"That kid walloped you good, huh?"

"Twice. That bitch was tough."

He laughed even though he meant to admonish her language. She limped off for the stairs but he called her back.

"Lara's still unconscious. She doesn't have any family nearby and I don't want her to wake up and find nobody there. We're rotating shifts at her bedside. Can you go sit with her after school?"

"I have practice at four."

"Right," he said. "I forgot."

"No. I mean I'll do it. I'll skip." Amy shivered. The house was cold. "I can be there by three-thirty. Stay till seven? That means you have to cook."

"Done." He smiled at her. The coffee maker gurgled and steamed, fogging up the cupboards.

21

GALLAGHER BYPASSED THE PRECINCT altogether and drove straight to the hospital. His gut told him to lower his expectations but he couldn't help hoping for some good news. He'd walk into the room to find Lara sitting up and wolfing down breakfast. Eager to get back to work.

She looked exactly as he'd left her. Unconscious and unresponsive. A little paler this morning. He pulled the chair up to the bed and spoke softly to her, updating her on the case and griping over the Lieutenant's temperament. He omitted Vogel's threat to pull the investigation out from under them but added some office gossip. When he'd exhausted his news, Gallagher sat quiet for a spell. Then he squeezed her hand and said he'd be back later.

The tired-looking nurse at the desk clicked through charts on her screen and told him there had been little change in Lara's condition. She was stable, that's all. Sorry. He walked back to his truck in the parking lot and dug out the phone number for Lara's sister, Marisol. He couldn't put this off any longer so he dialed Albuquerque.

Marisol Sparks sounded tired when she answered, then became panicked when he explained what had happened. She calmed when Gallagher assured her that her sister was stable and someone was sitting with her at all times. Marisol was an army wife, her husband stationed overseas in Kandahar. She was home alone with their four year old son, trying to make ends meet. Marisol fretted the details, she'd have to pack her boy into the car and drive up to Oregon, there was just no money for plane tickets. Gallagher told her to stay put, there was nothing to do for Lara at the moment. It took a few minutes to convince her but Marisol finally agreed. He promised her that her sister wouldn't wake up to an empty hospital room, her friends at the precinct were rotating shifts to sit with her and he himself would call her the minute there was any change in Lara's condition. Marisol sobbed quietly and then choked up a laugh. "All this time," she said, "I'm praying for my husband's safe return. It's like holding your breath, dreading a phone call about something bad over there in Afghanistan.

Instead, I get a call about Lara. It's almost funny. Or ironic, I dunno."

"She's gonna be okay, ma'am." He lied, unsure if it was for her sake or his. "Lara's pretty tough."

"She is. But dogs? My God, of all things."

"She doesn't much care for them, does she?"

"God no," Marisol said. "She hates dogs. Has ever since she was little."

"Why is that?"

"Didn't she tell you? When she was nine, she and a friend were attacked by dogs. This creep who lived at the end of the block, he had two pit bulls. Kept them locked in the garage all the time. I mean, all the time. The dogs had gone crazy being locked up like that, you know. Well they got out one day. Tore through the neighborhood. Went after two little girls playing on the sidewalk. Lara wasn't hurt but she saw her friend mauled by those two animals. She's hated dogs ever since. Scared to death of them."

Gallagher listened. Unanswered questions clicked into place and with it, a twang of remorse. Hell, he'd hate dogs too if he'd endured that. He gave Marisol the number for the hospital and the name of the doctor looking after Lara. His cell number too. He said everything would be fine and got off the phone. It was stupid to promise such things but he couldn't think of any other way to say goodbye after dumping such shitty news in the poor woman's lap. "Please," he said to no one, thin air. "Please don't make a liar out of me."

HE drove to the crime scene, rain pattering the windshield all the way. Detectives Rowe and Varadero had rotated to the graveyard shift so the incident was theirs. One unmarked car was still here, parked in the gravel beside the CSU truck. Water beaded on the vehicles, the lawn soggy from the overnight rain.

A uniformed officer stood on the porch, blowing into her hands to keep them warm. Gallagher nodded as he came up the steps. "They still here?"

"Yes sir." The officer stuck her hands in her pockets. "One detective is here, the other one went back. I think the CSU techs are almost done."

"Cold this morning, huh?" Gallagher watched her shiver.

"I been out here since four this morning," she said. "The dampness just seeps into your clothes, you know?"

"My truck's still warm. Go sit inside, warm up."

"I'm okay, sir. But thanks."

The CSU tech had finished taking pictures and was packing away his camera. The casings spun from Mendes's weapon had been collected and tagged, leaving only chalk circles on the floor. Blue latex gloves were peeled off sweaty hands and tossed in a bag.

Gallagher passed through the foyer into a tall corridor. Detective Rowe sat in a wicker chair sketching a floorplan of the scene into his notebook. A simple but elegant stick figure represented Detective Mendes, with arrows vectoring the angle of rounds fired. Rowe's face was serene as he sketched, losing himself in the simple craft of drawing. At his feet lay the carcass of another dead dog, its hide slick with jellied blood.

"How's Mendes?" Rowe asked without looking up from his drawing.

"Stable." Gallagher knelt over the carcass. Like the others, the dog was big and fierce, some breed he didn't recognize. But it was mangy too, with bald patches of hide and ribs poking through the skin. "Mean-looking bastard, isn't he?"

"Malnourished too." Rowe set aside the notepad and pondered the dead dog. "Look at the damn ribs on it."

"These dogs got a sweet tooth for eating people. Guess it's a long spell between meals."

Rowe chuckled at that, said, "I read your reports on this guy, how he runs with a pack of stray dogs. Look at these scars." His pencil ran along scar tissue scored on the neck and snout. "These dogs fight each other. These scars are a telltale sign of signs of some internecine scrap within the pack."

An eyebrow went up. "You an expert in wild dogs?"

"Saw it on the Discovery channel."

Gallagher rose and eyeballed the scene. "What do you got?"

"Well, it looks like detective Mendes had a hell of a fight on her hands. She put down this dog then spent her clip in that direction. She ran, got swarmed. See here?" Rowe waved his pencil at the blood smears on the floor. "She got taken down here, put up a fight. See the swipe pattern?"

A red snow angel on the linoleum. Gallagher pictured it in his head, running the events in vivid Technicolor.

Mendes, alone and swarmed by dogs, by the animals she feared most. He felt queasy and shook his head to disperse the looping images but they would not leave.

Detective Rowe closed his notebook. "What did you see, Gallagher?"

No response. Gallagher simply stared at the bloody smear at his feet. What the hell had he seen?

"You okay, man?"

"I saw a dog," Gallagher mumbled. "It took her down. Not this one." He nodded at the carcass. "Some other dog. Big one."

"I hear that." Rowe stepped over the mess and hovered over a red patch further down. "Look at this."

Gallagher stepped over the blood to where Rowe was pointing. A paw print of blood and dirt, like the others tracked over the floor but this one was clear and it was enormous. Twice as big as the rest.

"That is one big goddamn dog."

AMY liked hospitals. Which she knew was weird. She liked wandering the halls and peaking into rooms. She'd never had a serious injury or illness and so had no reason to fear them. But they were confusing and twice she had to backtrack her way, uncoding the department names and room numbers that seemed to make no sense.

Even when she found the number she was looking for, she wasn't sure it was the right room. The woman in the bed looked nothing like Lara. A nurse hovered, changing the dressing on the woman's arm. Amy took a tentative step into the room for a closer look. It was Lara, but she was so pale. She couldn't help but look at the exposed arm. Wet puncture wounds marred the flesh, the congealed blood dark against the waxy skin. Amy could smell it from where she stood on tiptoes.

"She a friend of yours?" The nurse didn't even look up from her task.

"Sorta. I was gonna sit with her. If that's okay."

"I think she'd like that." The nurse looked up and smiled. "Your other friend just stepped out for a minute."

Amy didn't know who she was talking about. The nurse smiled at her as she hustled out the door. Amy didn't move, unable to do anything but stare. How could that be Lara? She looks so small in that bed. She took a step closer then startled when she heard someone behind her.

A woman hurried in. Black and pretty. A Fendi slung on her elbow, phone in her hand. "Hello," she said.

"Hi."

"Are you the relief shift?" She put her bag on the table and rummaged through it. "I had to make a call so I went outside. I always thought you weren't supposed to use your cell in a hospital but I see plenty of people yammering away on them." She stuck out a hand. "Sorry, I'm Charlene."

Amy shook her hand, said her name.

"Amy?" Charlene cocked her head, trying to place the name. "Are you a friend of Lara's?"

"My dad is. I mean, they work together."

"Oh," Charlene snapped her fingers. "You're Gallagher's kid. Lara told me about you. Nice to meet you." She renewed the handshake with vigor.

"Ditto." Amy glanced at the bed. "Is she any better?"

"She's stable. We're just waiting for her to wake up. I hope you brought a book."

Amy lifted her backpack. "Homework."

"Smart." Charlene hooked the bag back onto her elbow. "I have to run. Shit is piling up on my desk, pardon my French, and I have to get back. You'll be okay? Who's relieving you?"

"I'm not sure."

"I'll figure it out. Bye Amy." She rushed out of the room and then everything was quiet. Amy sat in the chair. She got up and dragged the chair closer. Should she talk to Lara, like they do in the movies when someone's lost in a coma? Someone zipped by the open door and she stifled under self-consciousness and kept quiet. She pulled her backpack to her knees, thinking she should start her homework but didn't feel like doing it.

When she looked up, Lara's eyes were open.

"Lara? You awake? It's Amy."

Zero response. The eyes open but there was no hint of Lara in them. No recognition, no awareness. Amy waved her hand before Lara's nose. Nothing.

Should she call a doctor? Did it mean anything or was it an involuntary response? Full on creepy, Lara's eyes wide like a zombie. And she didn't blink. Wouldn't her eyes dry out like that? Amy gently, gently pulled the eyelids down. There, that was better.

The lids slit open and rolled back up.

Amy stepped back. Screw this. Call a nurse.

22

LARA STARED AT THE CEILING. THE florescent light singed her eyes. She was awake. In a hospital bed. Why? What happened?

And then it all came back. Prall, the dogs, pulling the trigger. The thing. Its teeth, the pain as it ripped into her stomach.

She screamed and tore the drip from her arm. Off the bed and sprinting full tilt down the hallway. At least that's what she wanted to do. She remained prone on the bed staring at the ceiling tiles. Something was wrong. Her muscles didn't work, her hands stone no matter how hard she wanted to flail. No sound came from her throat. She couldn't even move her eyes.

She heard a voice near her ear. Charlene, invisible outside her field of vision. Lara screamed for help but her lips never moved. Charlene was talking, telling her about work. Gossip. How could she not hear her? After a while, Charlene became quiet and the only sound was that of pages turning in a magazine.

A face swam into her sightline. A nurse. Lara screamed again but nothing happened. The nurse went away.

A new face crept into her field of vision. A girl. Gallagher's daughter. Amy's long hair swung and bristled her chin. She could feel it. Why couldn't she move? The girl's eyes were saucers of fright. Why does she look so scared? Oh god, how bad am I hurt?

Amy, help me. Please.

IVAN Prall leaned against a stump of deadfall, his back nestled into the soft moss. Legs sprawled before him in the pine needles. The Siberian lay coiled nearby, bedded down with its chin on its paws. The other dogs stayed close, sniffing the loam or lying sphinx-like on the forest floor.

They had withdrawn to the safety of the trees, the dark of the mountainside. Another den lost and Prall had only himself to blame. Going back to the halfway house was risky but finding it boarded up and abandoned was an unexpected boon. He would have wagered a day's earnings that the old house would have been razed for the hellhole it was. But it wasn't. No one cared. The house sat dark and forgotten. A perfect refuge for the pack since the pigs took their old den. He hadn't expected them to look there. He had underestimated them, the pigs. Especially the woman.

He scratched at a scab on his ribs. Blackened blood flaked away under his dirty fingernails. The Argentino mastiff nosed his ribcage and lapped its tongue over the scab, grooming it clean. Prall smacked it away, hazing it off with blows until it pouted off across the pine needles and joined the others.

Prall watched the dogs. The dogs wrestled and fought. Every animal in the pack unnerved by his mood. They nipped and trampled one another, the aggression growing into full blown snarls and snaps to the neck. The bitch was gone, blown to hell by the guns of men and the pack was feeling her absence. Without a female to nicker, the pack's aggression turned inward and the scrapping was getting out of hand. More than once, Prall had been set on by the younger males, testing his power. He had killed one and marked two others. That should have been enough to dismay the rest but aggression still festered in the ranks.

He looked up at the ripples of blue sky slipping in and out of the canopy of leaves and he questioned the wisdom of his plan. Chased out of the Gethsemane House into this garden, this Gethsemane. Doubting his course of action and recusing himself for the losses they'd suffered and the certainty of more losses to come before it was all over.

And there was the cop who'd found the den. The woman. He had no idea if she was alive or dead. This was a mistake, a sin never made before. What if she survives? Had he ruined his chances for redemption?

He leaned and spat into the dirt. There was no time for weakness. There would be more losses and more bloodshed but no tears would be shed. He could not cry, even if he wanted to. The reformation had sealed his tear ducts forever. Wolves do not cry. All that mattered now was the burning need for revenge and the lasting hope for salvation. Stay the course, the plan would provide both.

BEHIND the halfway house was a footpath that cut through the raspberry bushes into the trees beyond. Gallagher followed the track as it snaked around willows and dogwoods until it dropped to a creek bed below. He looked north towards the source then followed the stream as it trickled past him to where the creek bent leeways and disappeared behind some cottonwoods. The creek graded downward and fed into the river further down. A box turtle sunned itself on a rock. Gallagher climbed down the bank, slipping on the wet leaves and coming up with a damp ass. The turtle dropped into the water and vanished. He crossed the stream, eyes on the muddy banks for paw prints. Cutting for sign. That's what they said in the old cowboy movies. They went thataway. Gallagher couldn't see anything that looked like paw tracks or any kind of tracks at all. He'd make one shitty cowboy. Still, it made sense the dogs would flee this way. The footpath led directly to the creek and from here Prall could lead them further into the trees or south to the river and into the city.

When he got back to the house his knees were damp and his shoes muddy. The police tape had snapped at one end it twisted and popped in the wind. He went through the house again, top to bottom, hoping the fifth time would be the charm but there was nothing new, no overlooked gem that would lead him to the crazy son of a bitch. The techs had gone over everything, leaving dust smears and tape behind, the duffel bag and filthy clothes tagged and carted away.

Upstairs in the big room, Gallagher sat on the floor and studied the pentagram scored into the old sheetrock. He waited for some divine inspiration to drop a lead into his head, psychically cutting for sign that would lead to their suspect. He shivered from being damp. After a while he rose and quit the house.

At the office, he filtered through the paperwork and stuck the essential stuff into a folder to take home. Vogel stopped to inquire about Mendes's condition but he had no news and the Lieutenant grumbled and moved on. Gallagher thumbed through the mess on Mendes's desk until he found her notepad. Skimming through it, there was a note about the Gethsemane case files still held up in evidence. He called down to the evidence dungeon and barked at someone to locate the files detective Mendes had requested. He felt better for having hollered at someone.

He was late getting to the hospital. Amy was watching TV, feet propped onto the bed and her hand in a bag of pretzels. Mendes lay stiff and straight, unchanged since he last saw her. The only difference were her eyes. They were blinded with squares of cotton and taped into place.

"What's wrong with her eyes?"

"They wouldn't stay closed." Amy sat up, dropping her feet so her dad could move closer. "They just stayed open. It was creepy. The doctors thought her eyes would dry out like that so they taped them shut."

"Did you talk to her like I asked? Did she react at all?"

"She hasn't reacted to anything. Even her eyes. They were just like, lifeless." Amy wiped her fingers on her jeans. "Whose shift is up next?"

"No one. Everyone's busy."

"We can't just leave her alone."

"I know."

"Do you wanna stay?" Amy asked. "We can order a pizza or something."

He picked up her school bag and peeled her sweater from the back of the chair. "No. Let's go home."

"Dad. Are you sure? I don't mind."

He wrapped the sweater over her shoulders. "You've done enough. Let's get home."

LARA dreamt about sex.

Sex outdoors, the smell of damp earth and dead leaves. Stars sparkling dull against a black sky.

She had stared at that ceiling for so long, the dimpled tile with a water stain and the cruel fluorescents. Unable to shut her eyes against it, her pupils shrank and her vision blurred white. Snowblind until the doctor shuffled in and forced her eyelids closed. The feel of tape pulling the upper lid over the lower one and then the pressure of wadding packed against it. Darkness, merciful in its oblivion and she slept.

But now the dream of sex. It started as sensation, something against her skin. She was dreaming but conscious of the dream at the same time. Running through half-memories of all the times she'd done it outside. On a picnic blanket with the feel of mown grass under her shoulders. In a pool she and a boy had snuck into late at night. On the rooftop of a cheap hotel in Mexico with her last real boyfriend. His name was Matt. The breeze warm off the Caribbean and the sound of the beach below. Sand still on their bellies, pumicing their skin raw.

Above her was a night sky pinholed with stars. Beneath her a carpet of pine needles and the smell of dirt. The trunks of pines and elms at each point of the compass. Her palms flat on the ground, propping herself up. Her arms pale blue in the moonlight.

The man behind her. She thought it was Matt at first but it wasn't Matt. Too rough, the way he slapped her and gripped her hair. She looked over her shoulder but he tugged her hair hard, keeping her eyes off him. He was noisy. So was she.

She pulled away, leaving hair in his fingers. A cloud passed over the moon and blocked the light. Too dark to see his face. She didn't care, pushing him flat on his back. She picked up steam, feeling it build inside her. A breath away from coming, the clouds parted and his face shone pale. She knew it would be him but she couldn't stop now.

Ivan Prall clutched her arms and held her fast until she finished and wilted onto him.

She pushed herself up, found her hands were slick. Blood all down her arms, her stomach, her thighs. Prall lay stone still. His throat was open, the severed windpipe sucking wet air. His belly was gutted, ribs protruding through the meat. The cracked sternum rose and fell. His entrails squirmed between her thighs like eels swimming in blood.

She bolted off and crawled away. Her skin painted red and nothing to wipe it off with.

The crack of a branch caught her ear. Bootheels crunching pine needles. A figure pushed through the branches and stood in the moonlight, the face hidden under a baseball cap. He wore camouflage underneath an orange safety vest, the kind hunters wore to keep from shooting one another. Rifle in hand, an old bolt action topped with a scope.

She ran. Breakneck through the trees, skin clawed by branches and her feet bare over the earth. Cold teeth swallowed her ankle and she hit the ground. An old bear trap, the iron jaws biting clear through to the bone. She pulled at it but the iron jaws wouldn't give.

The sound of his boots. The hunter clomped forward and bore down on her. She clawed at the trap, clawed at her leg. The hunter seated the rifle to his shoulder and lay his cheek into the stockpiece. Even with one eye hidden behind the scope, she recognized his face.

Gallagher steadied his aim and fired. A clean killshot and her chest bloomed red when the bullet found her heart.

LARA WOKE. She didn't startle or jerk awake like she did from any other nightmare. She couldn't move and she couldn't see and the scream bubbling up inside her had nowhere to go. The paralysis, the cotton wadded over her eyes. How long has she been like this? What day was it?

She heard the creak of the chair, someone in the room. Who was sitting with her now? She knew they were taking shifts so she wouldn't be alone. Charlene and Gallagher and Amy. Even Kopzyck had taken a turn. He had yammered at her, complaining about how she got the homicide promotion over him. How unfair it was. Then he put his feet up and napped until he was relieved.

"You lived."

A voice she couldn't place. Someone else from the unit? Or a doctor.

Hands touched her face. She felt fingers peel the tape back and the pressure on her eyes lifted away as the batting was removed. A warm palm flattened against her brow, a thumb pulling up her eyelid. The voice again, rumbling low in her ear. "Sometimes surviving isn't the best option."

The light stung, dim as the room was. The figure hovering over her took on shape. His breath hot on her face. Prall.

She wanted to scream but could not. She wanted to stab her thumbs through his eye sockets into his brain but could not. Prall stroked her cheek, his fingers hot on her skin like he was burning a fever. Her face reflected back in the mirror of his sunglasses. On his brow, the cross-shaped scar was raw as if fresh.

"You know what happens now, don't you?"

Lara willed her muscles to do something, her hands to strike out. Her teeth, anything. And where was the nurse?

Prall leaned over her. He stank of sweat and dirty hair. A gamey musk, like wet dog. He said, "This is the scary part, the paralysis. It's like dying 'cept you're awake the whole time." His nostrils flared, taking in her smell. "What's your name, piggy?"

He reached over her, his hand coming back with a blue plastic card embossed with information. Ivan Prall looked at it for a spell, his lips moving slowly as he read. He tapped the plastic against his teeth.

"Mendes, Lara. Detective, Portland Police Bureau."

He flicked the card away and touched a finger to her lips. He traced his fingertip over her chin and down her neck, the rise of clavicle and down her sternum. His fingers circled her breast and spiraled round the nipple. He pinched and twisted.

"You're like me now."

In spirit, Lara struck out like a rattlesnake, bashing his skull against the floor until there was nothing but froth and bone chips. In body, she did none of this. Still as statuary.

"No more playing piggy for you. You're gonna change, Lara Mendes. And when you do change, you'll come to me. Take your place in the pack."

He slid the sunglasses off his nose. His eyes were all wrong. They were bloodshot and the irises glowed yellow around the pupil.

"Tell me something."

His coarse palm smoothed down her ribs and along her hip. Turned in to the thigh and slid under the hospital gown.

"Who's the little girl who comes to sit with you?"

The screams bounced around inside her skull with nowhere to go.

23

LI'L DEE LIT THE WICK ON THE LANTERN now that it was full dark. There wasn't a lot of kerosene left, he'd have to be careful with it now. That crazy bastard Reggie had used some of it, not for the lamp but to rub on himself. Dee had come back to the hovel to find the stupid son of a bitch stripped to the waist and washing himself with it, rubbing kerosene over his armpits and down his neck. Dee snatched the fuel can away and cursed him. The man was getting crazier by the day, you never knew what kind of nonsense the fucker would get up to next.

Reggie didn't even apologize. He pulled his clothes back on, wrapped himself in his sleeping bag and sat by the window. Watching. After a while, he started coughing again. He reached for one of his jugs, thumbed the lid off and spit into it. Great phlegm gobs spackled with blood and God knows what. He jammed the lid back on and slid the jug back amongst the others.

Dee sat and chewed a bun salvaged from a dumpster. The man was bugging and Dee considered moving on. He didn't want to give up the space but Reggie was beginning to scare him. He was sick, that was plain enough from the coughing and the moaning, the fever that rippled through the man. He was hot to the touch, burning up inside. And now this craziness with the cans.

Reggie refused to piss outside anymore. He collected a bunch of cans and jugs, anything that had a lid and these he pissed in, always sealing it up when he was done. The first time Dee saw it, he yelled at him to do it outside. Reggie refused but he weirdly encouraged Dee to piss outside, to piss a ring around their shack to mark territory and cover his scent. Dee just shook his head at the damn craziness. Reggie had taken to burying his shits too, like a cat. He'd go out behind the shack with a little shovel, to the spot where it was sandy and he'd dig a hole and do his business and backfill it. Pure craziness.

Dee weighed his options. Pack up his gear and look for a new squat or stay and watch Reggie go to pieces. Wake up one night to find the lunatic coming at him with a knife.

"I can't do it anymore."

Reggie had spoken, but not to Dee. He stared out the window and spoke to no one, to the night. "I just can't."

Now what? Dee watched as Reggie knelt over his belongings in the corner. He rooted into a satchel and came up with a few cards. Drivers license, something with a picture on it. These he stuck into a pocket and then turned to Dee and dropped the satchel at his feet.

"Here," he said. "Take this. I won't need it anymore."

Reggie shuffled to the door. He opened it, letting in a blast of wind and then he looked back at Dee. "Don't stay here. Find a new place. They'll find this place sooner or later. You don't want to be here when they do."

Dee said nothing, blinking his eyes. Reggie pulled the blanket tight and left.

Dee dug through the satchel. He found a can opener and a good jackknife. He dug into a smaller pocket inside the lining and came up with money. Not loose change but paper money. Three wrinkled fifties and two fives. Son of a bitch.

GALLAGHER knocked on doors, canvassing the area around the halfway house for the third time. Nothing useful had been pulled from the scene, just like the earlier squat in the industrial lot. The investigation had stalled out and Mendes remained in hospital. The Lieutenant had ordered him to back up Latimer and Bingham on a homicide up in North Portland. A white male found dead in a laneway behind a drycleaners. The victim's tongue bulged out the mouth and rope burns round the neck. No ID on the body and no cell phone to backtrack through. No witnesses. Another stone cold whodunit without a shot in hell of ever being solved. Every detective got one and this time it was wonder boy Bingham and cracker Latimer. So it goes.

Gallagher looked at his watch. Mendes was alone right now, caught between sitter shifts. As the days dragged on it was harder to find anyone available to sit with her. Including himself. The list was down to himself, Amy and Charlene but that wasn't enough to cover it all. All he could do was hope Mendes didn't wake up in the gap between sitters. If she ever woke up. The doctor he'd spoken to this morning mentioned the increasing risk of coma.

Walking back to his car with a handful of nothing from the canvas, his phone buzzed. On the display, *PABLO.*

After the animal shelter had been processed and the police tape taken down, Pablo had gone back to work. There was no one to replace him and the pens were full of animals that needed to be cared for, crime scene or no. Still in shock, Pablo did what most people do in crappy situations. He carried on. Gallagher had stopped in to see him two days ago with a request, asking Pablo to monitor all complaints that came in. If anyone called in about stray dogs, no matter how minor, Pablo was to call him immediately.

He put the phone to his ear. "What'cha got, Pablo?"

"Just took a call from someone over in Felony Flats, said her Corgi was almost mauled by a couple of pit bulls."

"Where exactly?" Gallagher scrounged for his pen and took down the address.

"I dunno how accurate the woman is," Pablo said. "I asked how she knew these were pits, all she said was they looked mean as hell."

"Good enough for me. Thanks for the heads up." Gallagher almost hung up there but lingered, letting the pause stretch down the line. "You doing okay? You should take some time off. Go fishing or something."

"You kidding me? Who's going to mind the store when I'm not here?"

Gallagher smiled. "I know. Just don't push it, man. You've been through a helluva shock. Deal with it now. Otherwise it just comes back to bite you in the ass later."

"Thanks, Oprah."

"Fuck you too, buddy."

THE ADDRESS of Pablo's caller was dark when he rolled the Cherokee past the house. The porch light out, all the windows dark. No sense bothering the lady who called. He'd be stuck on her stoop for half an hour listening to a longwinded complaint. Who had the time for that nonsense?

Most of the houses on the block were dark and quiet. A single window lit up on this house or that. A few homes were permanently dark, shuttered in foreclosure or short sale with a realtor's sign on the lawn. Further down, a rutted laneway ran the breezeway between a tidy craftsman four-square and a colonial with broken windows. He followed it down where the lane ended at a rough service road behind the neighborhood. On the far side, the ground dropped to a wallow of hemlocks tangled in morning glory.

He cut the engine, left the headlights on and got out. Looked down the seepway. They could have come through here, trailing the path of what was basically a wide ditch. A run-off path for the spring thaw. It was dark and most of the homes it buttressed had fences up, blocking it from view. Like a freeway for psychos. Or monsters.

He walked the edge, past reeds and dried up bulrushes. Nothing more. What was he expecting to find? Prall sitting on the bank casting a line into the dirty water? Just fishing, hoss.

He headed back to the glare of the Cherokee's headlights. Something scuttled across the parked truck, winking out one headlamp then the other.

Gallagher stopped. Could have been a neighborhood dog, sniffing out the truck disturbing its territory. Another shaped passed before the lights, tail up, and then another. Three dogs, at least what he saw was three. He squinted against the headlights, picking out the dogs around his truck. A pit bull brindled with black stripes and a Husky with a white belly and black topcoat. The third animal was thick and muscular but Gallagher couldn't place the breed. Satanic was his guess.

Two more animals appeared. None of them made a sound or charged at him. They trotted back and forth across the headlights and circled the truck. One by one, the dogs lifted legs and pissed on the tires. Marking territory.

Gallagher's palm pivoted on the butt of his Glock. How much trouble would he land in if he drew and simply shot down every last one of them? Of course, at this angle he'd shoot the hell out of his ride too.

The dogs kept trotting round the truck, watching him. Their heads up, tails high. That meant something in dog language but he couldn't remember what. The big Siberian ambled towards him and Gallagher tightened his grip on the gun. The dog turned back and leaped clear onto the hood of the Cherokee. Nails scratching the paint, it looked at him and pissed all over the windshield.

Okay. Gallagher understood that language. Dog speak for 'fuck you'.

"Fuck you too, Rover." He drew his weapon and leveled a bead on the biggest animal, that satanic-looking one. At this range he could put down one or maybe two without puncturing his truck. What he should do is call for back-up. If the dogs were here, then Prall had to be close by. To hell with it. Ivan Prall would be a lot less dangerous if he culled half the pack right here, right now. He thumbed the safety off.

The dogs bolted.

Like they knew what he was thinking. Maybe it was the sight of the gun. They were lightning fast too, already to the wallow and splashing through the reeds. He walked to the truck, the piss still steaming off the windshield. The whole thing stank to high heaven.

DEE counted the money again. One hundred and sixty and some change tinkling around in the bottom of the satchel. His patience with the sick man had paid off. Now the crazy bastard was gone and he had the hovel to himself. And this, cash in hand. He dug through his plastic bags, all he owned in the world, and came up with the bottle of Canadian Club he'd found three nights ago. Three fingers left sloshing inside the bottle and he was saving that but tonight was special. He unscrewed the top and toasted his fortune. Tomorrow he could buy more.

On the second pull, he heard the door thunk. He'd latched it shut when Reggie left but now someone was outside. Did the nutjob change his mind and come back? He craned an ear.

It wasn't him. Scratching at the door, nails clawing the wood. A dog wanting inside. Dee went to the window but saw nothing. The scratching at the door went on and then stopped.

He lifted the latch and eased the door back no more than an inch. A snout dove into the breach and popped the door back, knocking him on his ass. The dogs poured in and Dee crabwalked away. The dogs nudged him with their snouts, knocking him this way and that. They stood on him, pressing down with heavy pads.

They tore the shack apart, rooting through everything. They shook his bags to ribbons. Frenzied, darting back and forth like they smelled a cat hiding in the mess. They zeroed in on the jugs in the corner, knocking them over and scratching until the lids popped off and rank piss spilled out over the floorboards. They went crazy.

The floor shuddered under him and his eyes went to the door. The dogs lowered their tails and got out of the way.

It filled the doorframe, whatever it was, ribs scraping the jams. The weight of it shaking the tinderbox shack, bottles dropping from the window sill. His mind shut down at the sight of it. It was too big, too scary to be real. The outsized teeth and yellow eyes, like something out of a storybook he had as a child.

It slammed into him, pushing him whole across the floor, crumpling into the wall. He felt its teeth in his belly and opened his eyes to see the other dogs moving in.

24

LARA OPENED HER EYES. THE LIDS didn't curl up involuntarily like before. She could blink them at will. Panic rose up like bile. Another cruel dream or could she move? She tried her hand, felt the bedsheet on her fingertips. She could move.

She lifted her head but pain shot hot through her stomach. Every limb was jelly and her spine creaked. Take it slow. She rode out the pain, focused on her breathing. She took a gulp of air, bore down and sat up. The room swam, the equilibrium in her ear all out of whack. She fought down the urge to vomit. Okay. Everything's okay.

"Lara?"

She flinched at the voice, unable to find it with her eyes. Who was it? The dizziness evened out. There, in the corner.

Amy Gallagher unfolded herself from of the chair, dropping a book to the floor. "Ohmygod. You're awake."

Something touched her hand. Lara looked down to see Amy's hand folding over her own. She blinked, still skeptical it was all real.

Amy dipped her head, trying to find Lara's eyes. "How do you feel?"

Her mouth was cotton, the words gurgling out slow. "How...how long have I been out?"

"Three days. You had us scared. Thought you weren't ever going to wake up."

The number rattled around Lara's head like a roulette ball that wouldn't slot. Three days? She felt Amy's hand squeeze hers. Why was Amy here? Where was Gallagher? She looked at the girl sitting on her bed, saw the backpack and books piled on the floor. She swallowed. "What are you doing here?"

"Dad wanted someone here when you woke up. We've been taking turns."

"Taking turns?" Lara blinked. Nothing made sense.

"Your friend Charlene too," Amy said. "A couple of other people from work. Detectives, I guess. I think even your boss, Lieutenant whatshisname."

"Vogel."

"Yeah him. The big guy."

Lara looked at Amy and her heart dropped. The girl had come to sit vigil in a crummy hospital while she laid there like a vegetable. "Amy. I can't believe you're here. Thank you."

"No biggie. I'm just glad I was here when you woke up." She put her hand to Lara's brow. "Jeez, you're still kinda feverish. Are you okay?"

"I feel awful. But I want out of this bed. Where are my things?"

"Bagged and tagged. Evidence I guess." Amy slid off the bed and got her backpack. It was stuffed with clothes. "I brought these. They're just sweats and stuff. Figured you'd need something to wear home."

Lara smiled and pulled the t-shirt out. A grey V-neck with an orange tiger logo. "This is your basketball team, isn't it?"

"Lame, I know."

"No. I love it." Lara smoothed the shirt over her knee, admiring the logo. A small twinge of pride swelled in her ribcage. Silly. But still. Something buzzed around in her head. Words.

Who's that little girl who comes sits with you?

Prall. He'd been here, been in her bed while she lay comatose. Everything crashed back, a riot of sounds and pictures. It was no dream, he had been here. He had seen Amy. She swung her legs down and the cool floor hit her feet. It was bracing but felt good. Solid.

"Whoa. Take it easy, Lara."

She gripped Amy's bicep and squeezed. "You shouldn't be here. Go home."

Amy startled, confused. Lara felt a tug on her arm. An IV drip taped to the inside of her elbow. She stripped back the tape and pulled the needle out. Blood welled up in the little hole.

"Hand me those clothes."

"What are you doing?" Amy looked scared. "You need to rest."

"I'm fine." Something righted itself inside her head and the vertigo receded. The pain running down her back faded. "I feel great actually. Are you gonna hand me those or no?"

Amy chewed a lip, gripping the backpack in her hands.

THE cab ride home made her seasick. The driver kept glancing at her in the rearview, ever wary of fares losing their lunch in his backseat. As they turned onto her street, she was relieved to see her car parked neatly outside her front door. She wondered who drove it here.

Climbing out of the cab was slow and she eyed her reflection in the window. Her arm in a sling, dressed in a teenager's sweats. Ridiculous.

A figure sat perched on her stoop. Elbows resting on his knees, watching her come up the walkway. "You're supposed to be in the hospital," Gallagher said.

No 'hello', no 'how are you?' She stepped past him and slotted her key into the lock. "You're supposed to be hunting our suspect."

He followed her inside without being asked and looked the place over. It wasn't what he expected. Artfully decorated with nice things but there was no mess. No clutter, no tangle of shoes to trip over at the front door. Neat and organized, the way the homes of people without kids are. Gallagher envied the orderliness but it puzzled him.

"I don't get you," he said. "Your desk is a complete disaster but this," his wave sweeping the room. "This looks a model home."

She went on into the kitchen without answering or even looking back. He followed, leaning up against the doorframe. Like the living room, it was organized and clean. A cup and spoon in the sink, waiting to be washed.

"Amy called you?" Lara rooted the fridge for a carton of orange juice.

"She was worried about you."

"I'm fine."

He watched her struggle to pop the spout on the carton. He didn't offer to help, just nodded at her slung arm. "Yeah, you're in great shape."

The spout popped and she drank from the carton. "You want coffee, you can make it yourself."

He pulled out a chair. "Does it hurt?"

"A little. It's mostly just numb." She wiped her chin with the heel of her hand. "Did you talk to the Lieutenant?"

"Yup. Rowe and Varadero caught this one. They'll want to talk to you."

"What did you tell them?"

He stretched his legs, crossed one foot over the other. "Told 'em Ivan Prall sicced his dogs on you."

She looked at him, her face stone. "Did you see it?"

"I saw something."

Lara chewed her lip, considering what to say next. "It wasn't a dog."

He blew out his cheeks, shrugged. "I didn't know how to type that up in the incident report. 'Monster' sounded too vague and 'wolf' sounded too batshit crazy. I settled for 'dog'. He felt her eyes bore into him but didn't look up. He smoothed his palm flat against the table top. "I don't know. I dunno what I saw."

"Well I do. I saw it up close." She let her eyes drift to the floor. "It's crazy, I know, but why not just come out with it? Why keep it to yourself?"

"Vogel is itching to yank us off this. You were down for the count and he's looking for any excuse to shitcan me. What was I supposed to tell him?"

The question hovered there like a bad smell in the room. Lara wrapped a hand round her stomach and lowered slowly into a chair.

"You okay?"

"Just tired."

"Go lie down."

"In a minute."

Gallagher sat up, creaking the chair under him. "Okay. What now?"

"We go back to work," she said. Like there was any other answer. "We find him. And we stop him."

"You sure? You look like hell."

"Thanks. Asshole."

"Atta girl." He smiled up at her. She cracked a smile back, unable to stop it. "So. You know where we can find some silver bullets?"

"That's fairy tale stuff. We just need enough firepower to bring it down."

"Don't make it personal, Lara. Vendettas get messy. Clouds your thinking."

"Are you for real? All you do is make it personal. It's like, your schtick."

"It's not personal." Gallagher got up, opened the fridge. "I just like stomping shitbags."He tossed stuff onto the counter. Cheese, cold ham, lettuce.

"What are you doing?"

"Making a sandwich."

"Are you ever not hungry?"

"It's for you, dumbass. Amy said you hadn't eaten anything. Go lie down."

DETECTIVE Charlene Farbre sat on the bench in the lobby of Central Precinct, waiting. The shift change had come and gone and she should have been gone with it but her phone rang just as she was wrapping up for the day. A good portion of her week had been eaten up trying to track down a witness in a sex assault in Alimony Flats. A young woman had been assaulted by three men at a house party. Over seventy people crammed into this house but not a single one admitted to seeing anything. The victim had identified one of her assailants and Charlene had uncovered the names of his three friends also in attendance at the party.

Charlene had tracked the two who participated but the third one was dodging her. James Molliner had not been part of the assault but he was there. If she had any hope of nailing the other three, she needed to get to Molliner but the kid was slippery. Charlene had appealed to Molliner's mother two days ago. Two hours earlier, Molliner had called, said he'd come in to talk to her.

Here she was sitting in the lobby, eyes on the door. Ninety minutes in and tired of it. James Molliner wasn't going to show. She'd give it another half hour, then go on home.

The front doors whooshed open and Charlene looked up, hopeful, then sunk back down. This wasn't Molliner. The man that staggered in was ragged and sickly looking. Homeless. The threadbare blanket around his shoulders was wet, even though it wasn't raining.

Bored, Charlene watched the man as he stood dripping on the floor. He looked confused, unsure of whether to go on or turn around and leave. This wasn't unusual, crazies walked in all the time to annoy the desk staff with their crazy-ass nonsense. Charlene leaned back when the man's stink hit her. She knew the tang of BO and street-living but this was different. The funk was noxious and sharp. Not exactly pump grade gasoline or even diesel but it was fuel. Combustible. Kerosene. The man was dripping with kerosene. And he was shuffling towards the front desk.

Charlene sprang, hollering to wake the dead. "Get down! You, get down!" The two officers at the counter jolted up, caught off guard and confused.

"He's drenched in gas!" Charlene's hand instinctively reached for her belt but her sidearm wasn't there. She'd clipped off the holster and locked it in a desk drawer.

The man in kerosene-soaked rags raised his hands, palms out, but he didn't drop to the floor. His voice broke into a coughing jag. The two officers leaped over the desk, both drawing weapons and barking at the man to hit the floor.

"Wait," he croaked. "I want to turn myself in. Please."

Charlene glanced at the two officers. They looked back, just as confused. The sickly man waved his hands in surrender, gesticulating that he was no threat.

"I'm turning myself in. See? My name is Ronald Kovacks."

25

LARA COULDN'T SLEEP, BONE TIRED as she was. The effort of leaving the hospital, coming home and dealing with Gallagher used up the little strength she had. After losing three days in a hospital the last thing she wanted to do was go back to bed but she could barely move. Get some sleep, she told herself. Start fresh tomorrow.

But every time sleep crept in, she saw the wolf.

The attack was a cobweb of images and sounds, incomplete and out of order. She remembered the pentagram on the wall, the panic when the dogs tore into the house. The small relief when she shot the dog bearing down on her. The rest was spotty and unreal. The teeth. Pain. The weight pressing down on her and the gamey smell.

The wolf. It had other names but she couldn't bring herself to say any of them. Not out loud, not even in her head.

But she saw it. Up close. She smelled it and she touched it. The fur that stung her hands like nettles, like armor. Beneath that, muscle. Ferocious power. She knew in that moment she was going to die, that she was powerless to stop what was happening. It was the most sickening feeling she had ever experienced.

Not like this, she kept thinking. I don't want to die like this.

Her skin bristled and goosed under the bandages. The chafing gauze aggravating the itch and all she wanted to do was scratch and scratch and scratch.

Her bag was on the kitchen table. Someone at the hospital had cleaned the blood off of it for her. She scrounged up the painkillers and antibiotics and chased them down with a mouthful of tap water. The scissors were in the utensil drawer. She took them into the bathroom and cut away the irritating gauze.

The metal was cold. The flesh of her belly pale and oxygen-starved. The puncture wounds were angry red dimes surrounded by grey lifeless flesh. God, was it infected? She scratched at it, scraping off the patchwork of scabs. Release oozed all the way down her knees.

She cut into her bandaged arm, hacking the gauze like a paper doll. More red craters puckered round by dead flesh.

Was it gangrene? What did gangrene even look like? She ran the cold water and doused her arm until it was numb.

The tumble of images pushed back to the fore. The teeth and the fur. Hot breath and yellow eyes. Lara splashed the frigid water over her face, wanting to numb her brain.

Noise from the other room. A ringtone, not hers. But her phone was destroyed, wasn't it? A cell phone vibrated on the coffee table, one she didn't recognize. The display read PRECINCT. Gallagher must have left it for her, a replacement for the one lost at the halfway house.

"Hello?" Her voice hesitant, like it didn't belong to her.

"Hey, I heard you were back among the living." The voice rang unfamiliar down the line. "It's Hammond, we spoke a while ago about the Gethsemane case."

"Oh. Hi. How are you?"

"That was my question," he said. "Listen, I know you just got put through the grinder but something came up in the case, thought you'd want to know. It can wait, if you want."

"I'm fine. What is it?"

"You're not gonna believe this. You remember the perp in the abuse case? Ronald Kovacks? He's been AWOL for months, right? Get this, the guy just walked into central and turned himself in."

Lara faltered, processing the info. "He turned himself in?"

"He waltzes into the lobby, stinking up the place bad. Soaked in gas or kerosene. The sonovabitch is covered in the shit."

GALLAGHER bellowed at his kid, a banshee wail of rage boiling up from Irish blood. He'd come home to find a message from Amy's basketball coach asking where she was. She sauntered in an hour later and he demanded to know why she'd skipped practice. Amy simply shrugged, said she was hanging with friends. Gallagher smelled bullshit and hammered at her until she confessed she'd been out with a boy.

Amy stepped back, knowing she'd lobbed a grenade into the room. He detonated. Why, why, would she skip practice just to be with some braindead little peckerwood? Amy steamed at that, her dad's assessment of every boy she'd ever mentioned. He had never met any of them but that didn't stop him from dismissing every single one as a braindead peckerwood.

His cell kept ringing and ringing until he stopped yelling and answered it. Amy watched his face drop and saw his back as he marched out of the room. She knew from experience that something serious had come up and their fight was over. He'd be out the door and gone till morning.

He came back into the kitchen and fished his gear from the cupboard. He told her this wasn't over and they would discuss it in the morning. The door banged shut behind him.

Amy fetched a coke from the fridge and stewed, thinking of all the perfect replies to his hollering now that the fight was over.

RAFTON Correctional had been slated for closure twice but remained running despite its age and disrepair. Perched on a rise overlooking swamp land, it served as part lock up, part psychiatric facility. There was one road in off St. Helens Road and one road only, deep marshland on both sides. It was a pretty drive and Lara was glad she drove. Gallagher had offered to pick her up but that meant going out of his way. Faster if she just met him there.

He was late. Lara took a seat in the lobby and took out her phone. The replacement was newer than her destroyed phone and she was still getting used to it. She hated doing this.

"You need some help, ma'am?"

Ma'am? Lara looked up to see a correctional officer standing before her. He had to be in his twenties but he looked like a teenager. His smile was big and toothy. "I'm good. Waiting to interview a prisoner."

He sat down next to her. "Ah, you're with PD. Thought you look a little too serious to be a visitor. I'm Johnny." He held out a hand. "Officer Leto to the civvies."

Officer Johnny Leto proceeded to ask questions about what detective work was like, peppered with personal questions about herself like what her man thought of having a detective for a girlfriend. Lara couldn't tell if he was looking for professional advice or trying to pick her up but he was funny and charming in his awkward way. It beat trying to sort out her new stupid phone. When Gallagher came through the door, Leto reverted back to business but he pressed a business card into her hand as he said goodbye.

Gallagher watched the young man saunter away. "What was that about?"

"Not sure. That was either the clumsiest pickup I've ever seen," she said, looking at the card in her hand, "or the sneakiest."

"A correctional thug?" he sneered. "Mendes, please."

Detective Hammond entered the lobby and she rose. They shook hands, Hammond inquiring about Lara's health. He looked tired as he briefed them on the surrender of Ronald Kovacks.

"He's been in town this whole time," Hammond said. "Hiding out, living off a little cash he'd squirreled away somewhere. Playing hobo."

"You said he was drenched in gasoline," Gallagher asked. "What was he gonna do, torch himself in the precinct lobby?"

"No, he was just wearing it. He'd been smearing it on himself for days. Kerosene, oil, axle grease. The staff scrubbed him down three times but the sonovabitch still stinks."

"Why the hell would he do that?"

"To cover his scent." Both men turned their eyes on her.

"That's exactly what he said." Hammond's eyebrow went up. "How'd you know that?"

"Just a guess."

Gallagher turned back to Hammond. "So you've already questioned him?"

"Yeah. I didn't get too far. He's not all there, rambles a lot. And he's sick."

"Yeah. We know he's a sick fuck."

"Not that. He says he's dying."

"Of what?" Lara asked.

"Cancer." Hammond shrugged. "Or so he says. The nurse here said it's likely but they'll have to transpo him to a hospital for tests and stuff. How's that for luck, huh? We finally tag the sonovabitch and he ups and dies on us."

"Maybe it'll be slow and painful," Gallagher offered, but no one thought it very funny.

"Well, he's all yours. I told the warder you were coming, they stuck Kovacks in the box." Detective Hammond jingled his car keys from his pocket. "Go easy on him, huh."

RONALD Kovacks sat on a metal stool, shoulders sagging over a metal table. Opposite him was another stool, also bolted to the floor. The only other feature in the room was the camera mounted from the ceiling. Kovacks was a scarecrow of a man, shriveled up inside the prison jumpsuit. His arms were sticks spiderwebbed with raised blue veins. His cheeks hung sallow like he was missing teeth, the eyes small and deep set. An oxygen tube pinched his septum, the tube snaking down to a tank on a dolly.

The homicide detectives stood at the door. Gallagher stayed back, letting her take the lead. Lara took a step forward. "Mr. Kovacks, we're with the Portland Police Bureau. We're investigating your ex-wife's death."

Kovacks scrutinized Gallagher first, then Lara. "Sit down."

She took the stool, swung her knees under the table. Kovacks fixed his gaze square on her. Lara couldn't help but stare at the scar on his brow, a cross carved into the flesh. Not unlike the mark on Prall.

"How goes the investigation?" Kovacks smiled at her.

His gaze goosed the skin on her arms. She ignored it. "What do you know about Ivan Prall?"

"Who?"

Gallagher slid two sheets of paper from his pocket. One was a photo of their suspect at age fifteen, taken from Kovacks's own files. The other was Prall's self portrait. He slid these across the tabletop. "Prall, Ivan. One of the kids you destroyed."

Kovacks didn't even look down but he bristled all the same. "That's a vicious lie. I didn't hurt anyone. I loved those kids."

"Did you love Prall too?" Lara asked.

The red-rimmed eyes rolled back to her. He waved a hand, dismissing the idea like a buzzing mosquito. The effort seemed to exhaust him. He coughed up a wet hack and spit onto the floor. "Ivan Prall was a bad apple. Couldn't be saved. Lord knows I tried."

"You carved up his face," Gallagher said. "To match yours."

"To protect him from the wickedness, yes." Kovacks stared back at Gallagher, matching his contempt. "Didn't work."

Gallagher bounced a glance off Lara. This guy's a piece of work. "Ivan Prall killed your ex-wife, Bethany Kovacks.

He set his dogs on her and they picked her bones clean. Why did he do that? Why go after her?"

"The boy was troubled, like I said."

Lara studied the prisoner, looking for a tic, some chink in the armor she could drive a wedge through. "Prall wanted revenge for what you did to him. But he couldn't find you so he went after her."

"Oh, he wants much more than that."

She leaned in. "What does he want?"

"You want me to help you? What are you offering?

Her jaw set. She wanted to hit this man. Lara had no problem keeping her emotions out of her work but something about Ronald Kovacks set her teeth on edge. The way he spoke, the way he moved. Everything about him repulsed her. "This isn't a negotiation, mister Kovacks. It's a criminal investigation."

"Everything's a negotiation. Life is all negotiation. Haven't you learned that yet?" Kovacks held her eyes. "I'll help you catch him as long as this is held in consideration against my other...legal challenges."

No way in hell was this creep getting brownie points for answering a few questions. She was about to speak when Gallagher cut in.

"Done. Tell us about Prall."

Kovacks didn't acknowledge him, his eyes hard on the woman and the woman alone. "You know what he is," he whispered. "You've seen it."

Gallagher didn't like being ignored, cut in again. "He's a violent psychopath."

"I'm sorry, I thought you were serious about this." Kovacks turned to the door, hollered "Guard!"

"He's a wolf." Lara let it hang there.

Kovacks perked up. "Ding!" He mimed ringing a hotel bell, all smiles now. "Werewolf is the term we're looking for but we'll accept that answer."

"How do you know that?" Gallagher had spoken but Kovacks still ignored him. She repeated his question.

The prisoner's eyes lit up. "Who do you think turned him?"

Where the hell is this going? Lara didn't want to provoke the man into a psychotic rant and waste their chance. She leveled her tone. "You're a wolf too?"

Kovacks rang the imaginary bell again. "Ding. Another point for the good guys."

It was Gallagher's turn to grit his teeth. "Then why are you stuck in this hellhole? Why don't you go all wolfman and bust out of here?"

Kovacks still wouldn't look at him. "I'm sick. The change, it takes a lot out of you each time. The metabolism of the wolf burns brighter than that of man. It takes it's toll. And I'm old now. Ancient really, if you amortize it in dog years."

"Okay, we're wasting our time."

Lara didn't budge. "You said Prall wants more than revenge. What is he after?"

"He's looking for a way out. A cure. There's one way to exorcise the wolf inside you. And that's by killing the wolf that blessed you."

Gallagher didn't want to prolong this agony anymore but he had to ask. "So Prall thinks if he can kill you, he'll stop being the wolfman?"

"Yes."

"That's why you turned yourself in," Lara said. "To be safe from him."

Kovacks nodded and the oxygen tube swayed under his nose. "I was running out of tricks to hide from him. He'd sniff me out sooner or later. In here, I can at least rest."

Lara leaned closer. "How did it happen to you? How did you become a wolf?"

Gallagher shot a harsh look her way, wanting to end this bullshit but Lara wasn't looking at him. Why egg the bastard on?

Kovacks chortled, his teeth were yellow. "That's personal, sweetheart. Like asking when someone lost their cherry." The laughter convulsed into a hacking rasp. "Tell me about your first time, detective. What was it like? That boy fumbling his way into your virtue."

"I've never heard of that cure before. Killing the wolf that bit you." Lara could feel Gallagher glaring at her to end this but she refused to look at him. "Is it true?"

"It won't work for Prall. He's too far gone but he clings to his delusion. We all do, I imagine." Kovacks smeared the phlegm down his chin with his fist. He pointed a knotty finger at her. "But you, you're a different story."

She leaned back, bristling. Ronald Kovacks aimed his palsied finger at her slung arm. "He did that to you, didn't he?" A perverted smugness draped the corners of his smile.

"You're one of the blessed now too. But not confirmed, yes?"

Gallagher couldn't take anymore. He lurched forward, knuckles on the table. "Fuck you, Kovacks. And your deal." He propelled himself off the table towards the door. "We're done here, Mendes."

Lara didn't move."How do I find him?" Her good hand trembled, nerves or rage, impossible to say. "How do I find Prall?"

"You get back to me on my deal. Then we'll talk about Ivan Prall." Kovacks strained to his feet. "Guard!"

Gallagher wasn't exactly sure what happened next. He banged on the metal door and glanced back, saw Mendes hurl herself at Kovacks. She drove him into the wall, bouncing his melon off the painted cinderblock. The oxygen tank clanged as it hit the floor, the tube snapped free. Mendes shook him violently, screaming at him to tell her how to find Prall.

Gallagher barked at her to stop but she was deaf to him, deaf to anything but the sickly man jerking crazily in her hands. His head snapped back and forth like a broken bird. Gallagher grabbed her from behind but she was unmovable. She was five foot nothing but she would not let go, a mongoose on a cobra. He dug in and wrestled her off, legs kicking. Kovacks slid down the wall, his legs sprawled. A stupid look on his face.

The warder heard the racket from the hallway and opened the door. "Detective? Is everything all right?"

Detective Mendes stormed past him and just kept walking. Detective Gallagher smiled at the warder and bopped him friendly on the arm. "Get a mop," he said. "Shithead threw up on himself."

26

LARA DOUBLE-TIMED IT OUT TO THE parking lot. Every inch of her was shaking from the adrenaline juicing her nervous system. She wanted to hit something. She wanted to run. Just take off blind, bolting away from everything. What had she done?

Gallagher chased her down until he snatched her arm. He wanted to spin her around hard but she was immovable as a brick wall. All he did was slow her down. She stopped but didn't face him. "What the hell was that?"

"Isn't that how you do it?"

"Pick your moment, Lara." He stepped around, needing to see her face. "You don't do it in a goddamn prison." The panic in her eyes stopped him, knocking his anger off its axis.

Lara couldn't breathe, still riding out the adrenaline. She couldn't keep up with her own heart as it banged away against her ribs. Is this what drowning feels like?

"Easy." Gallagher took her arm, afraid she was going to keel over. "Catch your breath."

Lara doubled over, falling into him, and threw up all over his shoes.

AMY dropped her head into her hands and sighed. On the bed before her sat an open laptop. An old clunker of machine her dad had gotten from work. It was maddeningly slow and froze often. She hated it, cursing her old man for being so damn cheap. It had crashed again and she sat waiting for it to boot up. Again. That's when she heard the commotion downstairs.

She padded into the living room to see her dad and Lara stumble in. He was propping her up, her arm draped round his shoulder. He set her onto the couch. Lara looked green.

"What happened?"

"Get the bucket, honey." Gallagher looked up at his daughter. "And some water."

"Lara, you okay?" She took Lara's hand. "God, she's burning up."

"Amy? The bucket."

Amy ran to the kitchen. Lara shook off her jacket, put her head between her knees. "I'm sorry. I just need a minute."

"You need a doctor."

"No. No more hospitals."

Amy came back, passed the bucket to her dad. "I brought the Advil. It's all we have."

"Sorry for this, Amy." Lara kept her head down, worried she'd heave again if she looked up.

"It's okay." Amy looked at her dad. "Take her to the hospital."

"Tell her that."

Lara sat up, her face drained. "I'm okay. It's passed."

"Lie down."

Lara waved a hand. "I'm good, honest. Call me a cab, I'll get out of your hair."

"Lara," he said. "Just shut up and close your eyes."

She had no fight left in her. Her head touched the throw pillow and she dropped to sleep immediately. Amy got a blanket and covered her with it. They left the room without another word.

Amy leaned on the kitchen counter while he rifled a beer out of the refrigerator. "Did you eat?" Gallagher asked.

"I made a sandwich. Do you want something? There's tunafish."

He shook his head. Sipped the beer, then wagged his chin at her bedroom door. "You finish your homework?"

"Yes. How long has she been like that?"

"It just flared up. Let her sleep it off, see how she is when she wakes."

Amy crossed her arms. "The doctors were worried about infection from the dog bites. She could be really sick, Dad."

"Noted." He checked the time on the microwave. "It's late. You going to bed soon?"

She reached for the book she'd left on the counter, held it up. "I gotta read two chapters for tomorrow."

"What is that?"

"Lord of the Flies."

"Hm. Good book."

Amy said goodnight, promised not to stay up too late. Gallagher was amazed at how easily he lied to his own kid. He had never read that book, knowing it only by reputation. He hardly ever read for pleasure anymore. Who had the time?

The box was where he'd left it, in the mudroom. He emptied onto the kitchen table. Files and reports. The black notebooks of Ivan Prall's illegible ravings. He had reading of his own to kill.

LARA opened her eyes. The room was dark, the sofa underneath her unfamiliar. She tried to move but couldn't and she panicked, thinking the paralysis was back. Her hands moved, lifting to her face. It wasn't the paralysis, just a bone deep numbness in every limb. Sitting up was difficult, her legs dead weights clunking to the floor. Her hands frozen clubs. Sensation came back slowly and with it, the sting of pins and needles. There was nothing to do but ride it out.

She walked stiffly to the light coming from the other room. Her knee smacked into a table and Lara cursed, wondering who rearranged her furniture. Then she remembered where she was.

The kitchen was too bright. A radio playing somewhere. Gallagher sat with his feet propped on a chair. The table littered with notes and three of Prall's journals. A bottle of Jamesons next to a rock glass. "The dead have risen," he said without looking up from his reading.

"Sorry. I passed out."

His feet dropped from the chair and he waved at her to sit. "How do you feel?"

"Weird. Better." Lara eased stiffly onto the seat. She nodded at the mess. "What are you doing?"

Gallagher held up the notebook. "Trying to crawl inside this bastard's head. But this..." He tossed it onto the table. "This is all gibberish."

"I thought you didn't believe in profiling." She tried not to wince.

"I don't believe in werewolves either."

It had sounded funny in his head but voicing it out loud, it just came off ridiculous. So he shut up and the radio filled the empty space.

Lara spoke first, motioning to his glass. "Pass that over."

"You can have a glass all your own."

"Yours is closer." She took the glass and tilted it back. Cold water would have been the wiser choice but water doesn't seep into your shoulder muscles like this. "This is good. I don't even like scotch."

"That's because it's not scotch, it's Irish whiskey."

"There's a difference?"

"That's blasphemy."

She drank again, scaling the weight of the question in her head. She just blurted it out. "Do you think Kovacks was telling the truth?"

"Kovacks was playing you. It's what pedophiles do."

"I think he was telling the truth."

Gallagher took back the glass and sloshed more whiskey into it. "I think we both crawled too far into his head."

"So you think I'm just crazy."

"No. You've been through a violent trauma. Unconscious for three days. I think you're pushing yourself too hard to get back on the horse."

"I was awake the whole time."

That stopped him mid sip. He lowered the glass.

"I just couldn't move," she said. "Not even my eyes."

Gallagher set the glass down. Saw the memory of it dredging up in her eyes. The sensation of being dead. Her eye welled up and she wiped it away before it fell.

"That must have been terrifying," he said.

"You have no idea."

He took hold of her hand, felt it quaking. His thumb found the contours of her knuckles. "We'll fix this. You and me. Okay?"

Words. Just words. He held onto her hand, long after politeness required him to let go. The moment moved past awkward and became something else. Her eyes rose to his.

"John… "

"I know."

He pulled his hand away. She wanted it back. Their eyes bounced off each other's like repelling magnets, the awkwardness rushing back to fill the vacuum.

"Hey." A whisper.

She looked up and he was already leaning in. Already kissing her. Not some big explosion, just soft and tentative. Testing the waters. She kissed him back, her fingertips finding his neck. The water's fine.

Everything fell away in a sharp tiny moment. Bliss is one word for it. When the body takes over and stifles the brain and all its endless loops of second guesses and missteps.

A small thud snipped the moment short like scissors. Above their heads, footsteps on the second floor. Amy. The universe won't tolerate being shut out for too long and it rushes back in hard, returning all the petty details, unpaid bills and common bullshit that boil our brains every day. The universe hates bliss, snuffing it out whenever it bubbles up.

He pulled away and returned his ass to his seat. Amy's footfalls creaked the ceiling over their heads. Both reached for their glass, stalling until one of them had to say something.

"Gee," she said. "Awkward."

"Yup." His glass went back to the table. "Come on, I'll get you home."

"Are you okay to drive?"

"Hell no. Get your shoes."

THE dogs skulked through the trees. Restless, chasing woodmice. Ivan Prall sat cross-legged on the ground, chewing the end of a pencil.

The notebook was stolen from an unlocked pickup. The paper was lined and the first twenty pages were used to log hours and gas mileage. These were torn out but there was nothing to do about the lined paper. He penciled over it, sketching another drawing. A simple task that calmed him and focused his mind. He had no streetlight nor lantern to work by, here in this rocky clearing in the trees. He needed neither. The phosphorescent hum of a crescent moon and the pinhole of the lodestar were enough for his eyes to see.

The Siberian trotted up and nosed his ribs. He paid it no attention so the dog circled round and nested at his feet. The pencil worked over the paper, forming the outline of a face. His heartbeat slowed with each pencil stroke and his brain cooled, allowing clarity to his boiling thoughts.

The scent he'd been hunting so long for had suddenly materialized. Filtered up through the asphalt streets and wafting over the river, its signature tang rising up sharp from the city stink. This was the old wolf, the hated lobo. It had mired its scent in the filth of men to hide from him and suddenly there it was. But it was for nothing. The old lobo had hidden himself inside a prison, sequestered in a fortress of barbed wire and pot-bellied men with guns. The old wolf, the baptizer, had outsmarted him. He had disgraced himself by surrendering to the men but he was safe.

That was okay, Prall reasoned. He'd learned patience. He could wait.

His hand moved deftly over the paper, rendering a portrait with strokes true and economic. A woman's face this time. Prall clamped the pencil between his teeth and judged the rendering's merits. The eyes were real enough but the mouth was wrong. The mouth was always elusive. The slant of the corners and the furl of the lips, this was the true measure of a face but the hardest to capture and pin onto the page. The mouth in this rendering was close but not true. Overall, it was a passable rendition of the woman who had gotten in his way twice now. The woman he tore up and let live. That thought sickened him. He had no wish to pass the sin onto another but he had with her. And now she was damned too.

What was her name?

Lara.

27

GALLAGHER'S TAILLIGHTS FADED TO red pinpricks in the raindrops. Lara turned away from the window and kicked her shoes off. He had dropped her at the door like it was the end of some weird date. She kept thinking about the kiss. Where had that come from? She didn't like Gallagher. She even hated him sometimes. Yet he was the one who initiated it, ambushing her like that out of the blue.

Then again, maybe not. He wouldn't have done that unless there was something there. Had she done it subconsciously, sending signals without even realizing it? Go over the events, crack the details to parse the meaning of it. What if…

Stop. Her mind was ramping up speed, shifting through a million thoughts at once. A bad habit, overthinking everything until nothing makes sense. It's late. Go to bed.

She wanted another drink but all she had in the fridge was an open bottle of white that was at least a week old. She popped out the cork from the wine. A little stale but it would do.

The kiss kept replaying in her head, despite herself. She turned it over, examined it from all sides like a piece of evidence found at a crime scene. Brilliant. She pushed it away. There were would be no answers, no direction, until the morning when she saw him.

Pain zapped up her arm. Without even realizing it, she was scratching at the wound through the dressing. The itching was unbearable. Maybe the dressing needed changing. She went into the bathroom, unwinding the gauze.

It looked worse than before. The strangled flesh was jaundiced and the brittle scab tissue tore away with the gauze. The puncture marks leaked black blood and puss. It smelled awful too. Good God, was it gangrene? Is that possible? The whole hand looked wrong, the wrist bent. The knuckles looked swollen and the fingers twisted as if the bones under the skin had shifted.

She ran the palsied arm under the cold water, scrubbing it clean. The soap stung the raw flesh but the frigid water numbed the skin a little. She patted it dry with a towel and watched blood well up in the puncture marks. Angry red circles on her arm. And within those circles were tiny strands of hair lifting from the blood, sprouting from the wound itself.

ONTO Lovejoy, joining the traffic headed for the bridge. The column of vehicles backed up so Gallagher veered off, deciding to just drive for a spell. Clear his head. Try and sort out what had just happened.

It was stupid, he knew that. Disastrous too. Sure, Mendes was attractive. More than attractive, if he was honest with himself but he could deal with that. He had dealt with it, hadn't he? He never wanted a partner in the first place but then everything went screwy with the body on the riverbank. Mendes was a pickle and a stickler for procedure but they'd worked it out, got past that. Maybe—

No. This was a time-bomb waiting to blow up in their faces. He knew that from experience. There was Cheryl, of course. They were both young and convinced they had to stick it out for Amy's sake, blindly hoping things would just somehow get better on their own. It didn't. The divorce and the untangling of one life from the other while raising a daughter had been hellish. He was never going through that again.

Yet, dumb ass that he was, he got involved with another woman from work two years later. Pam was too young and he was too angry from the divorce. It was a mess from day one, both with wildly different expectations. Yet, small graces, it had ended cleanly. No lingering details, no fuss.

There were other women after that but none of them from work. No officers nor admin staff, not even a meter maid. He also swore off doctors, nurses and paramedics just to be sure. That cut about ninety percent of the women he met in a day from the potential dating pool. Normal women, the everyday population like the other parents at his kid's school, they just didn't appear in his world. Or he didn't appear in theirs. So his dating history was sparse and unremarkable. So why this thing with Mendes? Of all people, Mendes?

His eyes dipped to the speedometer. He'd been driving for twenty minutes without once paying attention to the road, lost in his own head. Where the hell was he? Cruising northwest up Front, following the river. The water on his right and the railyards to his left. No other cars on the road. He pulled to the shoulder and wheeled round onto the southbound lane. Something flashed in the headlights—

Gallagher braked, dipping the Cherokee's nose. A dog stood in the middle of the empty road, its eyes flashing in the halogens. It didn't bolt or even flinch at the oncoming grill, like the road belonged to it and he a trespasser on its pissing grounds. It was the Canario, that evil-looking hound with its cropped ears and muscular chest. He had looked it up after the earlier encounters, flipping through pictures of breeds till he found it. The dog eyed the truck, mouth open and then turned and trotted out of the beams.

One of Prall's dogs. Had to be. What are the chances? Gallagher wheeled onto the grade and killed the engine. Not much to see, the streetlights only threw so far into the empty expanse of railway tracks. His hand went to his belt but the gun wasn't there. It was in the cupboard, along with his badge. He had his cell. He could call it in, get a radio car out here to help look. For what, one dog?

Gallagher checked the road ahead and the road behind. No cars but on the far side of the road was an old sign listing in the weeds. Harvey's Garage. Why was that sign ringing a bell?

The body on the riverbank. This wasn't far from where Elizabeth Riley had been found.

The dome light came on when he opened the back. Gallagher took up the Maglite and found a field hockey stick under the stack of reusable grocery bags. He had told Amy a hundred times to move her gear out of his trunk but now he was glad she'd forgotten. He gripped it tight, testing its balance. The thing was deadly. He never understood field hockey. Why in the world would you arm twenty hormonal teenage girls with a bludgeon and send them onto a field to murder one another?

The dome light snuffed out and the Maglite went on. The beam didn't throw very far in the vast dark of the rail yard. His boots crunched the stone between the rail ties. Freight cars rusted on the lines, mammoth and silent in the darkness. He cast his eyes down the tracks, where they wound south into the core of the city. Was this how Prall was moving, running his dogs along the tracks? The tracks and the riverbanks.

The grinding stones were loud under his boots so he stopped on a creosote tie and listened. He could hear it, the dog, padding through the gravel somewhere between the cars. And then he heard the others skulking through the freights. He threw the light over the cars and caught their eyes in the beam. Up ahead and behind, to the right and to the left. Smart fuckers, surrounding him in the dark like this and him standing there with a schoolgirl's stick in his hand. Maybe they could play fetch? He tallied the dogs up, spotting the Siberian, two pits, the Canario and the Malamute. Where was the Rottie? And that big mastiff?

The dogs sniffed the ground, trotting sideways like shy ponies. None barked or growled. No need to intimidate the man. An easy kill.

Gallagher clocked the Cherokee and gauged the distance. Too far to outrun the dogs, not over these tracks. He stepped back slowly, hoping to ease the distance some. If they charged, he could brain one or maybe two of them with the stick. If he was lucky, the others would balk and he could make a run for it. But these dogs had killed before. They hunted as a pack and killed like one. The cell was still in his pocket but it may as well have been a brick for all the good it was now. And where the hell was Prall?

Show yourself, you creepy sonovabitch.

He sidled back towards the truck. The dogs matched his pace, neither closing in nor losing ground. His foot caught a rail and he stumbled, almost fell. The dogs jolted. The Siberian flashed its teeth, black lips stretching up the tartar-spackled fangs. The Canario broke ranks and rushed him. Gallagher dropped the flashlight, swung hard with both hands and clubbed the dog's skull. It yelped, rolled with the blow and ran off. The others stopped, watching the action. No other dog charged.

Gallagher kept moving, his heartbeat thrumming in his ears. The dogs watched but didn't pursue, tongues hanging from their chops. What the hell are they doing? Who cares. Keep moving. Don't fall.

Something big skulked into his periphery and lumbered in his direction. He knew what it was before seeing it. He knew then that all the rationalizations he'd constructed was all bullshit. The thing moving at him was bullshit too. It didn't exist but here it came just the same.

The lobo sklathed heavy over the rails. Snout to the ground, tracking him with yellow eyes. Hackles up, the fur like blades ridging the backbone. Christ almighty. How had Lara survived an attack from that?

The wolf charged in for the kill. If he ran, he was dead. He charged at it instead. Screaming out some banshee-kamikaze war cry as he rushed it. It worked, the lobo reared back and he cracked the club across its skull with everything he had. It snapped, teeth popping at him. He swung and bludgeoned it again. It reared and shook its head violently at the pain.

He ran. Gallagher ran like he hadn't run since he was kid, full tilt and blind. His feet somehow slamming between the rails, the truck getting closer. The thing was already on his heels, popping its jaws. He sailed over the last rusty spar and spun in midair, hurling the stick at it. The ditch was muddy as he crashed and rolled and kept running. No time to even glance back to see if he clobbered it, he just ran.

Fingers tearing open the door latch. He jumped under the wheel and almost snapped the key firing the ignition. The Cherokee roared and he slammed the shift into gear, kicked down the pedal. The truck lurched forward. The passenger window exploded. The truck sunk portside and lifted on its starboard side. The snout jammed through the window and snapped, slicing its flesh on the shattered safety glass. The truck lurched up and threatened to tip over onto Gallagher's elbow. He punched at it, kicked the accelerator. All four wheels hit the ground and the truck lurched forward and Gallagher didn't let up. Dragging the monster until its head slipped the window and it was gone. In the rearview, the lobo shook it off and chased after him. Gallagher punished the old V8, putting distance between him and it.

No.

He jammed the brakes and cranked the wheel, spinning the truck around. The lobo flashed in the headlights.. The truck shot forward and he aimed the grill right at the damn thing. The monster lunged leeways but he caught a piece of it, nailing the hind end. Like a brick wall, the truck buckled and spun. Gallagher bounced hard and fought to keep it on the road. The truck balanced out. His chin ached from slamming into the wheel. He spun the truck back around but the headlights threw down on an empty road. He saw the dogs loping away through the freight cars, darting past the Maglite he had dropped out there. Of the wolf, there was no sign.

The Cherokee started to clink and sputter. Gallagher couldn't catch his breath, couldn't think straight with the adrenaline still pumping his heart. Rain spackled the windshield. It pattered in through the shattered starboard window. He watched the seat darken with the raindrops, not knowing what to do next. Call the cops? Check the damage to the grill? Call the insurance company or just get it fixed himself?

After a while, he took his foot off the brake and rolled away.

AMY lay in bed listening to the radio. She didn't want to get up but any minute now her dad would holler up the stairs for her to get her butt in gear. She slid out of bed and shivered, looked for her robe. Coming downstairs, the house was quiet. No clatter from the kitchen, no smell of just brewed coffee. The kitchen was empty, the lights still off. Was he still sleeping?

"Dad?" she hollered up the stairs. She couldn't remember the last time she had to yell at him to get up. There was no note on the counter and the phone indicated no new messages. That was weird. There was always a note, a message explaining why he wasn't there. Don't panic, it's too early for that. He just forgot this time.

The coffeemaker gurgled and Amy waited for the toaster to pop. She wanted the newspaper but with dad gone, it would still be on the porch. She cinched her robe tight and unlocked the front door.

Dad was in the rocker, legs straight and crossed at the ankles. Asleep with his head down. Amy stopped, the porch cold under her bare feet. "Dad?"

He jerked awake, the rocker creaking under him. Something slid from his lap and clunked the boards. A gun. Not the one he wore for work but the bigger one he kept locked in a cupboard in the basement. It was black, she didn't know the name of it.

"Why are you out here?"

"What time is it?" He flinched under a stiff neck. Eyes bloodshot. He picked up the gun and returned it to his lap.

"Were you out here all night?" She folded her arms against the chill. She hated it when he blew off her questions. "Why do you have the gun?"

"It's nothing." He got up slowly, lightheaded. "Neighborhood watch stuff." He went inside without looking at her. She got the rolled-up paper from the step and followed him in.

28

THE BUMPER WAS KNOCKED LOOSE, hanging down on the driver's side. The headlamp was crushed and the grill punched in. Gallagher slotted the Cherokee nose first into a spot in the parking garage. He preferred to back in but he didn't want anyone seeing the damaged front end, didn't need any questions about it. There was nothing he could do to hide the shattered window on the shotgun side. Clear the shards of glass away, that's all. The truck looked like hell and he walked away from it in disgust.

He went to the desk sergeant, asked for all the incident reports from the night shift. There was nothing there. No reports of the dogs, no dog attacks, no 10-24's about a possible dead body. The desk sergeant went for coffee, letting Gallagher use the desktop to check the 911 calls. Again there was nothing here related to his case or what he encountered last night. When the sergeant returned, Gallagher asked if there were any outstanding reports waiting to be filed but the sergeant said no, everything was in. It had been a quiet night.

In the bullpen, Gallagher found his desk occupied. A flabby kid with a beard sat in his chair, tapping away at his desktop. A flat of unmade banker's boxes leaned against the wall, like it was moving day.

"What the hell're you doing?"

The kid turned round, nodded. "Hey man. I'm gonna be a while." He turned back to the screen.

Gallagher gripped the chair and swung the kid around. "Who the hell are you and why are you fucking with my work?"

The kid leaned back, getting distance from the cop. "I'm transferring all the files, like I was told to. Excuse me."

"Told by who?"

"My boss, Jim. Down in tech. He got orders to copy and transfer the open case files on this station and that one there." He pointed at Mendes's desk.

"Get outta my chair."

"Look man, I got to do this. Go talk to— "

Gallagher snatched the kid's ear and hauled him to his feet. "Get the hell away from my desk." The guy squealed as Gallagher propelled him out of the cubicle.

"Fuck you man!" The kid screamed but he kept walking. "You can't do that to me!" He bumped into Lara as she turned the corner.

Lara watched the kid huff away then looked at Gallagher. "What was that?"

"Someone told that creep to dump our case files."

"Who?"

He shrugged, took a closer look at her. She looked tired and strung out. "You feeling better?"

"Bad sleep." Her eyes went to the unfolded boxes tilted against her evidence board. "What is going on?"

"Lara, sit down." The tone serious, his voice like gravel. "We need to talk."

"Yeah. About last night. Listen, John, I know—"

"No. Not that." He rubbed his chin, hesitating. Groping for a way to say it. "You were right about Prall. About what he is."

She wasn't sure she'd heard him. "What?"

"It came after me last night. Not Prall, the thing."

"Are you all right?"

"My truck's banged up pretty bad, but that's all. He baited me, with his dogs. I walked right into it."

"Jesus. Where?"

"Not far from where we found Elizabeth Riley."

Lara sank into her chair, knocked down by what she heard. "You saw it? The wolf?"

"Up close. I'm sorry I didn't believe you before. I should have."

Neither moved. Phones rang in the background, the photocopier chunk-a-chunked in the corner. Lara felt a tug inside her, a twisted knot loosened and eased off at this thin life-rope tossed her way. She wasn't alone, she wasn't losing her mind.

"What do we do now?"

"We talk to the Lieutenant. This is bigger than us. We need a SWAT team. Firepower. We can get Pablo's help. Maybe some wildlife experts."

"The Lieutenant is going to think we're both crazy."

"I know. You got a better idea, I'm all ears."

She didn't.

They didn't have to wait long. The Lieutenant banged out of his office, calling for their heads.

MENDES and Gallagher sat before the desk like truant school kids. Lieutenant Vogel brought the wrath of God down on their heads. Lara's gaze drifted to the picture of Vogel in his glory days of wrestling, the tights and tall boots. She wanted to laugh, the whole damn thing was so ridiculous. The Lieutenant's neck cabled up as he bellowed and they had yet to even mention Prall's name.

"The warder at Rafton Correctional is livid. You two waltz in there and assault a prisoner? A guy dying of cancer!"

It was about Ronald Kovacks. What they had done to him. Gallagher had meant to talk to Vogel about it, to ward off any trouble. In the shitstorm of the last two days, he had simply forgotten about it. Time to pay the piper.

"It was just a little misunderstanding." Gallagher spoke. Lara seemed fixated on the picture on the wall, like she couldn't care less.

"A misunderstanding? Oh I see, I'm the asshole here." Vogel's face bloomed red. "Not only do I have the prison hammering on me, detective Hammond is furious. This is his prisoner, his case, and you two just fucked him on it."

Gallagher clenched his teeth. Lara had yet to say anything and he could only carry this one so far. They'd crossed a line, simple as that.

The Lieutenant caught his breath, amped up for another round. "You," his finger squared at Gallagher, "I'd expect this from you. But the prisoner stated clearly it was detective Mendes." He all but snarled at her. "What the hell did you do to him?"

She pried her eyes from the picture. "The prisoner was uncooperative. I needed answers."

"Are you fucking with me? I made you homicide so you could keep a leash on that sonovabitch." Vogel chin-wagged at Gallagher and hammered on. "Not turn into him!"

"Leash?" Gallagher spun to her. "The hell are you talking about?" She didn't return the gaze.

"Do you clowns have any idea the kind of hell this makes for me? Internal Affairs will crawl so far up my ass I won't know whether to shit or wind my watch." Vogel wiped the sweat from his lip. "As for you two, they're gonna drag you behind the sheds and burn you at the stake."

The rage burned off, leaving a vacuum in the room. Mendes and Gallagher looked at the floor. Vogel waited for some sign of contrition. The wall clock ticked away the seconds.

Lara spoke up. “We need to talk about Ivan Prall.”

“Who?” Vogel wasn't ready to change topics. “The dog guy?”

Gallagher groaned. Not now, not with the Lieutenant looking for someone to hang. Lara looked him in the eye, serious as death. We have to do this.

“What about him?” Vogel asked.

Gallagher cut in before she could continue. “Ivan Prall is extremely dangerous. We need to throw everything we got at this guy. And I mean everything.”

“What? Are you telling me you can't handle this?”

“We need more bodies working this,” Gallagher said. “We need a task force and a SWAT unit ready to hit this guy as hard as possible.”

Vogel wasn't buying any of it, that much was clear.

“Are you familiar with this suspect?” asked Lara. “The case file?”

“He's the crazy guy with the dogs. Thinks he's a vampire or something.”

“Werewolf.”

“Whatever.”

Lara sat up. Loud and clear with a straight face. “He isn't crazy. He is what he says he is.”

Tick, tick, tick. It was like someone had passed wind in the room. Lieutenant Vogel just blinked stupidly at her, then Gallagher and back to her. “What?”

"It's true." Gallagher had never gone skydiving, never jumped out of an airplane, but he imagined this is what it felt like. A freefall with no turning back. "We both saw it. The… uh… werewolf. That's what attacked Lara, not the dogs."

The Lieutenant waited for one of them to crack, to start laughing at this bad fucking joke but neither flinched. His detectives held faces of stone. Very well. "Collect your open case files, hand them over to Bingham and Latimer. Including the Prall case."

"Mike," Gallagher leaned in, "don't do this. Not now."

The Lieutenant raised a hand, ending the matter. "Both of you are suspended until I clear this up. Surrender your firearms and tin to the desk. Then get out of my precinct."

There was nothing left to say.

LARA went straight to her desk without looking back. What did she think was going to happen? Was the Lieutenant going to believe them? Stupid, stupid, stupid.

She took one of the empty boxes and placed it on the floor below her evidence board. She tore the photographs down, letting the pins fall around her. The pictures went into the box, no notations, no cataloguing. Next the sketches and journal entries photocopied from the notebooks. After that, the reports and notes. Pushpins tumbled and became lodged in the industrial pile.

"You were supposed to be my *leash*?"

Gallagher caught up. Lara kept her back to him, tossing pages into the box. "What the hell was that about?" he said.

"I wanted to work homicide. That was the deal."

"You should of told me."

"How? When you were busy ditching me? It doesn't matter anymore." She stepped past him to get another box. "Excuse me."

She scooped up the binders from the desk, one open case per, and dropped them in. He reached into a box and retrieved a sketch. Prall's self portrait. "We still have a problem."

"We have nothing." She snatched it from him, balled it up and tossed it in. "We don't even have jobs anymore."

"Fuck the job."

"We blew it." She took the box and marched past him. "You can go back to being a cowboy now."

DETECTIVE Bingham kept his ear to the ground all morning, sensing a change in the wind and an imminent internal shift within homicide detail. He'd heard the scuttlebutt about Gallagher bashing up a prisoner and even a blind man could see the Lieutenant had been pushed too far. He decided to move things along.

Ten paces south of the cubicle he shared with Latimer were two meeting rooms. Not interview boxes but utilitarian rooms for procedural meetings or interviews with families. The smaller of the two rooms was closed off for repairs after a grieving father trashed the place in his rage. No serious damage, just patching the fist-sized holes in the sheetrock.

Bingham had taken control of this room, intending to use it as an active workroom for his soon to be doubled workload. He had moved the contractor's material aside and set up the white board. By ten that morning, he'd been informed by Lieutenant Vogel that a team's workload would be dumped in his lap. One priority open case; the apprehension of Ivan Prall on two murder charges.

He and Latimer moved materials in and had a tech from downstairs linking laptops over three workstations. They had recruited a uniform from rookie hall to help out and said rookie was busy humping boxes in and dashing out on coffee runs.

Bingham stood before an enormous street map of Portland, circling crime scene coordinates in red marker. He turned to the tech hunched over one of the laptops. "How goes the battle, Jay? You about done?"

Jay the tech nodded without taking his eyes from the screen. "Almost there."

"Good," Bingham said. "When you're ready, I want these coordinates fed into the system. See what we got."

Bingham capped the marker and stepped back to view the big map. Pleased, he turned around to start on the files. Detective Mendes stood in the doorway. A box in her hands, watching the buzz of activity in the room. This was awkward. He nodded politely."Detective".

"What is that?" Lara chin-cocked the big map.

Bingham perked up. "Geographic profiling. We can analyze his hunting grounds and zero in on him."

"You won't find him that way."

Now that's just rude, he thought. He motioned to the box in her hands. "You can toss that over there."

More boxes were stacked unevenly against the wall, the cardboard corners crushed and the whole tower threatening to timber. Her work, dismissed and shunted aside. She dropped the box on the table and left.

TWO floors down, Lara Mendes placed her shield on the countertop. She slid the holster from her belt and withdrew her 9mm Glock service issue. The clip slid out and she placed it next to the shield. She racked the slide forward, double-checking that there was no round in the chamber and set it down. She pushed the shield and the gun across the counter to the desk sergeant. He scribbled details onto a form then spun the clipboard round for her to sign.

Gallagher stood behind her, shield in hand, waiting to go through the same humiliating routine. Their eyes met briefly as she passed him but neither said a word.

29

THE PETTYGROVE WAS QUIET when Gallagher pushed through the door and slid his ass onto a bar stool. Two daytime drinkers at the other end of the bar and three occupied tables. Gallagher checked each face in the room and tagged all but one of them as either a cop or ex-cop.

He needed to go home. Boozing down his shitty day in this place was just a bad idea. He had stormed out of the precinct, intent on going straight home when he remembered Amy was going to a friend's house for dinner. No need to rush home and fix a meal. So here he sat. Just one, to burn off the bad taste in his mouth. Was there anything more pathetic than anchoring his dumb ass at the bar to sulk a shitty day away? He didn't care. Country music spun out from two bashed up speakers, which didn't help matters. Like a license to get maudlin. He hated country music when he was a kid simply because his parents listened to it but had come around to it the older he got. Now he tortured his own kid with it and took no small pleasure watching her squirm when he sang along.

The woman behind the bar came round and called him by name. She knew everyone's name. He asked for a beer in a bottle, not the swill in the taps. The Pettygrove never cleaned their draft lines and more than one glass from the tap was lethal.

The ruckus with Kovacks was going to be a problem. He'd been down this route before, stomping heads when he should have kept his cool. He just couldn't help himself yet secretly relishing how much it drove Vogel up a wall. The funny part here was that he hadn't even touched Kovacks. Ha ha. Not that it mattered. He had history, Mendes didn't. He was the one the Lieutenant was itching to jettison from the detail. So it goes. Investigations like this would take weeks, plenty of time to worry about it later.

He tilted back half the bottle and let himself drift back to the real problem. The thing that came at him in the railyard. The thing that smashed his window and popped its teeth at him. It wasn't coincidence that had led him to it. The dog, the first one, had stood in the middle of the road waiting for him. How did it know where he was? He was driving, for Christ's sakes. The sonovabitch had waited for him to drive up and then lured him onto the tracks. It was a trap and he had walked right into it. Outsmarted by dogs.

They had laid a trap and waited. That requires intelligence and patience. What the hell was he dealing with? Did wolves hunt like that?

And then there was the thing itself. He could still see its teeth when he closed his eyes. The thing was fucking huge. It didn't move the way dogs do. It didn't behave like a dog either. It didn't bark or posture. The damn thing had locked on him and closed in fast, with purpose and intent. Like it was personal. Was some part of Prall still conscious inside that thing?

How the hell could something like that exist? How could it roam back alleys and riverbanks and no one know? He still couldn't utter the word, not even to himself. It was just too fucking crazy.

He killed off the beer and ordered another, along with a tumbler of Jamesons. He meant to nurse it but the whiskey went down too easy and he nodded for another. He'd just been given the axe. Didn't he deserve it? He studied the framed pictures behind the bar. Old black and white photographs of salty lawmen down the decades. Cops in stiff uniforms from the 1970's, all the way back to stone faced sheriffs in moustaches and waistcoats. His favorite picture showed two sheriffs in wide brimmed hats flanking a pineboard coffin propped vertically against a hitching post. Crammed inside the narrow box was a dead man with half-lidded eyes and a gaping mouth. Presumably some crazed outlaw that the lawmen had pursued and brought down with their gunblacked hands. Wagonyard justice.

The bar grew louder. Patrons shuffling in after the shift change. Gallagher glanced over his shoulder and clocked Latimer and Bingham settling into a sixtop with a crew from other details.

Shit.

"Two pitchers, Stephanie." Bingham leaned an elbow on the bar and nodded to Gallagher. "How ya doing, John? Hey, you wanna come join us?"

"Nope."

Gallagher drew circles with his glass, widening the little puddle on the bar. Bingham waited for his order, idly fiddling with a coaster. An awkward pall creeped down the bar. Bingham spoke up, needing to fill the void. "It's not fair, man," he said. "Vogel can be a real dick. Let me buy you one, huh?" Bingham waved his cash at the woman pulling draft. "Get the detective another round too, yeah."

"Fuck you, Bingham. And your drink."

"Suit yourself," Bingham shrugged, fronting. "I'm not the bad guy here, G."

"No, you're the weasel who snookered the case out from under me."

"You think I wanted this? I got better things to do than fix your mess."

Gallagher came off the stool in a snap. Itching for a fight and any excuse would do. "Like what? Beg the Lieutenant for a reach-around while he's pegging you to the headboard?"

Half the cops in the bar were on their feet, sensing the brawl about to spill open. Bingham felt all those eyes on him, he couldn't walk away now. "You're drunk, Gallagher. Go home before you embarrass yourself— "

The snap came. Gallagher plowed him against the rail and stove Bingham's face into the bartop. Hissed at him. "You think you can collar this guy?"

A rush to the bar. Hands grabbed Gallagher to pull him off but he would not let go, barking into Bingham's face."He will fucking eat you alive!"

An arm shot round his neck and choked him backwards. Gallagher punched out blind, looking to hit anyone. Everyone. The off-duty detectives hauled him off and pummeled him senseless with elbows and knees. Threw him out the side door. When he hit the alley, the fight had gone out of him and Gallagher slumped against the chain link fence. Of the four detectives who wrestled Gallagher outside, all knew what had happened to him and Mendes. Not one took it personally, not one got angry. Someone flagged a cab and they piled the sonovabitch into it and told the driver to take him home.

THE drive home was hellish. Twice Lara had pulled over fast to hurl but nothing came. She drove like a senior citizen the rest of the way home and crawled to the bathroom. Passed out with her forehead against the cold tile floor.

When her eyes opened again, the nausea was gone. In its place was a pulsating headache. She slid her phone from a pocket and blinked at the time. After ten. She'd been out for four hours straight.

Easing off the floor, she rifled the medicine cabinet only to find an empty bottle of Tylenol. Damn. She closed the cabinet and her face swung into the mirror. Yikes. She looked like the butt end of a three day bender. Puffy eyes and sallow cheeks. This is what meth heads look like.

There were no more painkillers in her purse. She'd have to go out because the knocking in her brainpan was getting worse. She peeled out of her work clothes and rooted for something comfortable. Anything would do, even the sweats Amy had leant her. She slipped on a pair of flip-flops and locked the door behind her.

The night was cool but the chill air did nothing to dampen the fire in her head. The streetlights hurt her eyes and the traffic stung. North two blocks to the corner store where she bought Tylenol and water and downed two pills right there at the counter. Back onto the street and six doors down, the painkiller kicked in.

Something wasn't right. Vertigo swam up and knocked hard, tilting her too far one way and then the other like she was drunk. Her ears stung. Every noise became too loud and too intense, like God had suddenly turned up the volume on everything. A couple passing by, yelling at each other. A car horn broke her eardrum. A dog tied to a post barked yipped at her, each bark snapping thunderclaps at her. Her palms stoppered both ears, running along in the stupid flip-flops.

Everything was too loud, too piercing. She couldn't think, couldn't breathe. There, at twelve o' clock stood a church. One bare bulb glowed over the arched door of St.

Patrick's Church of the Redeemer. She slid out of the flip-flops, gathered them up and ran for the doors.

Slipping through the heavy oak door, pushing it closed. The din outside muted to almost nothing as the door latch clicked. Soft light cast a jaundiced sheen on the wooden pews. Votive candles trembled beneath a gilded painting of Saint Patrick. Eyes cast heavenward. His hand held a crooked staff and at his feet were thousands of serpents.

Lara slid into a pew and exhaled. The church was quiet. She was still cognizant of the racket outside but it was tolerable. The smell of wood polish and wax was heady, bringing up memories of the church of her childhood. When was the last time she had even entered a church? Four years ago, when she'd flown down to Albuquerque for her nephew's baptism. How her mom would have disapproved. To her, a lapsed Catholic was one straw away from an ignorant heathen. Or an Anglican.

The click of metal as a door opened. She didn't bother turning around. Some other penitent looking for peace, shuffling reverently up the aisle behind her.

"Hello."

Lara flinched. For one tiny millisecond, she expected to see Ivan Prall. A priest stood in the aisle. He looked too young to be a priest. Her own age or maybe even younger.

She nodded, her hair falling loose over her face. She still held her flip-flops in her hands. Barefoot in a church. Her mother would have been mortified. "I'm sorry. I just needed a minute."

"That's what we're here for." His voice echoed softly in the enormous space. "Lots of people come in just to sit.

Gather their thoughts." He sat at the far end, the whole length of the pew between them. Folded his hands in his lap. "We could talk, if you like. About anything. The weather, or what's troubling you."

"Who says I'm troubled?" Her voice cut sharper than she'd meant but the priest either didn't notice or didn't take offense.

"No one comes in here at night if they're content." He leaned back, resting an elbow on the back of the pew. "But we'll stick to the weather. I think we're in for a storm soon. You can feel it in the air pressure."

She dropped her footwear to the floor, slipped them back on. "I shouldn't even be in here. I can't remember the last time I went to mass."

"I'm not a stickler for attendance. I like to see new faces in the church, anytime of the day."

"You must get a lot of crazy people in here."

"No, just troubled people. Folks with a lot of worries and heavy hearts."

Lara felt the tension in her shoulders loosen. The urge to run dissipated, her mortification sharp. She looked at the priest and wanted to ask a question but didn't know how to frame it. It just sounded so stupid.

"Do you believe in the supernatural?" She whispered it, as if lowering the volume made it sound better.

"Of course." He matched her whisper. "The Lord is supernatural."

"Of course. But beyond that, I mean. I..." Her voice trailed off, unable to finish.

"You're asking if I believe in ghosts and stuff," he said, picking up her thread. "Then no. Those bogeymen are human inventions. Projections of fears and hatreds, our bigotries made manifest."

"I see." Lara kept her head down. The numbness in her left hand returned and she flexed her fingers to ward it off. "What if I said there really were such things. Monsters. And that I saw one."

He didn't react, like he heard this all the time. "I'd be very interested to hear that."

Maybe he did hear it all the time.

"There's a man," she began, "who claims to be a werewolf. I assumed he was just psychotic and disturbed. He isn't. He was telling the truth. I saw the monster. It attacked me." She raised her injured arm, as if it was all the proof she needed.

The priest nodded softly, as if agreeing with everything she'd just said. "Go on."

"You know how the story goes, right? If you're bitten then you too become a monster. You become the wolf." She kept her eyes on the kneeler before her.

"I think you've been through a very traumatic experience. Physically and emotionally. What you knew of this man has colored your own thoughts. What you are experiencing now is spiritual trauma, and that is what brought you here."

"That's what I thought too. But something is happening to me. And I'm scared."

"What's your name?"

She told him her name. He rose and came down the pew to sit next to her. "Lara, there is nothing wrong with you. Nothing supernatural. Look at me."

She straightened up and pushed the hair from her eyes, folding it behind her ear.

"I promise you there is nothing— " His words choked off.

"What?"

"Your eyes."

They were amber. Incandescent around the pupils with an unnatural light.

A rictus of disbelief rippled across the priest's face.

She turned away. The look in his eyes answered her questions. She staggered to the door. He called after her, told her to wait but the oak door clicked shut behind her.

30

CARLY FARINO COULD ROT IN HELL. That was the conclusion Amy arrived at walking home from practice. She had confronted Carly about all the lies she'd been spewing about her. Carly denied it. Amy had shoved her hard to the ground and Carly's friends had jumped to her defense, hitting and kicking at her until Amy stormed away.

She had always hated her dad's temper. Hated it more when it bubbled up in herself.

But Carly. They used to be friends. Through middle school until high school, then they drifted. Where Amy played basketball, soccer and even field hockey, Carly was pulled into the sphere of the poser kids. The ones who made their own comic books and constantly formed bands and broke up said bands to form new ones. While Amy was put through drills by the coach, Carly was in someone's basement practicing on an imitation Fender bass. They had little to talk about anymore and by tenth grade they all but ignored each other.

A week ago, Amy learned of a number of nasty rumors going around. That she routinely screwed the older guys on the basketball team and blew doormen to sneak into clubs. Her friends told her to ignore it, everyone got their turn being rumor-slut of the week but Amy wouldn't let it go. She bullied and grilled everyone for the source of the bull-shit and learned it was Carly. Carly denied it. Amy shoved her so hard, Carly flew off her feet and hit the grass hard. Shoved back and booted by Carly's loser friends, Amy walked away. She didn't look back when Carly screamed names at her. Bitch, backstabber, phony, cunt. She didn't let herself cry until she was safely out of sight of school. She walked home.

Her tears dried halfway home and it was hot so she peeled off her jacket and tied the arms round her waist. She worried about what she'd find when she got home. Dad had come home drunk yesterday and made a quick dinner of grilled cheese and Doritos and they barely spoke through any of it. He said he was just tired. Later that night she found him back on the porch, sitting in the rocker. He just grunted the same crap about a neighborhood watch and kept rocking. The grip of the gun peeking out from a pock-et. She said goodnight.

Over breakfast, he was grumpy and his eyes were dark. He'd been out there all night but denied it when asked. Said he just hadn't slept well is all. He said he'd be home more now. He was taking time off work and maybe they could catch a Trailblazers game or go to the movies. Shoot some baskets.

None of it sounded right to her ears. Dad didn't just take time off work but he wouldn't budge when she asked why. Everything was fine, he said. Finish your breakfast.

Did he get fired? Did something bad happen, forcing him to take a leave? It would have to wait till tomorrow. She was too hot and too fed up to worry about anything else today. She just wanted to get home and curl up on the sofa with some bad TV.

Amy shifted the weight of the bag on her shoulder. Leaves rattled across the sidewalk and hit her ankles. The street was quiet. No cars, no pedestrians. Just the dog.

It sat on the opposite sidewalk, a big Siberian Husky, white with grey flecking. It sat straight, mouth closed and alert, watching her. Amy knew most of the neighborhood dogs but this one was new. No collar.

She walked on. Looked over her shoulder. The dog trotted across the road and sidled after her. She wondered if it was lost, if it would follow her home. She'd always wanted a dog but her dad never gave in. Amy turned back to see if it was still there.

There were three dogs. Two big brutish-looking dogs trotted dutifully behind the Husky, all following behind her. A fourth dog slipped out from behind a hedge and fell in line at the end.

Okay. This wasn't funny. The dogs weren't running and playing like normal, they followed her with a weird intensity. Tracking her. She picked up the pace. Don't panic, don't look back. Just get home.

Another glance over her shoulder, she couldn't help it. Five dogs now. And all of them getting closer.

Amy ran. And Amy was fast. She bolted across a yard and over a hedge. The dogs charged after her. She dropped the bag and ran faster.

Her house was round the next corner but she knew a shortcut, through the McNiven's backyard and the old man's tomato patch. Then a dead heat to her own back-door. She could hear the dogs panting behind her but didn't look back.

One thought repeated in her head. Please let it be unlocked.

GALLAGHER hauled in the grocery bags and dropped his keys into the bowl. He checked the shoes scattered at the front door. Amy wasn't home yet.

He still felt like crap. He considered going to bed after Amy went to school but knew he wouldn't sleep. He made a to-do list, all those annoying little jobs he never had time to do and drove to the Home Depot. He replaced the rotting downspout in the front yard and cleaned out the clogged eaves. He made a grocery list and drove to the Safeway. He didn't listen to the news, didn't look at a newspaper. He'd kept himself busy but now he was home and the house was quiet and all the bullshit of the last two weeks started roiling up in his head.

A loud thud scattered his thoughts, something hitting the backdoor. And then a voice screaming for help. Amy.

She was on her knees in the mudroom, locking the backdoor. Amy scrambled away, backing into the washing machine. Her face flushed and terrified.

“What's wrong?” He took hold of her, felt her quaking. Too winded to speak, too petrified to spit. He told her to catch her breath, take it slow.

“Dogs,” she finally said. “They chased me.”

He didn't see anything in the window. He told her to stay put and unlocked the door.

“Dad, don't— “

He stomped outside. Scanned the yard but there was nothing. No sound.

They materialized all at once. Dogs sklathing through the hedgerow, skulking in from the next yard. He counted six of them. Eyes locked on him, fanning out through the yard. Surrounding him.

His hand went to his gun, a reflex movement. It wasn't there.

The pack trotted through the grass, crossing each other's path. Traversing the yard in half-arcs. Watching him.

His eyes darted around for a weapon. A shovel or brick, anything. The Siberian passed right before him, taunting him. It snorted once then suddenly turned and ran. The rest followed, rattling the dry stalks of the hedge. In a flash, they were gone.

He heard the door click open. Amy ran out, clutching a Louisville Slugger in both hands. He coaxed it from her grip and wrapped a hand round her shoulders. Led her back inside.

THE pack raced into a culvert, splashing footfalls off the corrugated metal. Back into the daylight and further down a gulley to a stand of small trees. Where the alpha waited.

Prall sat on the ground and the dogs trampled round and nosed his hands. The Siberian trailed up last, dragging something in its jaws and dropping it at Prall's feet.

Prall scratched the husky's withers and whispered into its ear. He took up the schoolbag and dumped the contents onto the ground. His hand sifted through the papers and pens and clothing, spreading it all out before him. These he studied, as if divining some meaning from them the way a seer foretells the future from dove entrails. Their meaning eluded him so he scattered it away save for the clothing. He scooped up a shirt still damp with sweat and put it to his nose. He discarded this too and lifted the shorts to his face and breathed in their scent. This he tucked away into a pocket. The bag was hurled into the brambles. After a while he rose and quit the place, the dogs falling in line behind him.

AMY slouched in the passenger bucket, her feet on the dash. Her duffel bag was on the backseat, hastily packed. Clean clothes tossed in with the dirty. Her backpack, along with her homework, was lost. They had scoured the neighbor's yard for it but came home empty-handed. Then her dad decided to get rid of her.

Gallagher maneuvered through traffic, past all these turtle-paced drivers who clearly were in no rush to get anywhere. He glanced to the passenger side but Amy was still angry and would not look at him.

"You all right?" He tried.

"I'm not a kid anymore, you know. You can be straight with me."

"I know. It's just… It's not safe. Okay?"

"They were just dogs." She finally looked at him. "Why do I have to go back to mom's?"

"Humor me, okay. I'll come get you when this is all over."

Amy wanted to scream. She hated when he got vague on her. The more vague he became, the more important the issue. "When what is over?"

"Did you pack everything? The clothes in the dryer?"

"DAD!"

That got his attention. He looked at her.

"Don't talk down to me. What is going on?"

He turned onto Delaware and swung into the double-wide driveway of Cheryl's house. He killed the engine, shifted in his seat to face his daughter and came clean. "There's a guy out there. A dangerous guy with some nasty dogs. The dogs that chased you? Those were his."

Amy's mouth slacked, forming an 'O'. She hadn't seen the connection till now. "Oh my god, it's the guy you're after. The one who killed that woman. And attacked Lara."

"Yeah. But now he knows where we live. That's why you're going to your mom's." He looked up at his ex-wife's house. It was nice. "I need to stop him. Now."

"So go get him," she said. "You and Lara can take care of it."

"She's out of the picture."

That was news to her. "What does that mean? You're not partners anymore?"

"We're not anything. We've been suspended for assaulting a prisoner. Internal affairs is involved and it's gonna get ugly."

"Why didn't you tell me?"

He didn't answer, eyes roaming over the house. He popped his door and swung out. "Let's go."

He retrieved the duffel and crossed to her side. Amy hadn't moved. Hunkered down in the bucket, arms crossed. The way she did when she was little. He opened the door. "Come on," he said. "Out."

"What are you going to do? Go after this guy alone? That's crazy."

"It's easier this way. Partners slow me down."

"You say that, dad, but it's not true." She slid out of the truck. "You're not Clint Eastwood."

The light over the front door winked on. Amy took hold of the bag and dragged it up the interlocking brick. Over her shoulder, she said, "Call Lara."

"Say hi to your mom for me."

Amy stopped. "Do you like her?"

"What?"

"Lara. Do you like her?"

"We're not having this conversation now. Go."

"Tell her I was wrong."

He looked confused. The front door opened and Cheryl stood in the doorway.

"Just tell her. And be careful." Amy dragged the bag up the steps and into the house. Cheryl waved and he nodded back. That was all.

THE basement lights popped on. Gallagher crossed to a metal cabinet beside the workbench and slotted a key into the lock. He took down the Smith & Wesson and thumbed the release, ejecting the magazine. Full load. On the top shelf was a brick of 9mm rounds, a spare magazine and some oilcloth. He scooped a handful of cartridges from the box and fitted them one after another into the magazine. He set it down on the bench. A pistol and a spare magazine. It didn't feel like enough. What he wanted was an assault rifle, something powerful that would shred the thing out there. Hell, he wanted a fucking rocket launcher for what he was hunting.

He cast his eyes over the workbench, the tools hanging from a pegboard, the mason jars filled with woodscrews and nails. He pulled out a shoebox of blades, all exacto knives and carpet-cutters. None of it useful. Then he remembered something.

Rifling through the crappy Ikea shelves. Dusty board games, sleeping bags and the box of Christmas decorations. Under a stack of Amy's kindergarten artwork was a long box of lacquered mahogany with cherrywood inlay. He laid it on the bench, flipped the latches and folded back the lid. The utensils lay fitted in green baize. It had belonged to his mother, one of the few things she'd left him. He never used this stuff, not even on special occasions. It needed polishing, the metal oxidizing to a dull sheen. Who had the time? So it sat down here, hidden along with all the other stuff he didn't know what to do with. There were pieces for eight place settings plus serving utensils. Fixed to the inside of the lid was the sterling carving set; knife, two-pronged fork and sharpening rod. The knife slid out and he tested the edge against his thumb. The blade was thick and almost a foot long. The ivory handle was grooved with an ornate pattern but it was too thin and too slick to get a good grip. That could be fixed. He rooted up a roll of hockey tape and wrapped it round and round the handle until it was thick.

Gallagher tossed the tape and tested the new grip. Better, firm in his hand. He scrounged up a rag and buffed the blade to a sheen. He was fairly certain that the silver would have no effect on the thing he needed to kill but he felt better having it.

The cell came out of his pocket and he dialed Lara's number. She didn't answer.

31

LARA STOOD BEFORE THE DOORS of Legacy Emanuel, looking in at the emergency room. She ended up here after running from the church, from the horrified look in the priest's eyes. She needed help. There was something wrong within her and she couldn't deny it anymore. A full sprint here but she stopped short of the ER doors. What was she going to tell them? And even if they believed her, Lara pictured herself being poked and prodded like some alien specimen. Cut open and studied.

"Heads up!" Two EMTs coming up behind her, guiding a stretcher to the doors. A woman lay strapped on the gurney, her teeth visible through the oxygen mask. Her eyes looked terrified and those eyes seemed to plead with Lara as she floated through the ER doors. The naked panic in the woman's eyes brought back her own hospital stay. The paralysis.

Lara turned and walked back to the street.

She wandered home wondering what to do next. She didn't notice the mess until she turned the lock and stood in her living room. It was a disaster. Papers were all over the floor and the coffee table kicked over. The notes she'd brought home were shredded and tossed about. Had she done this? Trashed her own place and not even remembered?

The kitchen was just as bad. Food splattered on the floor. Broken jars and opened Tupperware flung from the fridge, the mess smeared across the linoleum. Leftover chicken was ripped from its foil and reduced to thin bones. A package of damp butcherpaper was torn open, the cut of meat ripped raw from the shank bone.

What the hell happened?

The question was rhetorical. She knew exactly what had happened and who had done it. She could still smell him in the room. His stink was everywhere. When was he here and what was he after?

A noise stopped her cold. The creak of wood from the back deck. He was still here, waiting for her to come out. She had no gun, no weapon. She wasn't even wearing shoes. She stretched over the counter and slid the big Heinke knife from its block and moved to the door.

Dark. The bulb that she never got around to replacing. Something stirred out in the yard. The dogs lay prone in the grass but now they sat up, ears swiveling in her direction.

Prall sat on the rail with his back nestled into the post. He held a bottle of Wild Turkey, propped on his lap. It was a Christmas gift from her CO back in the Fraud unit and the bottle had gathered dust since then. Prall tipped the neck to his craw and his adam's apple throttled up and down. He wiped his mouth with the back of his hand. His eyes went to the knife in her fist.

"You gonna use that or izzat just for show?"

One dog was on the deck, nestled under its master. The Siberian rose on all fours and uttered a low, sustained growl. Prall nudged it with his foot and it padded down to the steps to join the others in the grass.

Like before, he was shirtless underneath a rancid coat. The belly exposed. Lara judged the distance between them. Was she fast enough to drive the knife into his stomach? He was fast, she'd seen him move.

"Two paces, that's all." He grinned. "If you're quick, you can gut me."

"What do you want?" Her voice sounded weak in her ears.

"Kovacks." He swung his legs off the rail and his boots thudded on the wooden deck. "But he's in lock up. I can't get to him."

"You want me to help you?" Her gut told her to back up when he came off the rail but she stood her ground. "Are you crazy?"

"All I need is opportunity." Prall stood the bottle on the rail. "That lock-up is too hardcore for a sick man. They'll transfer him somewhere else, a hospital or the loony ward. I need to know when and where."

"And then what, you kill him?"

"You protecting that piece of shit, Lara?"

She winced when he spoke her name. Names hold power and the fact that he knew hers made her sick.

He kept talking. "That old fuck cheated me when he gave himself up. Thinks he's safe but I've come too far to give him up now." He tilted off the rail towards her. This time she backed up. "All I need is one shot. Then I'll be gone forever."

"And that will cure you," she said. "Killing him."

"It's all I got left."

She took her shot, slicing the blade at his guts. He feinted back. "What about me? What do I do?"

"I can't help you."

She slashed at him again, arcing the air with the blade. He moved fast, leaned out of it. The dogs were on their feet, agitated.

"Easy," he warned. "Anger just brings it on faster."

Lara stopped listening. All she wanted was to cut the leer off his face. It was simple really. To kill the wolf inside you, you had to kill the wolf that cursed you. That's all that mattered. Ivan Prall retreated, backing up against the rail. No where else to go.

She sprang at him, aiming for the face. He dipped left, knees crashing a deck chair. Lara swung again, fast. His left hand went up defensively and the blade sliced his palm and nicked the collarbone. He grunted once and lunged.

Sparks popped her eyes as he hit her. Fists clubbing her to the deck. She kicked out wildly but couldn't reach him. Her hair was yanked hard. He dragged her across the plank floor and threw her to the dogs.

Lara hit the ground and came up face to snout with the dogs. They circled round, lips curling back over teeth.

Panic stung her joints. A revulsion so deep it cooked the marrow of her bones. The dogs. Not like this. No way would she die like this.

The pit bull went for the face but caught her arm instead. More jaws locked onto her ankle. The Siberian clamped her bicep. The animals whipped their heads to and fro, near twisting the limbs off.

The pain was too much. Lara felt her mind shut down at its unending intensity as the dogs pulled her apart like a rag doll. And then something changed. The revulsion that iced her blood boiled into hatred, into a rage at what these filthy animals were doing to her. Something hot seared the muscle of her heart, shooting white heat into her bloodstream.

She shook the Siberian free. She stabbed her thumbs into the eyes of the pit bull. She snarled back. She popped her jaws the way they did. She bit down on the pit, tearing its ear off in her teeth.

The dogs backed off, tails between their legs. They sidled back and forth, confused and wary. What had she done? And where was Prall? She spotted him in her periphery, launching himself off the rail.

He hit her full freight and Lara flattened under the impact. Everything after that was a blur.

THE Cherokee blew through a red, forcing an Accord to brake and skid on the wet pavement. Gallagher clocked it in the rearview and sped away, putting the honking horns behind him. He wished he had cherries on the roof. All he had was the horn and the battered appearance of his truck, which told other drivers that he just didn't give a shit so get the hell out of the way. The other drivers, the ones who treated their vehicles like precious heirlooms, complied and he bullied them off the blacktop.

He drove straight up the sidewalk, popping two wheels over the curb. Lara's house looked empty, the windows dark. He still had the 'Police Vehicle' sign in his truck and this he tossed atop the dashboard. Vogel could take away his gun and his shield but no way in hell was he giving up that laminated sign.

He jackhammered the door and hollered her name. The door locked. Down the breezeway to the backyard where the gate stood open. He tried the backdoor.

The kitchen was dark save for a dim bulb under the hood fan. A mess of food on the table and the floor. Quarter-sized spots of blood trailed out of the room. More mess in the living room, the place trashed.

"MENDES!"

No sound at all. The bedroom door was closed. The gun came out. He pushed the door open with his free hand. Patted the wall for the switch.

"Leave it off." Her voice, lost somewhere in the pitch.

"Are you alright? Why are you sitting in the dark?"

"Stop yelling."

He wasn't yelling. The weak light from the hall grew warmer, allowing his eyes to adjust. Lara lay on the floor with her knees tucked into her chest, her hands clamped over her ears. Her whole frame shook with tremors.

"Christ." He put his hands over her as if to stop the quaking. Her skin was hot to the touch and damp with sweat. There was blood on her ankle. "What happened?"

Her wet hair clung to her face. "Go away."

"Where are you hurt?" He straightened her into a sitting position, unclamped her hands from her ears. He unglued the hair from her face. Her eyes finally rose to his and he saw unnatural light humming inside them. There was blood on her chin. More of it on her teeth. And her teeth were pointed. Her teeth were sharp, the way a dog's are. Or a wolf's.

"Jesus Christ." It was all he could get out. Her skin burned under his hands.

Lara winced at the crack of his voice like she'd been stabbed and covered her ears again. "Can't you hear that? They won't stop. Why won't they stop?"

"Hear what? Lara, look at me."

"The dogs." Her lip quivered but no tears fell. "They won't stop howling."

He heard nothing. A little noise from the street but that was all. He sure as hell couldn't hear any dogs. Gallagher felt his mouth go dry. He was in way over his head now.

He scooped an arm under her and lifted her to the bed. He ran a washcloth under cold water and folded it over her brow. Then he went from room to room closing every window and locking all the doors. Sealing off the noise from the outside world.

Lara had rolled onto her side. He touched her brow. Still hot. He dropped into the chair. What happens now? Would she actually change into that thing? Should he lock her up in this room until it's over? Or just put a bullet through her head.

He leaned back in the chair. Wait and see.

THE sky looked grey from the window. Gallagher sat up and his neck screamed from sleeping in the chair. The bed was empty.

"Mendes?"

He eased out of the chair and the screaming in his neck echoed down his spine. You're getting old, man. Stiff and slow to the bathroom and then the living room, calling her name. The kitchen was empty too.

She was sitting on the back stoop watching the sunrise. Folded up with her chin on her knee. She didn't turn when the screen door creaked open. Gallagher saw the mess he missed in the dark last night. The upended patio furniture and the kicked over planter. The red drops darkening on the pressure-treated boards.

"You all right?" He kept his voice low.

Her shoulders rose in a shrug but she didn't turn around. "I'm like him now."

"He's not human."

"It's almost funny, you know? Of all things, dogs."

He went down two steps and planted himself next to her. Eyes face front, away from hers. "How come you never told me about the dogs? When you were a kid."

She turned to look at this time. Her eyes were puffy and red. The strange amber color was gone. "Marisol told you." Who else would have known about that?

He nodded. "I pushed you too hard on this thing. I'm sorry, Lara."

She didn't know what to say to that. Barn swallows gathered in the yard. They watched them hop through the grass. When he spoke, it was slow and cautious, the way one spoke to a jumper on a rooftop. "We have to stop him. And we have to do it now." His mouth felt cottony. He swallowed and said what he had to say. "I can't do it alone."

"It's too late." She shook her head. Can't he see that? "I can't even help myself."

In his head, Gallagher flipped through a catalogue of assuring words and bolstering aphorisms, stuff he'd told his daughter over the years. Anything to prop her up. It was all bullshit now. What else could make a difference?

"He went after Amy."

That bit. Her fingers gripped his arm. "Is she alright?"

"Yeah. I packed her off to her mom's."

The swallows flitted up to the power lines overhead and chirped mindlessly at the morning sky. Lara broke the silence. “We're not even cops anymore, John.”

“I'm not talking about bringing him in.” His voice was level, resigned. “I'm talking about putting him down. Like a dog.”

She turned it over, what he was asking. To abandon everything they vowed to do as police officers as simply kill the bad guy. Kill Ivan Prall. “He was here,” she said.

It was his turn to clench her arm. “Did he hurt you?”

“He wants me to bring Kovacks to him. Get him out of lock up so he can get a shot at him.”

Gallagher shook his head. Ballsy fuck.

“He said he'd go away once Kovacks was dead.”

The sun rose over the rooftops. “Good. Let's do it.”

“What? No.”

“Yes. We get Kovacks out, use him as bait. Prall, or that thing, comes running. We put him down.”

“We can't just walk Kovacks out.”

“Details.” He dismissed it with a wave. “Prall thinks he can break the curse if he kills the wolf that got him. What if it works for you?”

Lara had a thousand reasons why that plan was the stupidest thing she had ever heard. But no words came out.

“Do you have a gun?”

“No,” she said. “But I know where to get one.”

32

MIGUEL HERRERA HAD FOUR TV sets stacked one atop the other behind the cage of Magic Man Pawn Brokers, each one cabled up to a separate DVD player. He loaded up all four machines and hit the play button. Tonight's marquee included *Ass Crackers 3, Jingle Ho's* and *Canadian Beaver volume 5* and *6*. Herrera had just opened a box of cannoli when the bell over the door rang.

A tall dude stepped inside and held the door for the woman behind him. His mouth dropped when he saw who she was.

"Shit, Mendes. I'm clean yo." He chomped the end off a cannoli and turned back to his screens.

Lara approached the counter and peered through the opening in the metal cage. "Relax. I'm just a customer today."

Herrera laughed, spewing crumbs. "Yeah dog, and I'm Mickey Mouse. You come back for a little mordida?"

"I need a gun. Something powerful and something clean."

"Shit. That is the lamest entrapment I ever heard. You losing your touch, querida."

Gallagher drew up alongside Lara. Herrera looked him up and down, dissed him with a laugh. "Who's this, the bad cop?"

Gallagher lunged through the opening, snatched a mittful of hair and collar and hauled the fat bastard through the cage. Gallagher meant to drag him clear through to the floor but the pawnbroker got stuck in the metal window. Herrera screamed and kicked his feet.

"He used to be the bad cop," Lara said. "Now he's just bad."

HERRERA sulked on a stool in the cramped workshop behind the cage. Mendes and Gallagher tossed the place.

"Fucking stealing my shit, yo." Herrera watched helplessly. "Ain't right."

Lara found a pistol on a shelf but it was a replica Colt Navy, something she recognized from old Westerns. Interesting but useless. "You're not big on irony, are you?"

"Fuck you," was all Herrera could muster.

"Bingo." Gallagher, from the other side of the room. Hidden under a horse blanket inside a foot locker, he slid out a shotgun. The metal was black and parkerized, the stock and slide flat black. He turned it over, inspecting the weapon from every angle. "Mossberg, the kind the Marines use." He handed the rifle to her, stock first. "The numbers are filed clean. It's got a matte finish too."

"No fingerprints." It felt heavy and solid in her hands. She checked the loading gate.

Gallagher dug deeper into the locker. He chin-cocked the pawnbroker stewing in the corner. "How do you know this guy?"

"He's my homey." She winked at Herrera. "Yo."

He pulled up a brick of twelve gauge shells. He handed it off to her and kept digging. "A-ha," he said. "It's a matched set." He held up a large knife, his fingers clamped to the blade.

Lara took it by the handle. The blade was eight inches of carbon steel, serrated near the haft. A Marine Kabar. It felt absolutely lethal in her hand.

"Semper fi," she said.

Gallagher wrapped the shotgun in the horse blanket and tucked it under his arm. Lara scrounged a fifty dollar bill out of her bag and folded it into Herrera's shirt pocket.

"Catch you later."

THEY took Burnside across the river, stitched over on Sandy then swung north to his neighborhood. Gallagher led her through the kitchen to a door off the mudroom and switched on the lights in his office. It was a small room, most of the floor space taken up by a desk and some filing cabinets. A long corkboard was mounted to one wall, pinned with photos and notes from old cases. Gallagher pulled the chain on a banker's lamp and opened a laptop on the desk.

Lara looked over the evidence board, noting the dates on the pieces. None of it was new, the most recent date she saw was from 2005. On the other walls hung plaques and picture frames; citations and commendations. The photos showed Gallagher smiling and clowning with other detectives and uniforms. One frame showed Gallagher and Lieutenant Vogel on a fishing boat, both beaming as they hoisted sturgeon for the camera. Like the evidence board, none of the photos were recent.

She compared the beaming Gallagher in the photo to the one at the desk. It was difficult to reconcile the two. "You and Vogel were friends?"

He looked up from the laptop. "A million years ago. I got partnered up with Vogel when I made Homicide."

"I didn't know that. He must of been a drill sergeant as a mentor."

"He stuck my nose in it when I fucked up. But he was pretty patient."

"Really? Must have been nice" she said, putting enough edge into her voice that even he registered the sarcasm. "So what happened? You two have a falling out?"

"Nah. Vogel earned up, became CO. Things changed. Hard to be pals with your boss." He moved out from under the desk and waved at her to sit down. "Do me a favor. When this piece of shit wakes up, key into the precinct site and look up Kovacks. We need his details."

She took the chair while he rifled a cabinet. The laptop creaked and ticked like it was dying a slow death. She looked over the pictures on the wall. "What happened, John?"

He looked up. "What?"

"All this stuff." She nodded at the pictures. "The citations, your evidence board. It all kind of stops. There's nothing new in the last five years or so."

He stuck his nose back in the drawer. "Cheryl and I divorced in oh-five and I became a single parent. Which, at the time, scared the bejesus outta me. This room has gathered dust since then."

"That must have been hard."

"Yup. Thing was, I couldn't balance the two, you know? Amy and the job. She was the priority and work took a backseat. I only had her on weekends that first year but I was scared shitless I was gonna screw it up and lose even that." Gallagher stopped digging and his eyes drifted off somewhere not here. "Something had to give. And it couldn't be her."

Lara watched his face almost crack. He shook it off and went back to the drawer. She wanted to say something but drew a blank on exactly what. The laptop limped to life, sparing her. She called up the PPB site, keyed her password and waited again. Ping.

"I can't log in. We must be blocked."

He came round the desk with a handful of crumpled paper and leaned over her shoulder. There was no other chair in the room. "Try Bone Slab."

"Bone Slab?"

"Vogel's password," Gallagher said. "His stage name from his pro wrestling days."

It worked. She called up Ronald Kovacks's sheet. His mug shot appeared onscreen. "Now what?"

He slid one of the pages to her. "We fill these out. Prisoner transfer requests. Then we fax it into the prison."

"And what, we just go pick him up? We're officially suspended."

"They won't know that. We say it's urgent and bullshit our way through."

"Using what for ID? Our Costco cards?"

He held out a small folder, a little bigger than a wallet. Inside was a PPB shield and ID. Gallagher's unflattering photo looking back at her.

"I lost mine three months ago, got it replaced. Then I found the old one under a floormat in the truck."

Some of the skepticism fell away from her eyes. But not all. "They'll still call the precinct to confirm the transfer."

"That's the point we need to rush it past them. How are your bullshitting skills?"

"Rusty."

"You can practice on the way over." He found a pen and began filling out the form. "Find the fax number for Rafton."

LARA knew this was a bad idea and said so for the third time when the security guard lifted the gate and waved them through. She would have mentioned it a fourth time but Gallagher marched on ahead to avoid hearing it. He was already arguing with the on-duty warder, a big man with de rigueur goatee and shaved head.

"Look, I wasn't informed of any prisoner transfer." The warder slid the forms back across the counter to Gallagher. "Come back tomorrow."

"My crime scene is gonna be stale by then. I need this guy now." Gallagher pushed the form back. "This was faxed through an hour ago. Check your machine again."

The warder folded his hamhock arms, refusing to even entertain the idea."There's a protocol here, detective. You can't just walk a prisoner out."

"When I got a crime scene going cold and the tech crew standing around waiting for me, I can do anything I need to. The prisoner knows the suspect and I need him on scene to confirm some details before it's picked apart. And I sure as hell can't bring the scene to him."

The man's mouth soured but doubt rippled across his eyes. "This is bullshit." He took up the paperwork and lumbered deeper into the office.

Lara watched the man cross into a cubicle further back and confer with another warder, presumably a supervisor. This man listened then glanced up at the two ex-detectives crowding the counter. Annoyed and suspicious.

"They're going to call the precinct," she whispered.

"Hang on."

They watched the supervisor dial a phone. The warder waddled back and huffed onto his stool. "No transfers after six PM. Unless it's an emergency."

A low growl uttered from Gallagher's throat. Lara took his elbow, worried he was going to pull his Wolverine schtick on the man. "Sir, we are three hours into a homicide investigation. That qualifies as an emergency."

The warder narrowed his gaze on her, hearing her speak up for the first time. "Then you need to warrant the request. And we need approval from your CO." He tossed back their paperwork. "None of that is here."

"Kid, get your fucking supervisor over here. Now!"

Lara felt Gallagher coil up under her grip, threatening to lunge. She anchored him to the spot. "Forget it, John. We'll come back."

"I didn't see your ID, ma'am." The bald man fixed his eyes on her again. "What was your name again? Mendes?"

"Next time." She peeled Gallagher from the counter.

"No, there's a problem with your clearance here. I need to see it, please."

Lara clocked the supervisor. Still on the phone but rising out of his chair, his eyes fixed on her. Gallagher tried to shake his elbow free but she gripped down and made him wince. "Move," she ordered.

The warder yelled at them to come back but Lara kept marching Gallagher out to the foyer. A guard on the other side held the door for her.

"Lara?" Correctional Officer Leto smiled at her, nodded politely to her partner.

"Hi Leto." She tried to be nonchalant but her tone was too hard.

"What was all that hollering about?" Leto shot a look at Gallagher.

"Procedural bullshit," Gallagher spat.

"We needed to see a prisoner." Lara leveled her voice. "But we didn't cross all our T's."

"Who? That Kovacks creep?" Leto chucked a thumb towards the exit. "Cause they just rushed that guy outta here."

"Kovacks? Where did they take him?"

"The hospital. Dude collapsed in his cell. He was turning blue."

Gallagher snapped at him. "When?"

"Not ten minutes ago. Hell, you can probably catch them on the road in."

Lara was already running for the door, hollering back her thanks to the correctional officer. "You're a peach, Leto!"

Leto watched them disappear into the parking lot then pushed on to Chesler at the front desk. There was still a hubbub brewing because the Supervisor had actually left his cubicle and came round to Chesler at the front desk.

"Whassup?" Leto said. Chesler and the supervisor nodded a curt hello and then huddled into whispers. Leto tried to eavesdrop but the Super was already walking away. The senior officer barked one last order on his way back.

"Get the central precinct on the phone. Homicide detail. Find out who's in charge there."

33

THE NEAREST HOSPITAL WAS BACK downtown. Gallagher swung out of the parking lot, hoping to catch the ambulance on St Helens. Lara looked out her window at the marsh passing by. The knot in her guts refused to slacken.

They found the ambulance one minute later.

It was cribbed to the shoulder of the access road, lights flashing but no siren. A paramedic stood in the headlights, looking down at the front end.

"Something's wrong." Lara felt the knot constrict her stomach more.

Gallagher eased the Cherokee past the stalled bus and swung to the gravel run. "Get the shotgun."

The ambulance's grill was busted in, the left headlight shattered. The bumper hung from one end like a loose tooth.

"Are you alright?" Lara approached the paramedic, the shotgun behind her back. She looked in the cab but it was empty.

The man's face was etched in shock and he couldn't stop rubbing his head in dismay. "I didn't see..." He stammered, tried again. "It came out of nowhere. Just ran out in front and bang."

She looked the man over. He was dazed but seemed unhurt. "You hit something?"

"Yeah. An animal. It was huge."

Gallagher went to the rear door and yanked it open. The bay was a mess of equipment and supplies heaved loose from the impact. The second paramedic straddled the stretcher trying to restrain the patient. Ronald Kovacks bucked and kicked his legs, thrashing about in a fit.

"You hurt, son?" Gallagher climbed in, pushing debris out of his way.

" I'm fine." The young man looked panicked. "Help me restrain this guy, would ya?"

Kovacks thrashed his head to and fro, tearing loose the oxygen line taped under his nose. His teeth chomped, trying to bite the paramedic.

"What the hell's wrong with him?"

"I don't know." The paramedic pinned one arm across the convulsing patient and reached for the restraints. "After the crash, he started screaming about someone trying to kill him."

Gallagher threw his weight onto Kovacks and the young man ran the belt over the thrashing man's shoulder and cinched it tight. A sickening pop came up out of Kovacks like his back was breaking. Pop, pop, pop. Kovacks chomped his jaw in a blur of teeth and gums. He caught the paramedic's sleeve and bit down. Gallagher froze as the pervert's teeth grew, elongating from the gums and tearing the young man's cuffs. Veins roped up his neck and swelled hot on his brow. The eyes dimmed and altered color, something not human.

"Mendes!" Gallagher's voice boomed through the bay.

Lara crawled into the cab, squeezing through the seats. She saw Kovacks's spasms, the maw of teeth growing sharp before her eyes. "He's changing," she said.

"What?" Gallagher felt the bones shift under his grip like some knotty parasite beneath the man's flesh. Kovacks flailed on. The clasp of the restraint belt bent, popped off. Gallagher pulled back, looking up at her. "What do we do?"

Past Mendes, he could see the first EMT through the cracked windshield. Still talking to himself, pacing back and forth before the bus. Something swallowed him up and he was gone.

And then everything went to hell, the world kicked off its axis.

The ambulance rolled. Hit hard on the leeside, crumpling the panel wall inwards. The bus tilted on two wheels and toppled over. Gallagher hit the far wall, now the floor, and the stretcher timbered onto him. Kovacks thrashed on him, his gnarled teeth grazing wet against Gallagher's ear.

Caught in the crawlspace between the seats, Lara spun and tumbled back into the cab. Off the dashboard, landing hard on the passenger door. Knees in the air, her elbow flat on the pavement that now filled the shattered window. Lara scrambled to get upright in the cramped space when something skulked past the front end. Dark pelage filled the windshield. The monster swung its head and looked at her through the glass. Yellow rimmed eyes held her own. Its enormity took her breath away. Terrifying in power and beautiful in symmetry, Lara Mendes was transfixed by the wolf.

The shotgun was angled under her, wedged between her back and the door. She squirmed in the floor well, trying to pry it free. The thing's snout pressed the windshield and fogged the glass. Lara clawed the shotgun up. No room to shoulder it, she simply fired from the hip. The fogged glass exploded, the boom punched out her eardrums. The wolf was not there.

The rear doors remained propped open, a square of night sucking the light from the interior. The wolf burst through, its maw stretched wide as if to swallow them all. The jaws sunk fast onto the legs of the restrained man, clicking as they locked. The EMT kicked out and screamed. Gallagher drew and swung the gun up to aim. The lobo pulled back and the gurney banged along after it. Ronald Kovacks was dragged, stretcher and all, out the door and into the night.

Gallagher blasted at it, the crack of gunfire booming inside the ambulance. Something told him to stop, to hold his fire for fear of hitting the victim. He ignored it, unloading five, six rounds at the damn thing but it was gone. He shot at nothing, at the night itself.

The young man scrambled away from the doors, slack-jawed in terror. Crawling right over Gallagher to the far corner, his mouth jabbering up and down.

"John!"

Gallagher's arms remained locked, the barrel still trained at the door. A hand shook his shoulder. Lara crawled over the terrified EMT into the bay and looked him over. "Are you hurt?"

He lowered the gun. "No."

"Move," she said.

THE ambulance lay on its side, two wheels in the air like some dead carcass. Gallagher banged out the door and swept the barrel left to right. Lara right behind him, crawling free of the dead bus.

The ambulance driver was on the pavement. He was alive but his breathing was shallow and his eyes were fixed, shock setting in fast. There was blood all over the road. Gallagher knelt over him. The man's left hand was gone and the open arteries pulsed hot blood onto the pavement.

Lara was already back inside the toppled bus, dragging the other EMT out. "Get out here. Help him."

He pushed her hands off. "No fucking way!"

She smacked him hard across the face. It didn't register so she hit him harder. The man looked at her in shock, anger. That was better. He took his kit and scrambled outside. Instinct and training took over when he saw his dying partner.

Lara chucked up the shotgun and swept the perimeter but all she saw was the road and the marshland beyond it. "Do you see him?"

"I don't see anything." Gallagher lowered his weapon. "Where are the dogs?"

A breeze ruffled the trees all around them but nothing moved, nothing sounded.

At their backs, the young man worked frantically to stop the bleeding. The face of the downed EMT took on the color of ash. "I need another bus out here," the younger man barked. "He's bleeding out."

Lara called it in, giving the dispatcher their location and relaying details of the injuries from the younger paramedic. When the dispatcher asked for her name, she hung up. She told the young man to hang on and looked for Gallagher but he wasn't there. She called out.

"Over here." His voice, further up the road. She jogged up and he chinned at something on the asphalt. "Look."

The oxygen tube lay coiled on the ground, flecked with blood. Gallagher dangled it between his thumb and finger. Lara crunched over the gravel shoulder to the ditch. She plucked a strip of fabric from the weeds, the same pale blue as the ambulance gurney. Another step into the long grass and her foot slipped down the muddy embankment. The ground dropped steeply to a gulley and beyond that, dark trees. Lara kicked her way back to the crest of the ditch. "Here," she panted. "Down this way."

He caught her hand and hauled her back up the grade. "Time to arm up."

From the back of the Cherokee, they took the two longhandled Maglites. Gallagher tore open the box of twelve gauge shells and Lara filled her pockets. She slid the Kabar into her belt and he found the carving knife, a dish-cloth for a sheath.

"What is that?" She eyed the knife with its crudely taped handle, took it from his hand. The sterling blade caught the light, unpolished as it was. An eyebrow shot up. "Silver? Seriously?"

"Last resort," he said. "You should see this bad boy cut turkey."

"You know silver doesn't work, right?"

"Yeah. But does he know that?"

She conceded the point. He shoved the trunk closed.

THE slope was muddy, their heels slipping in the wet leaves all the way to the bottom. The flashlights threw short against the dark. Beams hitting a few mossy tree trunks but little beyond that.

Gallagher fanned his light back and forth, already losing his bearings in that stygian pitch. He looked up at the sky, hoping to navigate from the stars but the night was overcast with clouds. Some cowboy you are, he scolded to himself. "Which way?"

Lara arced her Maglite round but seemed no more grounded than he was. "I don't know."

"Best guess?"

She aimed her beam north, then adjusted northwest. "This way."

They trudged off under that bearing, aligned with the pole star, their feet sucking into the muddy ground. Twenty sloppy paces in they found another strip of hospital linen. She pressed on, Gallagher following her lead. Thirty more paces and Lara stopped short.

"What is it?" His hand went to the holster.

She struck east, the beam of her light rolling over wildgrass until something pale poked up from the foliage.

An arm, torn off at the elbow. The gnawed ligaments and protruding bone drenched with black blood. The pulse monitor remained clipped to the index finger.

LIEUTENANT Vogel was supposed to be home an hour ago. This wasn't unusual for the commander of a homicide unit but his son was home from Washington State for the weekend and Vogel was looking forward to a big family meal and then a night of WWE on the flat screen. This was his son's second year at college and Vogel missed him dearly. His first year away had been a delight; the house was calm and there was no trail of dirty clothes. No one pilfering everything in the fridge. The novelty wore off by February and the house became too quiet, too clean. He and his wife found too much time on their hands without the trainwreck of their son to look after. This second year at college, the stillness was unbearable.

The Lieutenant had moved with grace and efficiency that afternoon; returning calls, shuffling paperwork and putting out fires all around him. He was wrapping everything up when the phone rang and a boatload of shit poured out of the receiver.

Correctional Supervisor Susan Dade called from the Rafton lockup and wanted to know why two of Vogel's thugs were not only still on the job but back here looking to have another go at the same prisoner. She was livid and Vogel asked her to back up and relay the details. His jaw set when he learned what had transpired. Vogel spoke calmly to Supervisor Dade, assuring her that this was a big misunderstanding and apologized for his officer's actions. He gave no details of their suspension from the unit, no information at all about the state of affairs within his department. He listened dutifully, said he looked forward to seeing her official complaint over the incident and promised to get back to her with some answers as soon as possible. When he got off the line, the roar issuing from his office echoed clear across the bullpen.

DETECTIVE Bingham sat in the makeshift task room comparing the big wall map to a corresponding map on his computer screen. He had put so much work into building a geographic profile of the suspect that had eluded two other detectives and now it just hung there mocking him. The profiling program had spit out nothing but erroneous estimates and the entire case had stalled out. His partner Latimer, refused to sink anymore overtime into this and went home on the shift change. Bingham had taken to simply staring at the map, waiting for God to drop a lead into his lap. He was still waiting.

He flinched at the roar bellowing across the cubicles. He went to the door and spotted the Lieutenant issuing orders to detective Rowe. The veins on Vogel's brow bulged, and that was never a good sign. The Lieutenant eyed him in the doorframe and marched right for him.

Shit. Bingham kept his smile light, his tone casual. "What's up, boss?"

Vogel shooed him back and closed the door halfway. "We have shit to shovel." He looked around the war room. "Where's Latimer?"

"He went home. Family stuff." Bingham didn't want to ask but knew he had to. "What shit are you talking about?"

"You're friends with Mendes, right? Have you talked to her?"

"No. Not since, you know, she got her walking papers. Why?"

"She and Gallagher are up to something." Vogel took a breath to calm the rage. "They tried to boost a prisoner from lockup. The one tied to this case."

"Kovacks?" Bingham blanched. That didn't sound at all like Lara. "Did they take him?"

"No. The warder smelled a rat."

"Why would they do that?"

"They're playing vigilante," Vogel said. "And digging their own graves in the process."

"Shit." Bingham reached for his cell. "Did you call her?"

"Neither one are answering their phones." Vogel leaned against the desk, leveled a finger at him. "We need to find them pronto. And we need to do it quietly. If this gets out, the whole department is in for hell on a popsicle stick."

"No shit. Let's get some uniforms, start tracking them down."

"No uniforms. We keep this in-house for now. Rowe's coming with us. Call Latimer, have him meet you at Mendes's place. Rowe and I will hit Gallagher's house."

Bingham followed the Lieutenant out to the bullpen. Detective Rowe marched up fast to meet them. "This just got worse," he said.

"That isn't possible." Vogel kept walking, making the detectives fall in behind him.

"That Kovacks guy was being transported to hospital but the ambulance never showed. A 911 call came in about twenty minutes ago. The bus was in some kind of accident. One paramedic is seriously injured, the other one's shaken up. But he said there were two police officers on the scene. Plainclothes cops."

Lieutenant Vogel stopped cold. "What about Kovacks?"

"Disappeared."

34

THE SMELL OF DAMP EARTH FILLED the dying man's nostrils. The musk of rotting leaves and the tang of earthworms cleared his senses. After the godawful stink of antiseptic floorwash and old paint and unwashed blasphemers, the smell of soil and weeds was a boon.

He lay face down in the dew, the restraints long gone. He clawed at the earth, trying to crawl away but the going was hard. The torn stump of his arm floundered in the muck like a tortoise's flipper. He was losing blood fast.

He had to change, had to become the wolf one more time even though it might kill him. The other lobo was still out there, circling in the darkness. Choosing its moment to strike. The bastard Prall.

Triggering the change took no effort at all. It was simply letting go, unclenching a muscle in the heart. Keeping the wolf down was the hard part. Any emotion could set it off, not just rage or anger. Fear, lust, hatred or jealousy, all of them poked the monster to life. All Ronald Kovacks had to do was let go and let slip the wolf.

The wolf's blood sang through his veins, pumped coarse through the ventricles of his venal heart. But it wouldn't be enough. The lobo in the dark circled closer and closer. At the first hint of the old man's transfiguration, it sprang.

GALLAGHER couldn't keep up. Even with the Maglite on the ground before him, the way was hard. The terrain was treacherous, jarring drops and dips hidden under the algae scum. Gnarled tree roots tripped him up. He'd already fallen once, scraping his palm bloody and losing even more ground on Lara.

Lara ran effortlessly through the dark, sidestepping every obstacle like she ran this course every day. She was breathing hard but not winded. Wanting to run faster but holding back to keep from losing Gallagher. Why was he so slow?

They pressed on like this for a while, Lara chasing ahead and Gallagher splashing slow through the marsh. He cursed her each time he fell, called out for her to stop but she was too far ahead. He trudged on and he thought he could hear the river up ahead. And then he saw her.

Lara stood in a hollow of black oaks. Her back to him as he caught up, her gaze fixed on the ground. Gallagher swiped a palm over his brow. She was still, not panting and heaving the way he was. Then he saw what held her eyes, the thing on the ground.

There was little left that could be identified as Ronald Kovacks. Or even human. What was there, in the mud and rotting leaves, was a butchered carcass, some godforsaken thing rendered into obscene pieces. Bone and meat and fur and all of it sopped in an impossible amount of blood. Webs of fur strung white with flecks of grey, the coarse coat of the wolf. The thing's entrails were strewn and scattered, its ribcage broken and snapped. Strung between the meat and splintered ribcage were shreds of orange cloth, prison scrubs rent over the gore like webbing.

The stink of it steamed into Gallagher's nose. It was all he could do to keep his stomach down. Lara hadn't moved, still as the oaks around her. She didn't even blink.

He turned away from it and spoke her name. Nothing. He touched her arm. She flinched like she'd been tasered, snapping out of her trance. Her eyes looked confused, like she didn't recognize him.

"Don't look at it," he said.

"It's nothing." She knelt down for a closer look, unfazed by the smell or the horror of it. "It's less than nothing."

What the hell was that supposed to mean?

Lara rose and stepped through the gore and knelt again. Studying something round nestled against a tree root. "Look at this."

The head. Neither the man nor the monster but some profane misalignment of the two. The thing's snout but the man's eyes, agape in what could only be terror. The jaw piece was missing, shorn away whole at the hinge. Lara reached down and gripped it by the hair and raised the dripping mass up to eye level.

"Jesus, don't touch it," he spat. "Put it down."

Her eyes met his and Gallagher saw nothing familiar in her gaze. She seemed some other person and her eyes put a chill down his back. She turned the head back and forth, inspecting it, then let it fall. It rolled onto its side in the mud, one wet eye staring up into the night sky.

"Get out of there, for Christ's sakes!" He barked at her the same way he barked at Amy when she was little. His anger coming out of nowhere. He stepped into the blood, snatched her arm and pulled her from the mess. "What the hell is the matter with you?"

She jerked out of his grip and stepped forward, eye to eye. "Keep your hands off me."

Her eyes seemed all wrong again. That weird flicker exploding in her irises. "Something is wrong, Lara. You should go back to the truck."

"No. He's too close."

He squeezed her arm again, he couldn't help it. "Take five."

All she meant to do was push him off but the shotgun was still in her hands. She crossbeamed it across his chest and he flew back as if hit by a bus.

"Oh God." It happened so fast, it didn't seem real. How could she have done that? This wasn't her. She wasn't violent, she didn't have fits of rage like this.

Gallagher rolled onto his hands and knees, the wind punched out of him.

"I'm sorry." She went to help him, to do something but her spine froze up and she became still. Something washed over her and tweaked the nose of her rage again. It was so alien to her senses that it took a moment to register.

She could smell Prall.

Turning her head, she could almost pinpoint the direction it was coming from, wind or no. Prall or the wolf, one and the same to her.

Gallagher kept his head down and gulped oxygen back into his lungs. He hated getting the wind knocked out of him, hated that moment of panic when you couldn't breathe like you're drowning. It had happened plenty of times, playing football or dust-ups on the job, but every time it spooked the hell out of him. When he looked up, Lara was long gone. But he knew she would be.

That sting of panic came back. Mendes had teetered on the edge but now she was slipping down the far side and he had no idea how to help her. He couldn't stop her, couldn't even keep up with her.

He was in way over his head with no clue of how to stop any of it. Who would? He was just a cop and his only real skill was threatening and pummeling people who were weaker than him until they told the truth. Or the truth he needed at that moment.

"To hell with you." He lowered his head until it touched the ground. He gave up. "I can't fix this so to hell with you."

Go get your kid. Go home. Lock the doors.

IVAN Prall knelt under the awning of a willow, its tendrils swaying over him like a jellyfish. The breeze that riffled the leaves cooled the sweat on his flesh and the earth was cold under his knees. Of that he felt nothing, only the hot tears on his face registered at all. The lecher Kovacks was dead and he emerged triumphant. He had spilled the blood of the old beast and its blood had cleansed him, washing away the sin of the wolf. He looked down at the object still clenched in his fist. The jawbone ripped from the head of the Kovacks-wolf, still warm in his fingers. A relic to verify the redemption of his sins.

He touched his fingertips to his tears, tasted the saltiness of it. Wolves cannot cry and Ivan Prall hadn't wept since his transfiguration all those years ago. Praise God.

Yet the tears didn't last long and his eyes dried and he wept no more. The flame of triumph flickered and snuffed, leaving a cancerous hollow inside him. He tried to remember the last time he had seen the bastard Kovacks. Some three months after he'd been attacked and fled the hospital. He had transformed twice in that time. His baptismal change had left him racked with guilt and shame. After the second transformation, he realized what had happened and what he had become. He had gone back to the Gethsemane house, that hateful pit for the wretched, to confront Ronald Kovacks. The man had chased him from his door like some rabid dog. He had never meant to pass the curse onto him, Kovacks had said. He had meant to kill him. He blamed Prall for his own circumstances, for being too stupid to just die. Prall ran alone and ashamed into the wilds of the mountain. And every day after that, he had cursed himself for not killing Kovacks on the spot, not gutting him with the knife hidden in his belt but the old man still held power over him and he ran away frightened. He didn't know it at the time but he could have ended the curse then and there. It wasn't until years later when he hit upon the solution, the ablution of the curse after so many attempts at other cures and still other redemptions. All that time wasted, all that suffering endured. His cross to bear.

So why did his heart ring hollow now?

Kovacks had begged for his life at the end. Like a mouse, like a woman. Caught halfway through the change, Kovacks writhed between man and lobo and begged like a leper. He tried to bargain for his life, promising that there were further mysteries to be divulged, hinting that there were others like them. Whole packs of their kind, running free somewhere north. Unafraid and unashamed of what they were. Prall was too far gone to hear. Even his wolf half knew Kovacks to be a snake and a liar, willing to say anything to purchase his life with thirty shekels of lies. His wolf showed no mercy, granted no clemency. How else could it be? The end had been written since the beginning and neither could deviate from their role. Only a snake could think it could slither out from under the paths God had set for them.

His ears picked up the thumping of pads and the dogs burst from the underbrush and circled him. The wolf had left them behind but when they saw Prall they nudged him with their snouts and licked his back and pawed his hands. Did they realize the wolf was gone? Couldn't they sense the alpha was dead and he was no more than a man now? If they did, the pack gave no hint of it. They nuzzled into him and leaned their ribs against him.

The Siberian came up last of all, trailing his clothes in its maw. It dropped the bundle at his feet, sniffed at him and suddenly jerked back. Prall reached out to scratch its ruff but the Siberian shied away. He wasn't surprised. The husky was the most intelligent of the pack, the beta. He would be the one to smell the change in him before the others. A sting of sadness pricked his heart at the thought, how the distance would grow between them now.

No time for that now. He pulled on the filthy jeans and rancid jacket. He was cold now, so vulnerable to the environment like all the other weak humans. The price to pay.

The wind blew harder, tossing the willow branches around him. The Malamute chomped at the dipping vines, playing. He smiled at its play, its youth but then something fired through his brain and knotted his guts. One single smell burned above all the million other odors in his nose. The tang of the woman, the one still hunting him. She was closing in fast through the grove.

And now the pack caught her scent. Every snout turned to her direction, ears up. They looked at him and then looked back south, downwind of the woman as they were. They ducked and circled round, anxious for some sign from him, some command to carry out. Would they withdraw or turn and hunt the female?

His brow creased. How could he still catch her scent if the spell was broken and the curse washed from his soul? Maybe some vestigial powers remained with him, he reasoned, after being the wolf so long. Maybe the beast's powers dissipated slowly over time rather than vanishing all at once. Something like this, some reasonable answer. The other implication was too awful to contemplate and he chased it from his thoughts.

The dogs grew restless, waiting. Prall made no move. He crossed his legs under him and straightened his back. None in the pack wanted this, just sitting and waiting for the enemy to come. Suicide. The pit bull leaned into him but he swatted it away. The Siberian barked in his face, openly disrespecting the alpha's decision. The others froze, expecting the beta to be brought down for its insubordination.

Prall stymied them all and did nothing. He picked up the jawbone from where it lay in the grit, thumbing the sharp contours of the teeth.

"Let the woman come."

LARA CLIMBED uphill, moving out of the marsh to higher ground. With the breeze at her back she was upwind of Prall. He'd know she was coming. It didn't matter. Nothing was going to stop her from blowing his rancid head off with twelve gauge buckshot. Not Prall, not Gallagher and not the goddamn dogs.

She crested the rise and saw a pinprick of light twinkling through the trees up ahead. The road couldn't be that far away. The smell of the river was close. Tracking him was easy now, his stink clear in the air like an arrow pointing the way. The dogs were with him

The ground was firmer here, hardpacked earth instead of the muddy slosh of the grove. She moved on through a stand of willows and up into a clearing.

Ivan Prall sat cross-legged on the ground watching her approach. Waiting for her.

“Hello,” he said.

35

THE DARKNESS WAS OVERWHELMING. Gallagher looked ahead and then back but it all looked the same, dark trees and uneven ground. He couldn't tell which way Mendes had run nor could he decipher north from south. The sky was clear and the stars visible, the moon a thin crescent. All of which was useless to him, a dumb-as-brick cop lost in the woods.

Pick a direction and march, he'll hit the road or a fence. The river. He knelt and patted the wet ground until he found the Maglite he'd dropped when Mendes walloped him. He couldn't believe how hard she'd hit him. She outran him, overpowered him easily. How far gone was she? To hell with her. She'd have to fend for herself now.

Ivan Prall would be long gone by now. The crazy sonovabitch got what he had come for. Now he would vanish along with his mutts and the file would remain open until someone consigned it away to the crypt of cold cases.

His fingers hit the flashlight and thumbed it on. He chose a direction and just started walking. He'd find his truck and drive to Cheryl's house. Make sure Amy was okay. That was all that mattered now.

And tell his daughter what? That he'd ditched his partner out in the swamp? He stopped and looked down at the muddy ground. What if Prall wasn't gone? Lara was chasing through the trees after a monster plucked straight out of a fairy tale. And the dogs, that pack of vicious dogs. How would he look his daughter in the eye and tell her he abandoned Lara to that?

Fuck.

He killed the flashlight. Cast into darkness, he listened. Nothing at first, then he heard it. The low murmur of the river. The river was north. Lara had fled north.

Orienting his way to the sound, he hit the light and started walking. Every twenty paces, he stopped to listen again, to keep his bearing straight. The ground was slick and uneven so he couldn't walk very fast. This was going to take a while.

LARA didn't trust her own eyes. Ivan Prall sat on the ground in a copse of willow trees. He made no move to run or even get up. Waiting for her.

She brought the shotgun to bear and drew a bead on his chest. The dogs, invisible until now, rose out of nothing. Ghosts that made no sound, baleful eyes that watched.

"Get on the ground," she ordered. "Face down. Do it slow."

Prall didn't move. "It's over."

"I will blow your head off, Prall."

"No. You won't." He tapped at the dirt with something in his hand. "Our business is finished. I win."

Lara inched further, eyes registering the position of the dogs. "Nothing is finished," she spat.

"Didn't you find Kovacks?" Prall raised the object in his fist and Lara tightened down on the trigger. No weapon. Just some bloody piece of bone. The missing jawbone. "Then you know," he went on. "The monster is dead."

"You're still here."

"But the wolf is no more. The hex is broken."

Lara scrutinized his face, his hands. He was human again. The bastard was even grinning. Could it be true? Was the wolf really gone? "Where does that leave me? Screwed?"

"No, no. Don't you get it?" He nodded at the barrel squared at him. "Lower the goddamn gun."

She didn't move.

"You're still playing cop?" Prall laughed. "What're you gonna do, arrest me?"

"I'm going to kill you. That's how it works, isn't it?"

"No. I killed the wolf. I'm healed. That means you are too."

Nothing moved. The ghost dogs watched the standoff, waiting for a cue. An outcome.

Her arm muscles constricted, the heavy shotgun quaking in her hands. Grit stung her eyes. Prall watched, divining the indecision in her face. "You haven't shifted yet. You haven't given in to it. You're healed."

"Then why do I still feel it?" The words spat through clenched teeth. "I still feel it. And I can still smell it on you."

"Because you got no faith."

"No." The rifle dipped, becoming heavier. She notched it up a hair and sighted the barrel square at his face. "Kovacks said it wouldn't work for you. You're too far gone to ever go back."

He looked right down the barrel. "Kovacks was a liar."

Movement in her periphery. She turned but it was too late, the Siberian launched at her. She fired but the shot went wild. The Siberian's weight took her down, landing on her as her shoulder hit the earth. A dull click as the dog's jaws locked onto her arm. The gun fell away as her free hand wrenched the dog's head round until something popped and the dog yelped in pain. She kicked it off and scrambled upright but Prall knocked her back down, pinned her with his bulk. One grimy hand locked onto her windpipe as the other ripped her hair and stove her skull into the earth again and again.

"Liar." He spat the words at her. His eyes bloodshot, his breath blowing fetid and hot. "You fucking liar. I'm saved!"

She recoiled from his stench, trying to breathe. She pushed back, locked onto his eyes and spat back at him. "You're deluded, Prall. You're still a monster. Still damned."

Her words stung. He screamed his rebuttal but the words came out garbled and gibbering and he smashed her face with his elbow. Her eyes flashed. He slithered up her body, pinned her arms under his knees and locked his filthy hands round her throat.

The air cracked. And then it cracked again. The choke-hold disappeared. Lara recognized the sound. Gunshots.

She rolled away, gulping in air and coughing it back up. Prall was gone, vanished from her field of vision. Further out, where the light disappeared into the grove, was the source of the gunshots. Gallagher, running in fast, the gun locked in his fist. Calling her name over and over.

She called back but her voice snapped into a coughing jag. Her arm went up, waving. Gallagher caught it, sprinting for her. Still calling her name.

He didn't see the dogs bounding up behind him. She called out but her voice was broken. She watched as the pack closed in fast and took Gallagher down.

LIEUTENANT Vogel swung his car to the shoulder, pulling in behind the one cruiser on scene. Detectives Bingham and Rowe were out the door before he killed the engine and the three of them took in the road before them. One ambulance, lights going round and round, with its back doors open. The other ambulance lay tilted on its left side, its lights dead. Shards of safety glass littered the pavement. The rear door hung open and debris trailed from it like gutted offal.

Detective Rowe let out a slow whistle. "Christ almighty."

Two EMTs strapped their bloodied colleague onto a stretcher, working a ventilator tube down his ruined trachea. The surviving paramedic slouched on the ambulance bumper. A uniformed officer patted his shoulder, telling him gently that everything was going to be okay.

Vogel marched for the uniform. "Is he hurt?"

"He's shaken up pretty bad," the officer said. "But he ain't injured."

The Lieutenant bent low to get eye-level with the trembling medical tech. "Son? Can you tell me what happened here?"

The young man didn't react. The uniform answered for him. "He hasn't said anything since I got here. He's in shock, I guess."

"When did you get here?"

"Ten minutes ago. Right on the ambulance's tail." The officer chin-cocked the injured man on the stretcher. "That guy? He was all over the road, sir. His guts, nasty."

"Lieutenant?" Detective Rowe leaned into the back of the lopsided bus. "Prisoner's gone."

Vogel paced the pavement. "They took him."

Bingham looked over the mayhem but couldn't hide his skepticism. "You honestly think Gallagher and Mendes did that?" He ran his light over the impact side of the downed ambulance, the way the panel crumpled inwards. "That doesn't look like any car impact to me."

"Then what was it?"

Bingham raised his palms. "No idea."

Vogel eyeballed the debris spilling out the back of the ambulance and trailing off to the far side of the road. "So what'd they do, drag the guy off into the woods?"

"The monster took him."

Vogel, Rowe and Bingham all turned their heads to the shellshocked paramedic. Vogel closed in on the young man. "What did you say, son?"

The young man kept his head down, his voice crackling out a whisper. "That thing took him. Ripped him right out of the back."

"What thing?"

"I dunno. It was big. All teeth." His head shook, trying to shake loose some image in his brain. "A fucking monster."

The Lieutenant traded looks with his detectives, all of them collectively weighing the kid's reason. The uniform offered up a condolence and said again, "The kid's in shock."

Vogel looked at Rowe. "Did you get ahold of Latimer and LaBayer?"

"They're on their way. They crowed about having to come back in but when I— "

"Hold up." Bingham cut him off. "Did you hear that?"

Ears cocked. A tiny pop pop in the night. Gunshots, cracking somewhere out beyond the treeline.

36

TEETH RIPPED INTO HIS LEG BEFORE he even hit the gravel. Face first into a puddle, brackish water up his nose. Gallagher felt their paws on his back, keeping him down with their muscled weight. Get up, get up, get up. He twisted round, trying to turn when more teeth clamped down on the back of his neck. The visegrip jaws broke the skin, a blast of hot dog breath on his ear. He snarled through muddy teeth as the animals pulled him apart.

No fucking way. The only cogent thought left in his brain. He roared up and bucked the weight off his back. He swung the pistol behind his head and fired blind. His eardrum burst but the teeth lifted from his neck. He swung the weapon down at the bastard ripping his calf and shot it through the head. The animal flopped to the gravel like loose dirt and the pack withdrew. He drew a bead on the Siberian and fired and missed.

With the teeth gone, the stinging in his blown ear took hold. Like a needle straight through the drum into his brain. Instinct clamped a palm over it, a natural but useless reaction.

When Lara erupted from the dark he damn near shot her, so crazed with pain as he was. She caught the wrist of his gunhand and pushed it down until he got his bearings. She spoke to him, her lips moving but none of it came through, nothing but the white hum stinging in his ear.

He slid his leg out from under the dead dog and she helped him to his knees. Her lips kept moving, eyes darting everywhere for the pack. There was blood on her palm, and more of it smeared across her cheek. He asked if she was hurt, unsure if he was even getting the words out right. He must have. Lara nodded and mouthed words he could lip-read. I'm okay, I'm okay.

She held up a palm, signing for him to stay put. Gathering up the Mossberg shotgun, she trudged off in the direction of the dogs.

No fucking way. He careened after her on unsteady knees, the balance of his inner ear blown off keel. She hollered at him to stay. A few words surfaced through the ringing in his head. Bad shape. Slow. Deaf.

Fuck that. Deaf and injured, no matter. He wasn't letting her go after that thing alone.

Lara looked at the mess he was in. Bloody teeth marks and torn clothes. Worst of all the fear in his eyes from being unable to hear. His fear was something new and it bounced back to her. He was yelling into her face, unable to gauge his own volume. He wasn't making any sense but every second word was a curse so maybe he'd be okay. She waved her hand at him, indicating she wasn't going to fight him. They would both go. She didn't want to leave him behind. She didn't want to go on alone.

They followed the gravel track, past a small boat on a trailer. More boats beyond that, some on trailers and others propped up in drydock. They'd come out of the marsh into the back acreage of a marina. She could hear the water lapping the concrete slip up ahead. The whole lot was a maze of boats and trailers, rain-battered fencing. A hundred places to hide and nothing solid to keep your back to.

They stalked through the boats, the hulls glowing dull in the gloom like phantom ships. A dog whipped between two hulls. Gallagher aimed but the thing was long gone.

Neither of them heard Prall slink into the open behind their backs nor did they hear the length of chain spinning in his hand. All Lara saw was the chain suddenly snap over Gallagher's throat and coil fast round his neck. Yanked hard off his feet. She chucked the Mossberg up fast and let it rip but Prall was already diving for cover.

That was when the pack charged, bolting from their cover and rampaging for Gallagher. Flat on his back, easy prey. No, she thought. Not this time.

She stepped into the path of the berserker dogs and barked at them. Her voice sounded all wrong in her ears, the timbre guttural and alien. The dogs skidded short, cowed by her roar. Confused as to who was suddenly the dominant animal.

Prall cursed at them to strike. To kill. Lara spun, tilting the shotgun from her hip and fired. The broad side of the barn.

The buckshot blew Prall off his feet and onto his back. He shot back up fast but suddenly pitched forward like a drunk. Face first into the grit. He didn't move and he didn't move.

Holy shit. She hit him. She hit him.

Lara bolted at him. She had no idea if Gallagher was hurt but she was not letting Prall vanish into thin air again. Gallagher would just have to survive on his own.

Prall clawed at the earth, slithering away on his belly. Looking for a place to curl up and die. She dove both knees onto his back, heard a snap. She slammed the business end of the Mossberg into the base of his skull. Disbelief churning into exuberance. "I got you! I FUCKING GOT YOU!"

Prall raked up fistfuls of dirt, pinned under her knees like a moth to a corkboard. Blood seeped through his rancid jacket where it was perforated with buckshot. Too enraged to form words, he curled his lips back and snapped his teeth.

Lara racked the slide, spinning off the spent shell. She pushed the barrel harder into his skull and curled her finger round the trigger piece.

Kingdom come.

Gallagher's hand came out of nowhere and shoved the barrel away. "Not here," he said. "Not like this."

THE boathouse was cavernous, all wooden beams and corrugated tin. Pleasure boats stacked in drydock. Most sheathed in tarps, the rest left to gather dust. The sound of water lapping the bay doors that opened onto the river.

A side door was pried open. They dragged Prall inside and propped him up against a post. Lara reloaded the shotgun while Gallagher found a length of nylon rope and lashed the son of a bitch to the beam. His head lolled sideways, unconscious but still breathing.

Lara's stomach roiled. The stench inside the boathouse burned her nose, the gas fumes and old paint making her sick. Her breathing was fast. She couldn't slow it down, couldn't ease her heart banging inside her ribs.

"No big bad wolf now." Gallagher's voice was too loud, still deaf in one ear. He thumbed back Prall's eyelid. The glassy eye rolled up to meet him, awareness seeping back in as the pupil dilated. "Just another asshole about to pay for his sins."

She said nothing. He turned to her and saw her hands shaking violently. Lara lay the shotgun down and folded her arms. "We have to do this." He touched her arm. "We can dump him in the river. Be done with it."

"No."

He watched her eyes dart between Prall and the shotgun but she made no move to pick up the weapon. "Do you want me to do it?"

"No. It has to be me."

He lifted the Mossberg by the barrel and held the stock piece out to her. Her fingers wrapped round the grip and the block slide. It felt too heavy in her hands, a dead weight threatening to pull her arm off their sockets. Gallagher stepped aside.

"Before this," she said, "I had never fired a round on duty." She saw him tilt his good ear to her. "How do I just shoot a man in cold blood?"

"He's not a man."

The door rattled in its frame, clawed from the outside. The dogs scratching to get in.

Lara took two paces towards the man on the floor but the barrel remained aimed at the ground. Too heavy to raise to the target. His head swung up and looked right at her and Ivan Prall spoke her name.

Lara

Hearing her name in his voice withered her. Palsied her grip on the rifle. He turned and spat, a bloodied glob on the floor, but he never took his eyes off hers. "Put it down, Lara. You can't shoot me now."

"Shut the fuck up!" Gallagher. His voice ringing off the tin walls. He didn't know what Prall was saying to her but it didn't matter.

"The wolf is gone, Lara." Prall ignored the man, his eyes on Mendes and Mendes alone. "You can't kill it anymore. You know that."

"Stop talking." Everything was too loud in her ears. Prall's rasp, Gallagher's hollering. The dogs scratching at the door. She brought the stock up and seated it into her shoulder. Whispered to him. "Just close your eyes."

Prall twisted and pulled against the restraint. Grunted at her. No, no, no. Blood pooled around him on the cold floor. "I've come too far. I will not be shot down by fucking pigs."

Gallagher hissed in her ear. "Do it. Do it now."

Prall's head flopped round and rotated upright. Eyes finding Gallagher's for the first time. "You. You're gonna get yours, pig. That little girl of yours? I'm gonna eat her real slow."

The S & W came up fast and Gallagher slammed it into Prall's head. Burnished metal against the cross-shaped scar. "Tell me something asshole, do I need silver bullets to kill a piece of shit like you or will any old hollow point do?"

"John," she warned him off. "Easy."

Spittle flew from his mouth. "Then fucking do it! Kill this piece of shit now!"

Lara notched the barrel sight onto Prall's eyes. At this range, his head would be blown clean off. "Don't look at me," she said.

Her finger inched back slow on the trigger piece.

The door burst open but it wasn't the dogs. Vogel and Rowe and Bingham hurtling inside. A uniformed officer bringing up the rear. Three guns went up in unison and drew a bead on the two armed people in the room. The ex-detectives, their weapons trained on the slumped figure lashed to a post.

"Drop the gun, Mendes!" Vogel's bark was sharp and unmistakable.

"Back off, Lieutenant." Gallagher barked back.

"Do it!"

A standoff. Everyone but the bleeding lump on the floor clutching a weapon. Gallagher chanced a glance at the open door but the dogs were gone.

Rowe raised an open palm, talking everyone down. "Just put the weapons down, people. Before something stupid happens."

What were they going to do, shoot three cops? Lara lowered her aim and Gallagher followed suit. Bingham moved in and took the Mossberg from her.

Vogel looked down at the man twisting against the rope, recognizing the face from the files. "Is that who I think it is?"

Ivan Prall grunted through clenched teeth. Vogel spun to Lara, veins bulging his temples. "What the hell were you going to do? Just shoot the man and walk away?"

"Yes."

"Hold on, Lieutenant—" Gallagher cut in.

"Shut up!" Vogel kept eye-fucking Mendes but she didn't look away.

Rowe knelt before the restrained man. "This guy's bleeding."

Vogel finally blinked, turned away. "Cuff these two."

Bingham didn't move, balking at the idea of cuffing another cop. Rowe's response was identical but the Lieutenant's nostrils flared like a bull and both detectives knew they didn't have a choice. The cuffs came out.

Bingham shrugged apologetically, "I'm sorry, G. You know the routine."

A racket from outside. Everyone turned as the dogs burst through the door. Barking and popping their jaws, the pack raced through legs and collided into knees. The pit bull snapped at Bingham's calf and he clubbed it with the shotgun. The uniformed officer kicked out at the animals and pulled his service issue. "What the fuck! What the fuck!"

Rowe fired a warning shot into the path of a rampaging dog. The animal tacked left and came around. The sound only crazed the pack further.

Lara's face sank and one word tripped from her lips. "Prall." The Lieutenant's bulk blocked her view and she elbowed him out of the way as the dogs kept darting and feinting, coming back for more.

The rope lay limp at the base of the wood post. A little blood but no Prall.

IT IS FINISHED.

The words buzzed through Ivan Prall's head as he scrambled away from the pigs. From the good book, the last words of a dying man. Those words gnawed and stung like a blowfly eating his brain. He knew it when the buckshot flayed his skin with leaden hail. He knew it lashed to the beam and his heart juiced faster and faster. When his tongue lolled through his teeth just to breathe. When the sight of more pigs gave him the strength to snap the rope.

He failed. A battle won but the war lost, lost, lost. He killed the lecher Kovacks, cleaved the bastard's heart in two with his teeth and ground his bones to paste with his molars. Spilling the monster's blood was supposed to cauterize the wolf from his own heart.

It didn't work. He'd miscalculated. He had been lied to. The 'why' of it didn't matter anymore. Kovacks was dead and now he was the only monster left. All other options ran dry after that. Heaven was closed off, redemption a cruel lie. Salvation was now a cocktease forever out of reach.

It is finished.

Fine.

The only door left opened onto a lake of fire. The only role now was that of the monster. Like a dirty Halloween costume dismissed by other children and left on the floor for him and him alone.

Fine.

He'd become the monster. Show them the gates to Hell. The woman would turn soon. She'll fight it at first but she would join them. She had nowhere else to go but the pack. The man was a different problem. Killing him wouldn't be enough. A violent pig would only welcome a violent death. But there was his kid. He got hard at the thought of eating the little girl.

So let the change come.

37

"SHOOT THESE DOGS!"

Lieutenant Vogel's last words, the dogs snapping and darting between his officers. He heard Mendes holler something, saw Gallagher go pale, and then everything else was drowned out by a sickening roar from behind the stacked boats. He'd never heard anything like it. It was obscene. Furious.

The dogs skulked out of the way, heads low and tails down.

It exploded from the dark, the lobo, as big as it was terrifying. Charging in, knocking them flat like tenpins. The Lieutenant's Glock was halfway from his holster when the wolf hit him, its leviathan maw opening. The jagged teeth bit, jaws clicked and locked and the man was jerked violently back and forth. His scream cut short by the snap of his collarbone.

Gallagher, gunless, bellowed at Bingham. "Shoot it!"

Knocked to the wet floor, Rowe watched in horror at the monster shredding his lieutenant. He felt something grip his wrist. Gallagher ripped the gun from his hand but the lobo was gone, dragging Vogel with it. The Lieutenant's fingernails left score marks on the ground.

Bingham blinked stupidly. Felt the shotgun tugged from his grip. Lara jacked the slide. She hadn't even got to her feet when she heard it coming back.

It launched in fast and low, spinning Gallagher off his feet and bowling Rowe. Trampling over Bingham, it knocked Lara flat. Its teeth clenched her neck without breaking the skin. Its yellow eye stared into hers, communicating something. Lara pushed it away, punched at it, anything to get it off of her. The wolf didn't budge, its eyes locked on hers. Waiting.

Lara Mendes felt something crack. Not bone or cartilage, some seal in her heart she'd been keeping shut for so long now. Looking into that yellow eye, the seal cracked and something bubbled to the surface.

She shut her eyes.

No.

IT WAS the uniformed officer who got the first shot. Knocked to his ass by the thing, he ignored the shock freezing his hands and took aim. Fired. It punched a small hole in the hind end. The giant wolf jerked and turned. He fired again but the shot was wild and the thing was on him. Wrenched back and forth until his neck snapped and the screaming stopped.

Gallagher fired as the thing loped through the open door. He missed and the thing was gone.

THE water lapped cold on her ankles. Lara splashed down the sloped concrete slip and pulled the body out of the water. The Lieutenant was gone from the waist down, bobbing obscenely in the water. Lara dragged an elbow up the slip and turned away from the appalling sight. The sound of the water trickling up and down the boat slip was calm and soft. Soothing almost. She'd lived in Portland for eight years and never spent anytime near the water. Why?

Gallagher's voice bounced off the tin walls until it found her. Calling her name and ruining everything.

The uniform was dead. Gallagher read the tag on his shirt. Dan Osteder. Detective Rowe was shaken but uninjured. Bingham sat on the floor with his legs tucked under his chin, lips quivering. Gallagher touched his shoulder and Bingham recoiled as if stung. He turned to Rowe and told him to find his phone. Call it in.

Lara retrieved the Mossberg from where it lay and waited for Gallagher.

Rowe clutched a throbbing elbow and barked at her. "Where the hell you think you're going? Put the shooter down and take a seat."

"We have to go."

"You're under arrest."

"Sorry." She turned to the door, Gallagher following.

"You bitch."

Bingham, speaking through chattering teeth. "This is your fault. You get the Lieutenant killed, the kid. And you just walk away. You make me fucking sick." He spat on the floor to underscore his point.

It stung and Gallagher saw it in her face. He pushed her out the door and when Bingham cursed them again, he squared her shoulders to stop her from looking back.

EVERYTHING was quiet outside the boathouse. The low rumble of the river and the creaking of insects. No wolf, no dogs.

"It's gone," she said.

He tromped forward and saw the river. Looked south to a grassy slope and then north, a stand of cottonwoods. "We'll find it."

"It could be anywhere by now."

"Can't be moving that fast." He walked back to her. "Not with the buckshot you unloaded on him. The kid clipped it too."

She dropped to her knees, let the rifle slip to the grass. "How?"

He watched her chin sink and he bristled. Hating it. Hating her for giving in."Get up."

Her shoulders sank further and then she didn't move at all.

He dove at her, grabbed her collar and yanked her eye-to-eye. "Didn't you hear him? He said he'd go after Amy. GET THE FUCK UP!"

She knocked his hands away, a sharp guttural sound erupting from inside her. That weird strength was back, that unnatural light sparking her iris. What he wanted.

"You can find him," he said.

"Stop."

He pushed. "You said you can smell him. Hear the dogs at a distance. You can track him down."

She hated him, anger like tinder to the flame in her eyes. "Like what, a dog?"

"Like a hunter."

"No."

"You have to. You're the only one who can find him now."

"Do you know what you're asking? The more you give into it, the deeper it takes hold of you. Don't you understand that?" He was about to speak but she cut him off. "I can't."

"Then he wins."

She backed away, shaking her head at what he was asking from her. He let out a long breath and spoke. "If there was another option, I'd be all over it. But this is the one we're stuck with."

She hated him for that. Her guts already roiling and the fever coming back, it was all she could do to keep it down.

To hang on. How could he ask that of her? If she gave an inch now, the thing inside would take a mile. More.

Her hand braced against a small boat, the hull stained green with river algae. She felt dizzy and sick. She looked up and saw more than just frustration in his eyes. There was contempt. Not pity, not compassion. Just bitter contempt. She wanted to slap it from his face. She wanted to hurt him.

"Fuck you then," he said. "I'll do it myself."

He turned his back on her and stomped for the cottonwoods. The gun white-knuckled in his fist. He bellowed out the bastard's name, screaming it into the void because he didn't know what else to do.

Prall.

Prall.

Prall.

Lara shut her eyes to keep the earth from spinning under her feet. "Shut up." Gallagher's screams rippled around her, spiking her vertigo. "Shut up!"

She opened her eyes and saw Gallagher out in the cottonwood trees. He'd stopped screaming, stopped hollering to all points of the compass. Head down, broken. Out of options.

Then the wolf broke from the void and dragged Gallagher into the darkness.

38

THE TREES BLURRED PAST, EVERYTHING spinning. He was raked roughshod over the ground at terrible speed. Bounced hard, dragged over knotweed, shredding his shirt until his back was scraped raw. His leg clamped in the maw of a monster.

Its pelage smoothed flat in the wind, muscles pumping through the dark fur. Somewhere in the distance behind him, Gallagher could hear the pounding of more paws as the pack thundered after them.

The gun was still locked in his fist. He brought it to bear in both hands but the monster changed direction, twisting and rolling him crazily. Canarygrass cut his face. His back splitting under the drag. He swung the sight back onto the mass of rippling muscle and fired.

The jaws let go. He cartwheeled through the muck, tumbling and rolling. His fingers sunk into the dirt, anchoring to a stop. Disoriented. Lost. The pack thundered up on him and he struggled to aim through his double vision. The dogs skirted round and kept running, ghosts without barks, chasing the lead. As quick as they came, they were gone.

He got to his knees but no further. Too seasick to stand, his calf crushed from the wolf's maw. Eyes whipping round, no idea where he was. How far had the thing dragged him? How far away was Mendes?

He waited out the vertigo until he could stand without keeling over. His leg hurt like a son of a bitch but he could walk. He had to. The moon frosted the groundcover with quicksilver but gave no clue which way to go.

A noise, sharp and close. Behind him somewhere. And again, now to his left. Pads trampling twigs, no attempts to be silent. The noise arced round him from aft to stern. The damn thing was circling him out there in the dark, keeping out of the silver trace of moonlight. Round and round it stalked, a monstrous satellite in his orbit.

Fine. That meant it wasn't tracking down Amy. His daughter's name caught in his throat. He wouldn't get to say goodbye. He stood no chance against this thing, this wolf, werewolf, whatever. He reconciled that but Amy… Their last words were angry, he'd yelled at her. Christ, why had he been such a prick? He still had his phone. Did he have time to call her? Just tell her he loved her and hang up? What if that thing sprang at him before he could hang up? She would hear him die over the line.

John Gallagher mumbled something. Prayer or plea, hard to tell. He pivoted around on his good leg, tracking the noise with the barrel of the gun. With any luck, any whim of God Almighty he could put a bullet in its brain before it killed him.

Amen.

MENDES ran breakneck through the trees, bounding over mossy deadfall and ducking low under the hanging pines. No flashlight but never stumbling in the pitch, her feet hitting solid purchase every time. Something had clicked inside her, locking into place. Reason, logic, intellect; all of it pushed aside and pure instinct took over.

She couldn't see in the dark but somehow sensed what was in front of her, feeling her way through like some mad Braille. She could read Gallagher out there in the darkness, read the wolf and the dogs. Where and how far away. She followed their precise path, every turn and change in direction.

When she realized what she was doing, she fell. Reason pushed back, smothering instinct. She was tracking Gallagher by scent, faint as it was. Smell and sound were the Braille she was reading. Instincts other than her own had taken over. Her heart knocked crazily, pushing something more than adrenaline through her system. The other, the feral embryo coiled up in her heart sluiced through veins and into the marrow of her bones.

And now she couldn't move. The same deadening paralysis she suffered in the hospital struck her down faster than venom, ossifying every ligament. Her jaw locked, a rictus of horror flashfrozen to her face. Like before, her mind was trapped inside a shell of stone. Cruelly aware, alert.

A voice carried downwind and bounced off the trees until it hooked in her ears. Gallagher's voice, screaming and cursing and worst of all, calling for help. Calling her name. Calling for a partner who would never come.

His voice was chased away by the drum of paws pounding over the forest floor. Snapping twigs, snagging burs. The dogs charging in fast. She couldn't move, couldn't scream, couldn't swing the Mossberg up to blast the filthy bastards to pulp. They would be on her in a heartbeat with their teeth and jaws.

They broke the underbrush and she braced for the impact but no teeth came. The pack jostled around her, stepping on her hands and nosing her face. Snouts prodding and poking her, nostrils blowing hot in her ear but they held back their teeth. Were they toying with her? Were these killers capable of that?

Their tang was overwhelming. A stench of wet fur and musk and rancid meat breath. But all of that was surface tissue, a wrinkled skin over boiled milk. Underneath the musk, she could pick out their moods as easily as reading words. No malice or aggression, no hatred nor enmity. There was confusion at first, then curiosity. Acceptance and finally camaraderie. One of their own. A raw fledging pack member.

One, two, three heartbeats before the full horror of it bansheed over her mind. Her heart stopped and skipped like a needle on vinyl, violently changing tempos. Her core temperature spiked and wet fire roiled up her bloodstream and cooked her brains inside her skull.

The tiny fetal wolf incubating in her heart unfolded its wet limbs and stretched to its full length. Like lashes to the back, her heartbeat pounded out thirty-nine ticks and it was finished. Lara Estela Mendes ceased to exist.

THE wolf came at him full bore. Gallagher wheeled the gun up and got off one round, punching a dark hole into the blue grey fur but the monster didn't stop. It slammed into him as he squeezed another round. Hurtled backwards into the dead leaves, he kicked out in a panic, pedaling mad to keep those snapping teeth at bay. He fired into its bulk, at the heart but the wolf roared in stronger, its maw widened and bit down over his ribs. He clubbed it between the eyes with the pistol butt and the thing shook him violently, whipsawing him through the dirt.

He spun, thrown from the teeth and thudding hard into the ground. His hand was empty. He groped the dead leaves for the gun that wasn't there and still wasn't there. The great wolf sklathed forward with no hurry, no rush. An easy kill.

No gun but he wasn't weaponless. He remembered the blade bundled inside his jacket. He tore it free, pulled away the rag. He wanted the silver to flash clean and bright. Wanted the wolf to see it. The wolf lumbered in slow. Limping, one shoulder dipping as it trotted.

Gallagher pleaded with God one more time. One clean shot, the eye or even the heart, the underbelly. Just one clean cut with the blade.

The wolf stopped cold, as if stonewalled by the prayer, and swung its massive head south. Ears up at what was coming. The wolf heard it long before Gallagher but their eyes caught it at the same moment. Another wolf, big as this one, loping between the oak and ash on newborn legs. Hurtling at them both, this lobo was pale, the white coat mottled black and grey over the crest. The tail held high, lips curled back at the sight of the blue-grey wolf. Its intentions were clear.

The grey wolf rose up to meet it. Two leviathans collided in a blur of teeth and chops. Eyes wide in aggression, clean with intent.

Gallagher watched, useless. A bystander of no significance, the knife a toy in his fist. The question glared white hot but the answer was simply too hard to bear. His gut knew it was her but his head refuted that truth.

The pale wolf roared up and the grey cowed, as if to submit but it was no more than a feint. It shot up fast and took the white down, jaws locked onto her throat. Pinning her down, forcing submission. The pale lobo twisted and snapped. The pack thundered in and the dogs raced round the warring monsters, yammering and howling. Insane, lost.

The one clean shot Gallagher prayed for was suddenly there and he took it. He came up underneath it, the blade in both hands and slit its belly open. The monster howled and bucked but Gallagher drove the blade harder, arms to the elbows in its guts, sawing at it. Coring it hollow. Blood spackled hot in his face and the intestines spilled out of the wolf's belly, slick ropes of gore until he was tangled in it.

The monster loped away from the pain. The pale wolf rolled to its feet and shook its head. Dark blood stained the ruff of its throat, its snout ripped and dripping. It chomped its teeth at him and Gallagher reared backwards, slipping in the coil of guts still on the ground. The ropey intestines slithered underneath him, snaking away in the dirt as the grey wolf ran.

Gallagher snatched it up, wet and slick, and wound the intestine round and round his fist. Holding it fast like an anchor. The gut cord snapped taut, dragging Gallagher through the dirt. It slipped through his fingers but he clamped down, refusing to let go.

The dogs charged the strange wolf in their territory, their fealty to the alpha intact. The lobo lunged for the Siberian, the beta, and took it down in its jaws. A bone snapped and the Siberian relented, rolling onto its back. The others slunk low, tails down. Rolling onto their backs before the pale wolf. They whined submission. The pale wolf leaped over them and bounded after the grey, following the twine of guts into the night.

The dogs twisted up and shot after it. The Siberian took two steps and fell down. Its forepaw broken, dangling useless. It whined at being left behind and got up again and then dropped. Clinging to the slick rope, Gallagher watched the animal try a third time to get away. It hobbled in a pathetic jerk after its pack.

The cloud cover melted off and the moon came out again, tinting everything blue. A metallic flash in the wet leaves, a familiar shape. The lost gun. He tightened his grip on the intestines and groped for it with his free hand, clawing the loam but it was still out of reach. He shifted his weight and reached again but the cord suddenly went slack in his fist. The tension gone.

The roar of wolves fighting in the dark. A godawful sound to bear witness to. The popping teeth and the monstrous snarling. Sharp and vicious, like nothing he'd ever heard. The baying of the pack as it circled the combatants.

He snatched up the gun and got to his feet, never letting go of the slack gutrope. Trailing it up like cowrope, following it to the sound of that terrible scrap. The intestine ran out, severed at the end. He could still hear them fighting but could see no more than six feet. Shapes darting past in the weird light, no more. Groping forward slowly, gun out before him and then the racket of snarls and pops ended. He heard the dogs stop and become still. Then all hell broke loose as every dog barked mad and snarled, their pads running. The dogs tore in to finish off the wolf that went down.

Twenty paces on and he could see them, swarming over the carcass like piranha. Their heads jerking this way and that, rending flesh from the bone. The lamed Siberian hobbled in on three legs, spent and clumsy until it dropped and simply watched the others tear the monster apart. Gallagher's bootheel cracked a twig and their heads turned to him, chops slathered with gore. He expected the pack to snarl and pop at him, like any feeding dog but they didn't. The animals slunk their heads low as if shamed and they sidled in confusion and finally trotted away from the dead thing.

There was little left that resembled a wolf or werewolf or whatever the hell the thing was. Cords of stringy meat stretched like webbing. The innards hung between the cage of ribs and dark blood drenched everything. Steam vapored up from the carcass into the chill air. There were pieces of hide scattered about but all of it slaked with so much blood the color of the fur was unreadable. Was it a grey or pale coat?

It has to be him. It can't be her. It can't.

He tripped over the thing's skull. Crushed and rent, the lower jaw shorn clean away. A swath of pelage was yet dry, a tuft free of blood. A bluish grey. Through and through it was grey.

Thank God.

Wind riffled the leaves and cut cold across his face. His head whipped round north and then south. Where was the other wolf?

Two pinpricks of amber fire flickered out in the dark and he realized they were eyes, watching him. The yellow fireflies hovered in until he could make out the form of the pale lobo. It trotted slowly to his left, keeping its distance and circled him counter-clockwise. She was limping bad, her hide dappled with blood. The snout was torn up badly. Round and round it slunk, sniffing the air of him.

He pivoted as it went round and he spoke to it. Spoke her name.

Lara.

The wolf curled its lips, creasing the gored snout into a snarl.

He spoke to it again, soft and low. Whispering her name. The lobo charged in, snapping its jaws then withdrew. It resumed its circuit, circling him just as the other wolf had done. Just before it went in for the kill.

Why did he think he could speak to it? It wasn't Mendes, it wasn't even human. The gun came up and he drew a bead straight between the lobo's eyes. For a moment, he hoped that the sight of the gun would spook the thing back but it circled in closer and closer.

"Please," he said. "Don't."

The wolf stopped pacing. Bared all its teeth at him. It coiled back, ready to spring.

"Lara, come back. Just come back."

His hands were steady, the sight true. At this range he could drop a slug right between its eyes but the eyes were the worst part. They were amber and lupine but there was something of her in them. Or maybe he just wanted to see her in them.

The gun went down, resting against his lap. The beast's snout flared and then the pale lobo turned and loped away, bounding over the carcass. The pack followed it, their new alpha, but the wolf whipped back and chased them away so they wouldn't follow. It swung its head once at Gallagher and then ran into the darkness of the trees and it was gone.

The pack paced and whined, abandoned to the dark without the pack lead. The mastiff bolted south back towards the marsh and the others followed. Left behind, the Siberian tried to crawl after them, kicking at the dirt, but it gave up. Tongue dangling between teeth, it whined and turned to look at the man left behind.

Gallagher knelt in the remains of the grey wolf. He looked at his hands, the gore slathered up his arms and let the gun fall away. He wiped his palms down his shirt but it too was foul with blood. He heard the lame Husky whining after its pack. It watched him and he watched it. A sudden urge to pick up the gun and shoot the dog dead but it passed and he hid his face in his hands.

The dog watched him and ceased its cries.

THE road was blocked off by two cruisers, cherries flashing. Further up the pavement was an unmarked Cutlass and the ambulance.

Detective Bingham sat in the cab and refused to get out. He hadn't moved from the floor of the boathouse until Latimer showed up and coaxed him outside. Sitting in the back of the unmarked car, he still hadn't spoken a word.

Detective Rowe was treated for the gash on his head but shooed the paramedics away when they wanted to put him on the stretcher. His head was still a fog and he remembered very little after rushing into the boathouse with his gun drawn. And now he and Latimer trampled through the underbrush into the trees, their flashlights rippling over the scrub.

Three uniforms were already on scene, marking the boundaries of the site. Gallagher had been walked out of the woods by two EMT's but he said nothing when Latimer spoke to him. The detective didn't push it, eyeballing the state the man was in and he watched Gallagher limp away towards the road.

Rowe and Latimer looked over the mess on the ground, the blood and the offal and the torn carcass. The bones scattered about, the meat all but picked clean. Latimer hovered over the ribcage for a closer look while Rowe found the broken skull. The detective slid a pencil from his pocket and tilted the severed head to one side. The face was torn away, the eye sockets red and empty. The skull, along with the rest of the remains, were clearly human.

"Christ on a stick." Latimer turned away from the gore. "What did that?"

Rowe shrugged. "Dogs must have got him."

Latimer threw his light over the ground, the trees. "What dogs?"

A uniformed officer called out and the detectives came running. Lit up in the lightbeam was a dog. Its foreleg shattered but trying to crawl away to the treeline. The dog stopped as it was surrounded by men. Someone suggested they call animal control.

39

THE SUDDEN DISAPPEARANCE OF detective Lara Mendes was lost in the long shadow cast by the death of a ranking police lieutenant. Lieutenant Mike Vogel had made the ultimate sacrifice, killed on duty, and was afforded honors befitting his rank. A full dress service was held on Tuesday, with almost every officer in the city turned out along with nine hundred officers from every state in the union. Delegations of police from Mexico, Canada and even the United Kingdom flew in for the procession. The widow Janet Vogel collapsed during the eulogy and was led out of the cathedral by her son.

John Gallagher attended the funeral. In light of his recent suspension, he was requested to dress civilian and not in uniform. He turned out in his spit polish blue, drawing visible ire from the commissioner, a captain and two sergeants. His former colleagues in Homicide Detail were polite as the day demanded but Gallagher could hear loud and clear the suspicion in their tone, see the blame fired at him in the set of their eyes.

Also in attendance was detective Adam Bingham but he looked pale, a wraith in his dress uniform. On leave since the incident, Bingham left halfway through the ceremony, unable to bear the crush of mourners. He had given a brief, sealed statement about the events of the night of September 26 and then cleared his desk and left. After consulting with his union representative, Bingham went home and spoke no further on the matter of the Lieutenant's death.

The investigation of homicide suspect Ivan Prall continued with Detective James LaBayer coming onboard to replace detective Bingham. LayBayer and Latimer worked in conjunction with detectives Bauer and Varadero who were charged with separately investigating the death of Lieutenant Vogel.

Detective Rowe gave his statement to both teams. Rowe remembered very little after hitting his head on a hull and Officer Grainge recalled the chaos when the dogs charged into the boathouse but little after that.

Suspended homicide detective John Gallagher gave his statement and then was questioned twice by the LaBayer-Latimer team and three times by Bauer and Varadero. Under the rules of internal police investigations, he was required to give a written statement and no more but he agreed to the questioning. Gallagher stated that he and detective Lara Mendes knew that their suspect would attempt to kill prisoner Ronald Kovacks during the transfer to the hospital. Prall did just that, attacking the ambulance with his pack of dogs and dragging Kovacks into the woods where he turned the dogs loose on the prisoner. He and Mendes pursued the suspect into the marsh but became separated. He found the dogs on the north end of the marsh. They had turned on their master and torn him limb from limb. No, he didn't know why they did that.

LaBayer and Latimer pressed him about a "giant dog" seen by one of the eyewitnesses. Gallagher guessed this witness to be Bingham but never knew for sure. The witness claimed that this giant dog had killed the Lieutenant. In fact, the witness had even sworn that this animal was a wolf. Gallagher shrugged it off, reminding them that Ivan Prall's dogs were all big and vicious strays. One of these dogs was a bull mastiff, a breed known for its height and mass. Gallagher could only assume that the "giant dog" seen by the witness was in fact this same bull mastiff. A monster of a dog to be sure but still, a dog.

"And what about detective Mendes?" asked Rowe.

Gallagher sat in the small room used for the Prall task force. LaBayer and Latimer had given him the courtesy of interviewing him here instead of the box where they grilled the smokehounds.

"We got separated in the dark." Gallagher tilted his head, working a kink out of his neck. "That was the last I saw of her."

Latimer rubbed his eyes. "Okay," he said. "That still doesn't help us. Why don't we go back to the beginning and start over."

A cord flexed in Gallagher's neck as he bit down the urge to reach across the table and throttle the fat son of a bitch.

"No. That's enough for now." LaBayer leaned forward and closed the open folder on the table like a referee blowing a whistle. "Thanks, John. You can go."

Gallagher nodded to the older detective and left the room. He marched through the cubicles of the homicide unit, enduring a gauntlet of accusatory eyes on the way. He bypassed the humiliation of waiting for an elevator and banged through the exit door, taking the stairs down to street level. He knew he would never be back. The only question now was how this was going to play out. They would either ask him to resign quietly or he'd be dismissed.

If asked to resign, he could probably negotiate some portion of his pension but if they sacked him, he'd be fucked. With his pension, even a fraction of it, he could probably hang onto the house and he and Amy would be okay. Without it, they would both be screwed. He'd have to sell the house his daughter grew up in and find something cheaper. The thought of it, cobbled into some low rise piece of shit where the halls stank of fish fry and God knows what, was too much to bear. Amy would give up on him and move in with her mom for good.

Under normal circumstances that would have been the worst fate possible, being alienated from his kid. But these days, normal was hard to come by.

THE medical examiner filed her reports on the two separate remains found at the crime scene. The first set of remains were positively identified as Ronald P. Kovacks but the second remains could not be identified with any certainty. The hands were too mutilated to render fingerprints and no previous DNA samples existed for Ivan Prall to match to. The remains were marked thus; *PRALL, IVAN (TENTATIVE).*

With no next of kin to claim the remains, the bodies of both Kovacks and Prall were sent to the Prager Funeral Home, contracted to the Multnomah County Coroner's Office since 1982. There the remains would be cremated and the ashes shelved for one year. If unclaimed, the ashes would be dumped in a small hole along with the cremains of every other unclaimed soul collected by the county that year. A sign fixed into the ground would bear only the year of their collective deaths.

With that, the file on Ivan Prall was closed. Detectives LaBayer and Latimer typed up the last of their reports, sent copies to the appropriate offices and sealed up the evidence boxes. The task force was disbanded and the equipment removed from the small meeting room. Latimer and LaBayer rotated back into their regular shifts.

The only file remaining open was the disappearance of homicide detective Lara Mendes. Her apartment had been searched and found untouched since the night she went missing. No tossed drawers or hastily packed clothes. Her luggage remained undisturbed in a hall closet under a pile of folded sheets. The records provided by her cell service showed no calls after the night of the twenty-sixth and her bank accounts remained untouched.

She was listed in the missing persons manifesto and flyers were printed up bearing her official police photo and physical description, details about her last known whereabouts. Gallagher helped distribute the flyers, handing them out to every door in the vicinity and papering every lamp post. Amy helped out too, volunteering to distribute flyers after school.

There were no leads, no witnesses and no calls to the tip line.

"DID you call the hospitals this morning?" Gallagher looked up from his newspaper when Amy padded into the kitchen, toweling her wet hair.

"Yeah," Amy said. Her breakfast was made and waiting for her on the counter. "No news. Except for Vincent Medical. They left me on hold. I'll call back after breakfast."

Every morning for the past week, Gallagher and Amy had called all of the hospitals in the city asking about any Jane Does who'd been admitted. Hoping someone matched Lara's description.

"Sit down and eat." He cleared away the paperwork, making space for her. Amy took her fruit and toast to the table, munching as she looked over her dad's mess. A fresh stack of missing persons flyers and a map marred with scribbles. She watched him making notes on the map itself. The bruises on his face were slow to fade and he was still limping. He looked tired and he looked old and it scared her a little.

"You want some OJ?" He got up and retrieved the carton and a glass, limped back to the table. "The forecast is calling for sunshine the next few days. Think I'll go see Pablo, get started on that backup plan."

She frowned. "Dad, you need to rest. Take it easy."

"I need to keep looking."

She crunched her toast and he skimmed through The Oregonian. A dry crackle from down the hall, the police scanner in his office was turned up loud so he could he hear it out in the kitchen.

"Dad?"

"Mmm."

"It's been a week."

That brought his eyes up. "And?"

"I dunno." Her shoulders went up in a shrug. "It's just— It's been a week. That's all. You've been going so hard on this and it's… " She shrugged again without finishing.

"You think I should give up? Face facts."

She let her spoon clink against the bowl. "No one's seen her. She hasn't been to her place, hasn't used her phone or touched her bank account. Do you honestly think she's, you know, still alive?"

"I wouldn't be doing this if I thought she was dead."

"I know." Amy chewed her lip, looking for the right words. "It's just, you're pushing yourself too hard. You need to recuperate. Look after yourself."

"And who's looking out for her?" His tone was too sharp and he regretted it immediately. "I know what you're saying, honey." He patted the back of her hand. "And I appreciate it, I do, but I gotta keep looking."

"It's not your fault, you know." As usual, she cut through the fog to stick a fork in the problem.

"Finish your breakfast," he said.

THE Multnomah County Animal Shelter was back to its hectic pace since the break-in and Pablo was grateful for it. Reuben Bendwater's death still hung over the place but the grim atmosphere lifted bit by bit with the return of injured pets and stray animals. The staff had pooled some money together and framed a picture of Reuben for the lobby, the words In memoriam etched below.

Pablo had spent the morning euthanizing an aging Australian Sheepdog named Boots. The family was in attendance, a father with his two sons. The boys smoothed their hands down Boots' ruff as Pablo administered a sedative and then the pentobarbital. The boys cried and the dad clenched his jaw to keep his own eyes dry and then he put his arms round his sons and led them out of the room. Pablo was washing his hands when Gallagher appeared in the doorframe.

The kennel exploded in barking as they pushed through the swing doors and moved past the rows of cages. Kenneled dogs had simple reactions to strangers, they either liked them or they didn't. They definitely did not like Gallagher, Pablo concluded.

They strode down the row of big dogs and little dogs and Pablo stopped at the last cage on the end. "Is that him?"

"Yeah," Gallagher said. "That's him."

The Siberian didn't even lift his head until the two men stood before his cage. The left foreleg was wrapped in gauze. He raised up on his elbows and let his tongue fall out of his chops. Waiting to see what would happen.

Gallagher knelt and nickered at the dog. "Here boy," he said.

The dog backed away as far as the cage allowed.

"Guess he don't like you," Pablo said.

"No shit. You got a muzzle for this beast?"

Pablo rubbed his neck, unsure about the whole deal. "I don't know about this, G. I got court orders to destroy this dog come Friday."

"Don't sweat it, Pablo." Gallagher rose up, hands on his hips. "I'll have him back by tomorrow. I just need a muzzle on this sonovabitch so he don't bite."

The dog let Pablo harness his snout with the leather muzzle and collar the lead. Pablo walked the dog out of the building before handing the lead to Gallagher. "Here," he said. "Walk him a bit."

The Siberian jerked and recoiled the minute Gallagher took the leash. Gallagher cursed and dragged the mutt along but he needed Pablo's help getting the damn dog into the back of his Cherokee. The dog turned and tried to bite Gallagher through the muzzle. Gallagher smacked it across the nose. "Behave," he snapped. "And don't even think about pissing back here."

He slammed the gate shut and saw Pablo laughing. Pablo handed Gallagher a plastic shopping bag. "Don't forget, if he goes, you gotta pick up his business."

Gallagher grunted out something like a thank you and climbed under the wheel. He checked the rearview. The Siberian panted and squeezed its snout out the crack in the window.

THE dog whined and scratched at the door when they got close. He pulled off the main road onto a gravel spit and parked in the shade of a maple tree. He opened the gate slowly to keep the animal from bolting and reached in for the leash. The Siberian backed away, forcing him to crawl in after it. It fought him at first, tugging and digging in its heels. Gallagher yanked and pulled and kicked the animal along, traipsing through the uneven ground of the marshland.

The sky was clear but little sunlight penetrated the canopy of trees inside the park. The trunks of the aspens were vibrant with moss and more moss carpeted the lengths of fallen timbers that crisscrossed the forest floor. Man and dog both limped, making an odd hobbling spectacle to see but they saw no other hikers.

The Siberian kept fighting him and Gallagher sat down on a length of mossy deadfall and spoke to the animal. He blew off his frustration, speaking calm and even to the dog the way one does to a toddler. When he rose and continued on, the animal sidled in beside him and fought no more.

Twenty minutes in and Gallagher worried he had taken the wrong path before spotting the strip of yellow tape on the ground. The animal became agitated, pulling on the lead again. He reigned it tight to his knees and patted its ribs. From his pocket, he pulled out a plastic freezer bag and opened the seal. Inside it was a T-shirt he had nicked from the laundry hamper in Lara's apartment. He put it to his nose and could smell her on it then he kneeled down to the dog's level and held it up. The Siberian was uninterested so he pushed the damp shirt into its nose.

"This is her," he spoke to the dog. "Find her for me. Show me which way she went."

The dog put its nose to the ground and pulled him a ways and then lifted a leg and marked a tree stump. It looked up at him and then watched a bird flitting over the pine needles. He tried again, putting the garment to the animal's nose, until the dog seemed to understand. Nose to the ground it meandered through the ferns and underbrush, tracking a scent. Gallagher ran out the slack on the leash and let the dog lead him where it would.

They hobbled along, man and dog, until they crested a rise and disappeared into a thick of hemlocks.

The story continues…

Three months after his partner mysteriously vanished, detective John Gallagher remains haunted by his encounter with something that should not exist. With no clues as to his partner's disappearance, detective Lara Mendes is presumed dead but Gallagher refuses to give up the search. Like a man possessed, he pushes himself to the brink to find her.

At a downtown firing range, 17-year old Amy Gallagher is taught how to fire a gun by her father. She goes along for his sake but Amy is increasingly troubled by her father's instability. His nightmares, paranoia and obsession with finding his missing partner are clear signs of post traumatic stress but her pleas for him to seek help fall on deaf ears. Chafing under his strict rules, Amy struggles to save her dad before he pushes himself over the edge.

Two hundred miles away, a woman with a terrible secret hides in the vastness of the Oregon wilderness, desperate to outrun her fate. Banished into self-imposed exile with a worsening condition, ex-detective Lara Mendes has exhausted any hope for a cure to her cursed existence. With no options left, her last chance at peace may be to take her own life.

Stalking her through the pines is a primordial nightmare plucked straight from a Grimm's fairytale. It wants Lara Mendes and will stop at nothing to get her.

The only question that remains is who will get to her first, and what will Lara do when they come?

ABOUT THE AUTHOR

Tim McGregor is a novelist and screenwriter. *Bad Wolf* is his first book. His produced films can usually be found in the discount DVD bin. Tim lives in Toronto with his wife and children.

Made in the USA
Las Vegas, NV
11 March 2023

68928376R00226